Hidden

Book I of The Twisted Boeman Collection

A. Ryan MacGibbon

@thewritersembrace

Copyright

@thewritersembrace

www.thewritersembrace.com

Dedicated to Mom,
who showed me that a mother's love has no bounds

"Where am I to go,
Now that I've gone too far."

Golden Earring

Part I
Revenant

1

Daray Horvac was brought back from the brink of slumber by the sound of his whistling kettle, completely unaware that his preconceptions of reality were about to be splintered on what was seeming to be a typical Friday night in. He awoke on his pleather living-room couch, the dim light of the evening moon shimmering through the window as an old re-run of *Jeopardy* played on his thirty-two-inch television. It took Daray a mental pause to remember where he was. Only seconds ago, he was on the verge of a dream, the imagery in his mind quickly fading from existence as he floated back to reality.

"Who is John Laurens?" a contestant on the television said from behind her podium, giving a question to the answer Daray had missed in his dazed state.

"Correct," replied Alex Trebek, one of the few TV show icons Daray could tolerate in large doses. The lady followed up with a $1600 answer, Trebek promptly reading the clue. "It's the colourful term for a misleading clue in a murder mystery."

"Intentional red herring," Daray spoke quietly to himself in the loneliness of his tiny living room.

The contestant on the show buzzed as Daray spoke the answer, quickly following with the same response. "What is an intentional red herring?" the woman said, adding to her score and increasing her separation from the other two contestants.

Daray could *probably* answer about forty-to-fifty percent of the questions correctly in any given round of *Jeopardy*. He always wondered what it would be like to be up on stage, the camera zooming in on your face while the rest of the world judged your intelligence as a person based on how quickly you could remember a useless trivia fact. There was more to intelligence than one's ability to answer a trivia question, as Daray *or any other academic* would argue. There was always that thought in the back of his mind that the contestants on Jeopardy got a little too much credit for being 'geniuses.' — credit that wasn't always given to scholars in fields of study that weren't math or physics. Of course, that didn't change his opinion of the show. He loved watching, and although he would never admit this to anyone, it made him feel a little superior when he could answer the clue correctly before any of the contestants. He supposed this was a little hypocritical—*but who cared?* It's a hypocritical world.

Daray tossed his thick blanket off to the unused side of the couch, standing up and peeling his eyes away from the shimmering screen, his ears remaining locked upon each clue Trebek read to the contestants. He released a vicious yawn, echoing through his small suburban home on the edge of Wolfville, Nova Scotia, looking over toward the window, watching as a heavy autumn rain began to plummet from the heavens above, blocking out the shimmering moonlight as the sky shifted from a dark grey to soulless black.

He was glad it was a Friday. Otherwise, he would have had to go outside and face the brutal November storm to get to the office. Daray worked as a postdoc in psychology at Acadia University, a school with a student body of only four-to-five thousand youth during any given semester. The University wasn't far, but his undersized home didn't come with a garage, and even the short sprint from his front door to the car would leave him soaked head-to-toe on a night like tonight. But it was the weekend, and he was perfectly content to stay in the comfort of his home, watching movies and re-runs on the television as the rain drizzled and poured outside.

From the kitchen, the kettle's whistle was growing louder and harsher by the second, calling for Daray as he fought away the grogginess. He hadn't been asleep for long, only turning on the stovetop a few minutes ago and then accidentally falling asleep on the couch while waiting, but he felt like he just awoke from a week-long snooze, his mind struggling to keep up with his body. Slowly he made his way toward the stove in the other room, flicking on every light along the way as the night grew darker, the rain pattering on. He lifted the old kettle from the burner and poured the steaming water into his favourite mug, a tea bag already inside to welcome the boiling water, the faint smell of chamomile starting to lift him back to consciousness. Daray wasn't sure if this was his fourth or fifth tea today. It seemed the entire afternoon had passed by in a hazy blur.

But he was okay with that.

He needed a day like today.

The amount of work he'd been doing over the past few months to pump out a few research papers and get his name recognized was enough to break any man. He couldn't remember the last time he went out to the bar, saw a movie in the theatre, or even ate a meal that didn't come with an aluminum foil top and microwave instructions. His research was exhausting; half of the original ideas he had devised himself, but the rest was composed of monotonous *lacky*-work thrust upon him by his supervisor, Allan. Daray had worked incredibly hard to get to where he was today, but it was reaching the point where he didn't know where one project ended and the next began. They were all starting to blend, like the edge of two oceans colliding with no land in sight.

Was it worth it?

3

God only knew—*not that he was a believer in the man upstairs. He was a scientist, after all. He preferred to base his beliefs on tangible evidence.*

Daray felt the warmth of his tea-mug resting in his hands, the soothing aroma of Chamomile filling his nose as he returned to the solitude of his living room. But he barely made it to the heavy indent in his usual spot on the couch when a loud chime echoed across his home, the ring of his landline breaking the balanced silence he had nurtured throughout his lazy Friday. He considered not answering, letting the machine take the call instead. They'd leave a message if it was important. Otherwise, it was probably just a fluff call or some after-hours telemarketer. He hadn't talked with anyone since he left the office late yesterday evening, keeping to himself as he enjoyed the solace of his quiet home. He seldom got calls this late on a Friday, his job very much a nine-to-five sort of gig in terms of internal communications. The remainder of his work mostly needed only an empty room and a laptop screen. Little else was required for him to push through much of his research.

The phone continued to ring as he considered leaving it unanswered...

>   ...*it rang*...
>   ...*and it rang*...
>   ...*and it rang*...

Unfortunately, curiosity got the better of him, perhaps a side effect of the nature of his profession. Daray placed the mug on an end-table, careful not to spill the hot brimming liquid on his hands, and lifted the phone from the jack on the wall, pressing the cold plastic to his ear. Later, Daray would think back to this simple and ordinary moment and wonder how his life would have turned out had he not answered this single phone call. But how could he have known that answering would tear apart his very beliefs of reality, flipping his ordinary life upside down, and replacing it with something a little more hectic…a little more unpredictable…and just a tad bit—*sinister*.

He couldn't have known.

But he shouldn't have answered.

"Hello?" Daray said hesitantly, his usual response to what would turn out to be a phone call far from ordinary.

There was no answer, only quiet silence between his greeting and the lack of one to follow, hushed static scratching at his ear. He waited a moment, listening for anyone on the other line, half-expecting a telemarketer to speak out and try and sell him the next significant breakthrough in some junk he cared little about.

"Hell—" Daray's second greeting was immediately cut off by the shrieking screams of a man, his cries and howls nearly blowing his ear-drum half-to-bits. He withdrew the phone from his ear, thrown back by the deafening response. Daray's heart began racing, catching up with the adrenaline ignited by the overpowering screams shattering his quiet night to pieces. The unknown man's harrowing cries continued through the earpiece, splitting the silence as Daray cautiously raised the phone back to his ear, leaving a gentle distance between the speaker and his skin to protect what was left of his aching eardrum.

"Hello?" Daray said again with a little more urgency, unsure if this was some sick prank or twisted joke. "Hello? Are you okay? Who is this?" He spattered out the first things that popped into his head, the grogginess of his mind replaced with adrenaline as if it were injected by the portable phone itself.

"Can you hear me? Hello?" Daray tried again, each callout returned with terrifying shrieks of pain and panic emanating through the telephone.

Daray tried calling out several times, praying someone would speak, but no words were returned. Only cries of agony hidden behind a restricted telephone number screeched out. Daray was half a second from clicking the 'end-call' button when a familiar voice spoke through the earpiece, nearly inaudible as if a large amount of static interference was scrambling the line.

"Daray? Is that you? Please, God, are you there?"

Daray knew the stranger's voice in an instant.

He was no stranger at all, Daray having worked alongside him almost every day for the past several years. The voice belonged to Dr. Allan Springs, head of the Psychology Department at Acadia University, and a longtime mentor, instructor, and supervisor to Daray Horvac. But Daray had never heard his supervisor's voice spoken with such distress and concern. He knew right away something was seriously wrong.

"It's me, Allan. What the hell is going on?"

"It—mar—dead—save—," Allan failed to respond, his voice jumbled and broken amongst the increasing static. "Help! Pleas—come—!"

Daray barely heard what his supervisor had said beyond the shouting, his heart racing faster and faster, the rain pouring calmly from the sky.

"Wh-what's going on?" he stammered out. "Do you need me to call the police?"

"No police—you—hel—"

The line died.

The empty dial tone lingered, the thunderous static still echoing from ear to ear as Daray processed the phone call that lasted all of nineteen seconds, every thought imaginable running across his now far-from-groggy mind.

Was this some sick joke? Daray didn't think so...

A prank? That wasn't like Allan…

No police? What could Daray do that the police could not?

What the hell was going on…

It didn't matter. Allan was in trouble, and he had asked *Daray* for help.

After a moment's hesitation, breaking away from his straying imagination, the young postdoc raced to his closet, yanked out the first pair of sneakers he could find and slipped them on without even typing up the laces. He grabbed the car keys hanging from a hook nearby, then raced out the front door, slamming it behind him as he braved the treacherous rain outside, his pyjama bottoms and university hoodie becoming drenched along the way. He hopped in his car, water dripping from his nose, and jammed the key into the ignition, bringing his tiny Ford Focus to a rumbling start. He then yanked the gearshift into reverse and tore out of his driveway, squealing his all-seasons as he swung out onto the main road of his tiny subdivision.

Fortunately, his supervisor didn't live very far from him at all. *Perhaps that's why Daray was the one he called.* Allan lived within the same sub-division as Daray, in the furthest corner lot next to the children's park where the forest's edge meets civilization. He only had one neighbour to the right, the rest of his lot extending into the trees for an added level of privacy. It was a nice lot, one that could only be afforded on a tenure salary. Allan's house was less than a kilometre away, yet it felt like the longest drive of Daray's twenty-eight-year life. He had no idea what to expect as he raced down the quiet suburban streets, his entire body shaking, his trembling hands barely able to grasp the wheel. Daray tore down Chestnut Avenue, reaching the end of the road and skidding onto Skyway Drive, blowing beyond the stop sign and drifting into the T-intersection. He raced to the end of the road, at the corner of Skyway Drive and Kent Avenue, and slammed on his brakes, swerving into the last driveway on the left.

Daray's headlights shone through the heavy downpour, illuminating the front of Allan's home.

Every light in his house was off, and despite Allan's car sitting in the driveway, nobody appeared to be home.

He was home, right? Daray thought to himself, questioning if Allan had even called from his house, or possibly somewhere else. The lights may have appeared to be out, but his front door was wide open, nothing but shadows glaring from beyond the threshold.

Why was their door open?

Had someone broken in?

Or did they leave without closing it?

Every streetlight down the road was burning bright — every light except the one in front of his supervisor's place. Daray didn't overthink it. His eyes were fixated upon the open front door, the dark black of his supervisor's home gazing back at him, greeting his arrival to an unknown horror.

"*Fuck,*" Daray whispered to himself, every goosebump on his skin telling him to turn around and drive away, the loyalty to his supervisor guiding otherwise. Daray flicked off his engine, pulling out the keys while simultaneously swinging the driver's side door open, exposing himself once again to the harsh autumn elements. He jumped out, the wind whistling through the trees surrounding Allan's house, not a soul in sight on this dreadful Friday night, hesitating as he stared blankly toward his supervisor's lifeless home.

Did he really want to go in there?

Not a fucking chance…

But what choice did he have?

Daray took an anxious gulp and trudged forward, making it only halfway across the lawn when the headlights in his car behind him cut out, drowning him in complete darkness.

"*Christ,*" he whispered, teeth beginning to chatter with no way of knowing what was about to happen. "It's now or never."

Daray reached the front porch, cautiously climbing each step, listening for the shouting and screaming he had heard over the phone minutes earlier.

But there was nothing.

Just the silence and his heartbeat pounding over the rain.

Cautiously, he pushed forward, reaching the top step and taking cover under the roof's edge where it was dry and cold. He stared ahead through the open entrance, the dark hallway inside barely visible, with no signs of Allan in sight, nor his wife Erin.

Where was she?

God only knew, and even that, Daray was doubtful.

"Hello?" Daray yelled out, needing a response but getting nothing but the wind's bristling howl.

"Allan? Erin? *Anybody?*"

If it were warmer outside, he may have heard the loud chirping of hidden crickets. But it was too cold for that. Only a deafening silence lingered in their stead.

"Fuck, Fuck, Fuck, Fuck," Daray mumbled repetitively, stepping forward over the threshold, the house somehow colder than it was outside. "Please...*anyone*...are you there...?"

Nothing.

Daray guardedly pressed further into Allan's home, the silence growing louder the longer he lingered. The living room was completely lifeless, the couches vacant, the television off. Daray's hand fumbled for the light switch in the dark, but the ominous stillness was broken only by the silence of the unresponsive lights above.

"Hello?" he yelled again, making his way into the kitchen, as empty as the room before. "Anyone?"

Silence.

He felt like a broken record, spinning in the abyss.

Where was he?

Daray's mind was traversing from anxiety to straight-up fear. Allan had only called him less than ten minutes ago and in that time, the power from his house had been cut and his supervisor was nowhere to be found. Whatever was going on, it had to have been—

A hollering scream split from the basement and resonated through the house like a fog horn in the dead of night.

Daray recognized the harrowing voice instantly.

It was his supervisor's scream.

It was Allan's.

The shriek lasted only a few fleeting seconds before abruptly coming to a halt.

There was no time to waste.

Against his better judgement, Daray rushed to the basement door, twisting the knob and swinging it open, a rush of freezing air immediately greeting him as he glared downward toward the darkened basement from atop the stairs. The air reeked of rot and sulphur, as if a wild animal had somehow crawled within Allan's basement and died months ago, never touched, never buried.

What was waiting for him below?

What hell was he walking into it.

He would find out soon enough.

Daray began his descent.

As he sunk into Allan's basement, the stench grew stronger—*thicker*—sticking to his skin like disturbed asbestos, mildew and dust forcibly rushing down his throat. A dim beam of light shone onto the bottom stair, the dust particles swirling in the dark as Daray descended onward, and as he reached the bottom and turned the corner, not even God Himself could have prepared him for the events that unfolded next.

There were two horrors that would greet Daray Horvac in the stiffening darkness of Allan's basement. Two unfathomable horrors that would soak within Daray's every thought for the remainder of his days...a blight on his forever scarred consciousness, images he would never be able to shake from his waking eyes.

The first horror that would greet Daray Horvac in the stiffening darkness of Allan's basement was a newborn baby wrapped in white sheets stained in what Daray assumed was blood, his tiny body wiggling and squirming silently on the concrete floor, its wails and screeches echoing through the basement as if it understood the terror it found itself in. Daray ran over to the baby, a few steps from the edge of the stairs. Chunks of blood and goo seemed to be slathered over the baby's skin, the baby itself looking no older than a few days. *Jesus Christ,* Daray prayed to himself as he stared down at the gruesome scene. *He knew Allan's wife Erin had been pregnant but didn't know she had already delivered the baby. He didn't think she was due for another month or two. In fact, he was almost certain of it.*

Had she delivered early?

It didn't matter.

Erin wasn't around to be asked.

And the baby was by itself.

Why was the baby by itself?

Why was it covered in blood?

Where was Allan?

Why was any of this happening at all?

These are the thoughts Daray thought silently to himself, wishing more and more that he could retreat to his home and call the police, sensing with each passing moment that he had made a mistake coming here. He searched around the room, his eyes struggling to cut through the thickening dark, barely a single slice of light peeking through the tiny basement windows.

"Allan?" he called out above the baby's sporadic cries echoing across the room.

No answer.

"Allan?" he called out once more, his voice audibly desperate and trembling, his entire body feeling like it was going to cave in on itself.

Daray scanned the furthest corners of the room, searching for anything else that may give him clues as to what was going on, praying there was some sort of reasonable explanation to this inexplicable situation.

And that's when Daray saw him…

Laying on his back in the furthest corner of the room…

Choking and wheezing in the putrid darkness…

The second horror.

Allan Springs appeared to be visibly clawing at his own throat, struggling and fighting to breath as if an invisible shadow was on top of him, wrapping his hands around Allan's neck, squeezing the life out of him pulse by pulse. Allan's body was soaked in mud and dirt, his legs were kicking and thrashing about, and his hands were scrapping at his jugular, desperately trying to break free whatever it was that was suffocating him.

Daray remained utterly still for a moment, knowing he should rush over and help his supervisor, but wholly petrified at the sight of the scene before him.

The bloodstained baby squirmed and cried at his feet…

His cries amplified across the echo chamber that was the basement…

And Allan lay in the darkest corner of the room, muddy and gagging, clawing at his own throat, struggling for any inch of breath he could achieve...

Daray didn't move.

He watched.

Because that's all he could do.

That's all his fear allowed him to do.

But after processing the fragmented chaos before him, Daray finally fought for the courage needed to break away from his paralyzed state and raced to the aid of his supervisor, who continuously gasped for air. Daray kneeled beside his supervisor, his eyes locking with Allan's bloodshot gaze, Allan's hands clawing at his own throat as if something was tearing away at his jugular from under his skin.

Daray had no clue what to do.

He had no idea how to act.

He was a Psychology postdoc, and except for a two-day CPR class he attended back in his junior year, he had *zero* medical training.

But it didn't matter.

As Daray reached down to try and help his supervisor, Allan immediately released his hands, taking a long and exasperating breath of air as if his throat had magically unclogged, his airways finally breaking free. Daray's supervisor coughed and wheezed as colour drained back into his face drop by drop.

Daray was the first to speak as his supervisor continued to cough and regain control. "Allan. Wh—What's going on?"

That's all he was able to spit out.

That's all he had the strength to say.

He had to wait a few seconds for a comprehensible response, the freezing basement air stewing within the rotten dark. Allan lifted himself into a sitting position, his breathing traversing from erratic desperation to controlled tribulation. His face was riddled with fright, his eyes darting back and forth across the room beyond Daray as if he was searching for something behind him. Daray turned around but was met with the complete emptiness of the dimly lit basement.

"Allan?" he repeated himself to try and prompt an answer. "What happened? Who did this? Please. We need to get help."

Allan's gaze shifted back to Daray, periodically scanning the room like prey wary of a hidden predator. He began to speak, his voice raspy and broken, every syllable trembling with hopeless strain.

"*She's...here*," Allan stammered out, his eyes searching behind Daray and around the room. "*...she's dead...but...she's here...*" His voice was barely audible, as if his throat had been completely crushed. "*Leave, Daray. Leave now!*"

Daray could barely hear what his supervisor was saying, let alone make sense of what Allan was telling him.

She?

Who was Allan talking about?

There was no one else here...

They were alone...

...weren't they?

"What the *fuck* is going on?" Daray said aloud, letting his thoughts slip across his tongue. He knew Allan had issues with mental health in the past, but nothing to this caliber, and nothing anywhere near a psychotic break.

Allan didn't respond. His gaze had entirely averted to the baby bathed in blood, white sheets wrapped around tiny wiggling limbs in the center of the concrete basement. Daray's gaze did the same. He could see the baby's tiny little fingers reaching up to the sky, calling for its unknown mama, with no answer to be given.

"Allan…" Daray spoke, examining his supervisor's widened pupils as they frantically searched the darkened rooms of the empty basement. "Is that your child?"

He gave no response. Only a blank stare and fearful expression filled Allan's soulless face, as if he didn't understand where he was, or who he was.

It was madness.

He had gone mad.

That was the only explanation Daray's troubled mind could come up with.

Of course, madness was the phrase given to problems unexplainable by those without the means to understand them, and there was nothing in this world that was truly inexplicable—not if you had the patience and determination to do the work…*to do the research.* That had always been Daray's guiding star as he struggled his way through life just like everyone else, and that would remain Daray's heading for the years to come—*because as fate would have it,* the events that were about to unfold over the next thirty seconds would not be without faith-defining consequences.

Allan looked back toward Daray, his mouth opening as if he were about to answer Daray's question of whether or not that was indeed his child, though he would not get the chance. Allan was halfway through the first syllable when he was abruptly cut off by a death-defying screech, echoing louder than humanly possible as the entire house began to shake and tremble. Dust plummeted from the ceiling and the walls shuddered uncontrollably as if the first earthquake in Wolfville's quaint history had cracked the crust. Tiny pebbles trembled on the concrete ground among the blood as tools, paint cans, and other garbage fell from their perches amongst the shelves surrounding the basement walls. Daray had to shield his ears to protect them from bursting as the screech pierced through the putrid air, his own scream nowhere near as powerful as what erupted throughout Allan's shattered home. It sounded like a woman's scream, splitting the night like cannon fire lasting what felt like an eternity.

But it was more than just a scream.

Screams are the logical response to fear—a *natural response*.

But this wasn't a shriek of fright, nor was it natural in any sense of the word. This shriek was the roar of enmity, ripping across the basement, shuttering every square inch of concrete and dust, the blood-soaked baby squealing alongside it. Allan was also covering his ears, his eyes darting back and forth once again, searching the darkness as the ground shook, cracks splitting across the exposed foundation, every wooden beam, shingle, and nail trembling in the dark. *Daray included.*

Then slowly and without natural cause, the shrieking began to diminish, the rumbling of the basement decelerating, a ringing quiet replacing shuddering screams. Daray looked over to Allan, his ears reverberating in immense pain, their bodies covered in dust and soot. "What in the Christ was that?"

Allan responded, his throat still raspy and coarse, his words barely audible. Daray didn't know these would be some of his last to him. "Retribution," Allan whimpered, "God forgive me."

There was a moment's pause as Daray carefully plodded over Allan's choice of words. Daray was looking directly at Allan, but his supervisor was not returning the stare. Allan was looking beyond him, over his left shoulder and into the darkness of the basement, his eyes fixated on whatever lurked in the shadows.

Daray slowly twisted around to see what captivated Allan, his ears still ringing, his mind racing inexplicably.

The temperature of the fetid air dropped by the second.

The smell of rot and decay became nearly unbearable.

The tiny hairs on Daray's arm and neck began to rise, and once he turned and realized what Allan was staring at, he understood why his supervisor seemed to be slipping into madness.

Lingering behind him in the very corner of the dark basement room, materializing out of thin air, was a woman. Daray had to squint to focus, his pounding heart nearly bursting through his chest. Her face was almost entirely covered by her long dark hair, drooping down from her scalp. The woman's hair was split and filthy, as if it hadn't been washed in years, and a small chunk looked like it had been ripped from the side of her head, a peeling flab of skin exposing an exposed piece of skull above her left eyebrow. Only one eye was exposed—*her left one*. It was near impossible to see in the flickering dark, but it almost appeared as if it were hollow, the details of her face concealed by shades of night. The smell of rot also seemed to emanate from the same corner, rising through the chilled air like the carcass of forgotten roadkill left to decompose. The woman's clothes were utterly tattered and shredded, and her skin was riddled with cuts, bruises, dirt, and gashes.

It took Daray a few more seconds to notice what seemed worst of all, the part that separated what could exist in reality from that which could be explained—*from that which had no anchor in this natural world.*

Her blackened bare feet weren't touching the floor at all.

They were hovering less than an inch above the ground as if her entire body were dangling from invisible threads.

Daray's entire body began to shake even more as he stared at the drifting woman in the dark, her hair-covered face staring blankly back at him.

He felt the frog in his throat build, fear and confusion replacing his ability to speak. Daray managed to swallow his fear long enough—*if only for a second*—to stammer out a few weak words.

"Who…are you…?"

"Shut up," Allan responded, his eyes never drawing away from the mysterious woman. "It's me she wants."

Daray wanted to respond, but the fear blocking his throat had built up again, impeding his speaking ability. All he had were his thoughts, and even those were starting to become more erratic by the second as he failed to piece together the horrors before him.

The rotting stench grew more putrid by the second, flowing across the room and reaching every corner of the God-forsaken basement. Each fleeting moment felt like a lifetime, each inhale shallow, every exhale staggered and broken.

"Do it," Allan strugglingly whispered, his voice mirroring that of sandpaper and cigarettes.

Daray looked over at Allan, kneeling on the cold ground beside him, his eyes locked in on the monstrosity before them. He wanted to ask Allan what was happening. He wanted to know if there was any sense or logic to whatever it was that hovered before his waking eyes.

Was this a nightmare…?

Was this Allan's doing…?

Was this real…?

Was this even possible…?

Or was this something humans were not yet meant to understand…?

These were the questions that Daray could not answer in his supervisors' final moments.

These were the uncertainties that would race across Daray's mind throughout endless sleepless nights for years to come, that would slowly drip in the back of his mind like a leaky faucet left unattended.

These were the questions Allan would never have the opportunity to answer.

Here Daray was, face-to-face with a creature—*levitating in the corner of the basement*—the ground trembling at the sound of her desolate shrieks. All Daray could do was kneel next to Allan...*wait...and stare...*too scared to do anything else...The fight or flight response seemed to only apply in situations explained by nature...but this was something else...something beyond what Daray's years of science seemed able to comprehend...*fight* was replaced by fear...the natural response of *flight* was nowhere to be found.

She was floating.

She was actually floating.

How was she...

The creature let loose another scream, not as loud as the first but loud enough to completely stop Daray's thoughts in their tracks. But it wasn't the scream that frightened him this time, *at least not entirely.* The woman began to drift forward, her hair brushing off to the side over her dislocated shoulder, revealing the horror that was her misconfigured face.

The woman's nose was bashed and broken, her skin bruised and peeling. Her eyes were glowing black and hollow, as if the pupils had glazed right over any colour, filled instead with an emptiness unlike anything Daray had ever seen before. There was no rosiness in her cheeks, no life crawling under her peeling skin, her face cold and pale, black, and rotting. But worst of all was not her nose, nor her skin or eyes—but her jaw. The bottom half of her jaw had been utterly snapped from her skull, dangling by only the tiny remnants of her decaying muscle tissue and string-like skin. Daray watched as the woman's yellowed teeth wobbled back in forth, swinging within her unhinged jaw as she slowly inched closer from across the room, her scream emerging from what seemed like every direction, not just her deformed mouth and soul.

Daray wanted to run. He wanted to rush up the stairs, out into the rain, hop in his car and drive as far away from here as he conceivably could. He wanted to wake up in his bed and learn this was all some horrible dream—a twisted nightmare.

Daray wanted many things.

But he could only sit and watch as this twisted, demonic woman slowly approached him and Allan, stopping mere feet before them, floating inches above the ground like a weightless apparition as blackened skin hovered above streaming blood.

Too scared to run. Too frightened to fight.

Daray simply prepared for his end.

The woman sluggishly began to reach out her arms, the smell of decomposition radiating from her corpse-like figure, dead skin flaking to the ground like evening rain.

"Do it," Daray heard Allan say again as he watched the misconfigured woman reach out with bone-exposed fingers. "Do it."

Daray didn't know what to expect as the corpse-like woman wrapped her dead hands around Allan's skull, Daray watching from right beside him like a scared little child. He didn't know what would happen, but when it did, he was relieved it wasn't inflicted upon him—*even if only for the moment.*

This horror replaced all others.

This horror was beyond anything Daray could have ever even imagined in the darkest of nights.

The woman wrapped her rotting hands around Allan's skull, and not even a half-second later, he began to scream. At first, Daray could only hear the popping sound inside Allan's body. But then, as his supervisor's shouting grew louder and harsher, Daray could see what the broken-jawed woman was doing to him. Inch by inch across Allan's body, Daray could see his bones begin to protrude from under his skin, jutting out like broken twigs from the branch of a dying tree. One-by-one, Daray watched Allan's bones begin to explode from within, pushing their jagged way through the tissue-like skin, filling his entire body with bloody holes and contusions. It started in his arm and hand, his wrist becoming completely deformed as every bone split into a hundred pieces and pushed its way through his shredding body. It spread across his entire frame, reaching Allan's shoulder and stretching into his chest and face. Allan's screams grew completely out of control, the pain seemingly unimaginable as the lingering woman held a death grip on Allan's skull, each dead hand wrapped around his face like a rotting vice grip. The screaming lasted all of twelve agonizing seconds before it finally ceased, Allan's jagged arms dropping limp, his body irresponsive to the splintered bones falling out of his skin to the floor.

Daray stared up toward the corpse-like woman, terrified of what she might do to him, his feet unable to muster the courage to run or fight, all urge to flee overcome by fear.

Then, as if to add one final piece of terror, the woman let out a short shriek and crushed Allan's head like a ripened tomato, bursting blood and brains across the room, bits of his supervisor landing on Daray's face and tongue. The drifting woman then released Allan and let him drop to the floor, the lifeless body of Daray's supervisor sounding like a sack of broken eggshells as it connected with the dust and concrete below.

There were about ten seconds of silence, the woman blankly staring at the now contorted and motionless body lying on the floor, her hallow gaze locked on the corpse under her blackened toes. The ghostlike woman then shifted her gaze to Daray, her matte-black eyes fixated on his pale face as if deciding what to do with him.

"*Please...*" Daray begged, swaying back and forth in petrified angst. "Please...let me live..."

Another ten seconds of silence followed Daray's plea to live, each second lingering longer than the last. It only took twelve to shatter every bone in Allan's body. God knows what the creature would do to Daray.

Or *why*, for that matter. *But it didn't matter.*

Because the woman spoke two simple words, barely audible as her jagged voice and swaying jaw whispered directly to Daray, who cowered on the floor next to Allan's deformed body.

"*...Keeeep...Saaaafffe...*"

And that was that.

Daray watched as the spectre-like woman dissolved piece by piece. After a few extended seconds, her body had dissolved to pale dust, swirling in the musty air as if an invisible draft pushed her across the darkness. Eventually, her entire body had diminished to soot-like ash, floating around the basement like a swarm of mosquitoes before surrounding the baby lying on the floor in bloodstained sheets.

Daray's body trembled in fright, waiting for the evil spirit to return to reality and turn his bones to mush. He waited for the spectre to reappear and finish the job, splitting every bone in his body and letting him crunch to the floor like a sack of broken eggshells as Allan's body did —*but it never happened.*

Calmly and peacefully, the rotting dust particles swirled around the toddler, blanketing the baby in a thin coat of ash, then slowly sinking into the infant's skin like the simple spray of sunscreen on a summer afternoon. Daray could hardly believe he was alive as he watched the last ghostlike particle disappear under the crying baby's smooth and bloodied skin. Then, once the final pale particle injected itself into the young boy's body—*as if God had magically intervened and saved Daray's life*—the lights came back on, illuminating the remnants of the woman's ghastly horror.

To Daray's right, his supervisor lay in tatters, bones sticking out his liquified skin, his face crushed into a million bits.

The room around him slowly transitioned back to normal, the smell of rot completely dissipating, the freezing cold disappearing in a similar manner.

And just out of reach, a bloodied newborn baby lay crying on the cold cracked concrete, all remnants of the demonic spirit now hidden under his flesh.

Daray wasn't a religious man, but from then on, he would pray every night that he never sees that God Forsaken creature again. And he wouldn't for thirteen more years—*then the true horror would begin.*

Part II
Discovery

2

A roaring jet engine couldn't have been heard over the thunderous applause emanating from the crowd of what must have been five-hundred-strong public attendees. Every man and woman across the auditorium were on their feet, clapping their hands to the wisdom of Daray Horvac, who was soaking it all in at the front of the stage, waving his hand to the applause and smiling from ear to ear as he listened to everything he had worked for the last thirteen years finally come to fruition. Not in all his years had he seen such a sight at a public lecture. Typically, when an academic gave a talk on their research—*watering it down for the average ear to take in*—it would be concluded with a generic polite applaud, followed by the shifting of feet eager to get home to their sports and Netflix shows. Not this time, however. This time, not one person was making their way toward the exit, all of them staying for every drop of information they could soak in. Daray could tell that all in attendance were brimming with questions and awe, each of them thirsting for more as if Einstein had just unveiled his mass-energy equivalence principle.

Daray couldn't believe it. He knew his talk was revolutionary, but not in a million years did he expect quite the response he was receiving here tonight. And it wasn't just your ordinary public audience of high-school teachers and late-blooming scholars. *Everyone* in Wolfville was there. The Dean of Acadia University, Leslie Hedera, was sitting front and center, smiling proudly as the audience applauded alongside her. Sheriff O'Connell was somewhere off to the left supporting his friend and community member, and even Mayor Jillian Adams was in the top row, looking down upon the half that voted for her—*as well as the half that did not*. And even some prominent businessmen had taken the time to listen in on Daray's thirty-two-page PowerPoint presentation, including Igor Jefferson, owner of several local car dealerships, and Alex MacInnis, head of the largest bank in the region. It was the kind of crowd every scientist dreams of when sharing his life's work, but few seldom get the luxury of indulging in.

And among those in attendance, standing off to the corner on the near-left aisle, eyes blue and smile glowing, was his wife, Janene, clapping as if it wasn't the hundredth time she had listened to him deliver his big speech. Every morning for the past month and a half, Daray would set his alarm an hour earlier than usual, pour a half-dazed cup of coffee, and begin to practice his speech.

He would practice it in front of the mirror while his wife showered and prepared for the day.

He would practice it at the dinner table, asking her for suggestions and improvements.

And he would practice alone in his basement office, manically altering and rearranging his major talking points, focused on nothing else but performing justice to thirteen years of complex and relentless research. Slide-by-slide, he would vocalize his well-combed words, pausing between key points, obsessively editing the text in the slides, as if a grammar error would take away from the internationally-renown importance of his research. Then, once he had honed down his speech, editing everything to unattainable perfection, he would make his way back upstairs, mumbling the words under his breath as his wife and son prepared themselves for bed—*if they weren't asleep already.*

Janene had been there every step of the way, from his time ending as a postdoc to his stature as a world-renown scientist in the field of Cognitive Psychology. And now here she was, standing in the front row as Daray reached the pinnacle moment of his tenured career. She had sacrificed a lot for him to be here—*too much.* Daray understood that, and he would make it up to her and their son, Amon. There was much to do still, but he would make up for so many long nights alone, locked away in his basement studying that which had never been researched before, breaking barriers no one thought would ever be broken.

The entire capacity-exceeded room was still performing its resounding applause, a few even whistling, not a single soul yet to leave the room. *It had all been worth it,* Daray thought quietly to himself, standing at the front of the Acadia University Auditorium, hand outstretched to his astonished crowd, waving in complete euphoria as if this was the most important thing that had ever happened to anyone.

Perhaps it was.

Who knew what the ramifications of his research would be? It would roll the head of every man and woman across the planet. Scientists will immediately swarm into the field like moths to a flame, and those more religious will cement onto this work like magnetic Velcro. And once the summarized version of this paper was officially published in every magazine across almost every category, there would be many more souls flocking into their local churches, *no matter the denomination.*

It took about two entire minutes for the roar of the applause to slowly suffocate, each person sitting down one by one until only the reporters were left standing scattered across the auditorium, notepads and pens at the ready. Usually, a speaker would be lucky to get even one reporter to write about a public talk. Now there must have been at least a bakers-dozen in attendance, all of them eager to ask their questions and write their articles, all of them knowing they were witnessing something that could elevate their careers—*even in the small University town of Wolfville.*

But before the questioning period began, there was to be the final courtesy statements given by the head of the department, who, as of three months ago, was Dr. Gregory Dunlop, a genius in Developmental Psychology and a true leader in his relative field. But after today, his research would compare to Daray's like a child's macaroni painting compared to the Mona Lisa, though Daray didn't think his colleague was bitter about it. There hadn't been this much stature and publicity at this university in its entire hundred-and-fifty-plus years of history. Dr. Dunlop was more than happy to walk out on stage and shake Daray's hand in front of key members of politics, his salary most likely about to raise ten-to-twenty percent, the flashes of cameras illuminating their friendly embrace for all to see. Daray received his handshake firmly, returning Gregory's smile as Daray released his grasp as gave up the podium for his departmental superior. Dr. Dunlop adjusted the microphone to his level, being about half a foot shorter than Daray, cleared his throat, and began his concluding remarks.

"Ladies and Gentlemen," he paused, scanning slowly across the entire crowd as he recited his scripted words. "Please join me once more in congratulating Dr. Daray Horvac for his positively galvanizing speech."

And just like that, the crowd was momentarily back on their feet, applauding the masterful presentation they had just witnessed, filling the entire room with boisterous applause one more time. This applause was shorter, lasting only a few seconds before everyone sat down for a second time, the reporters content to stand, virtually drooling to get their questions out.

Once the clapping of hands had halted entirely, the department head continued his closing remarks, Daray standing off to the side, awaiting the questioning period.

"Thank you, all, for taking such deep interest in the immense academic efforts of Dr. Daray Horvac. I can imagine you're all still processing the research that Dr. Horvac shared with you, and I imagine you'll be thinking about it for some time, discussing the implications with friends, colleagues, family, and all those you see throughout your daily lives." He paused a moment, looking up from his notes as if going off script, adding a few words from his own heart. "One of the great drivers of humankind is our divine desire to understand our place in the universe—*to understand our purpose*. Many claim to know, yet I would argue that very few, *if any*, have offered evidence or confident hearsay about what our purpose truly is. What it *truly* means to be alive. Daray..." Dunlop said, looking over toward Dr. Horvac, "...what you have just shared today may not define our purpose, *I don't know if anyone could ever do that*, but it certainly hints that life warrants more than what we currently understand today. You give me hope that there is more to uncover, more to learn, and a deeper truth to understand beyond that which our current models can explain. I do not pretend to speak on the meaning behind what it is you have uncovered, but know that you have given an old man joyful hope toward what lies in humanity's future, and folks, I assure you, that is no minuscule feat on its own." Dr. Dunlop turned back toward the crowd, his eyes shifting back toward his notepad, the train going back on track. "These revolutionary results, as you all very well know by now, will surely ripple across the world, forever changing the way the human race regards nature for generations to come. Dr. Horvac, as a token of Acadia University's utmost appreciation, please accept this humble gift as recognition of your years of hard work and unquestionable success and devotion."

A second-year psychology student, whom Daray quickly recognized as one of his students, Cindy Collins, hopped up from the first row, carrying a small gift bag and bouquet of flowers, traditionally given to the speaker of the room on occasions such as today. Daray accepted the gift in front of the crowd of hundreds, shaking the girl's hand as cameras flashed, whispering a small *thank you* before she nervously made her way back to her seat. The gift bag was heavy for its size, and he was eager to open it, but would refrain until the questioning and festivities were over. The night was still young, and he was excited to crack open a bottle of chardonnay to celebrate.

Dr. Dunlop continued at the podium, Daray placing the gifts gently off to the side of the stage where his wife could grab them and take them to the car once the crowd began to disperse.

"I will now open the floor to those eager to pick at Dr. Horvac's brilliant mind. Remember, only one question per person, *please*; otherwise, we'll be here until the cows do indeed go home." The crowd snickered and chuckled amongst themselves, Dr. Dunlop doing an excellent job lightening what had previously been a heavy and intense presentation. "There will be thirty minutes for Q&A, followed by a two-hour social gathering in the main foyer, where our incredibly gracious mess-hall staff have whipped together a plethora of snacks and Hors d'oeuvres for you to enjoy. Daray, please take your spot at the podium and let the questioning period begin."

Daray stepped away from his spot in the corner, shaking the department head's hand once more in front of the cameras, then hopped back before the spotlight to face the fervent crowd. He adjusted the mic back to his level, then began to speak as Dr. Dunlop shuffled back to his seat next to Cindy Collins. "Thank you, Gregory," Daray said, clearing his throat and taking a sip of water from his bottle sitting on the pedestal. "I guess we'll do this the old-fashioned way. For those with questions, please raise your hand, and I'll do my best to answer those that I can in the time we have. And if I don't have the answer, it was a bad question!" The crowd chuckled at his half-witted joke, half of them quickly raising their hand to try and extract a piece of his mind.

Daray scanned the eager crowd, selecting a young woman in the fourth row to go first. He could tell the lady was nervous, but she mustered the strength to speak out before the lingering audience.

"Thank you, Dr. Horvac," the lady said, speaking as loudly as she could so he could hear. A runner with a microphone quickly passed it down across the row, amplifying her voice across the loudspeakers so everyone could hear. "Forgive me, I am no scientist, but if what this research is suggesting is true, then this is going to completely rattle the spiritual and scientific community. Were you hesitant to publish these results for the masses to see? I mean, *don't get me wrong*. Your studies are breathtaking, but are you nervous about what may follow?" The lady handed the mic back to the runner, who was already running up the row for the next audience member.

Daray welcomed the inquiry. He thoroughly expected the audience to have such questions, having prepared an extensive list of responses in advance.

"Thank you for the question, miss...."

"Dawson. Amy Dawson," she said, her voice now harder to hear without the microphone.

"Thank you, Miss Dawson," Daray said, acknowledging the young woman. "Yes. You could say I was weary of showcasing the findings, more for my family than for the implications of the work. Many people won't be happy with what I have to say. I'm aware of that. But then again, what kind of man would I be to stand in the way of the frontier of science? I'm a strong believer that if you have something that's new to the world, something meaningful, then you have the moral obligation to share it with as many people as you can, no matter the general public's opinion. Science cares not for the opinions of humanity. Just ask Galileo. Great question."

The next to speak out was an older gentleman standing closer to the back row, his bearded face and plaid shirt matching his grey hair and wrinkled face. The runner handed him the mic, and even with the amplification, Daray struggled to hear every word.

"Dr. Horvac." The man said, his voice scratchy as if he had smoked a pack of cigarettes every day for the past thirty years. "My entire life, I have questioned the existence of God. I am not one to skip church or lose my faith, but there was always the scratching feeling at the back of my mind that we were truly alone and that there was no purpose to life. You've shown me today that that is not true. And I can take comfort in knowing that someday, I'll see my wife again."

Daray didn't respond right away. This was the fun part about giving a *public* lecture. Science was never about jumping to conclusions. It was about showing, with as much certainty as you could, the true nature of the world around you. It wasn't until the public began reading between the lines, did you get gaps between well-tested truth and wishful hope. But if what

Daray had talked about today helped the older man sleep at night, then it wasn't his place to steer him otherwise.

"Thank you, sir. And I'm sorry to hear about your wife," Daray answered. "If there's no direct question, may we move on to the next person?"

The grey-haired man nodded, handing the microphone back to the runner, who quickly passed it off to someone Daray recognized. It was one of the older veterinarians at the local animal hospital. Sadly, it was the lady that had put his dog down a few months ago when the pup got too old to stand. He couldn't remember her first name, her name tag simply reading Dr. Mullins pinned on her white overcoat. She grabbed the mic from the runner's hand, smiling at the crowd as she began to speak.

"Thank you, Dr. Horvac, for your eye-opening research and awe-inspiring work shown here today." She paused a moment, looking for the right words as her moment in the spotlight quickly went by. "I know this is only slightly related to your work— but from what it said in your slides, every test was completed on male children between the ages of three and thirteen for the sake of limited variability. Do you—*and I know this is stretching a bit*—but do you think these same results might also apply to the animal world, not just the human one? And if so, do you plan to expand this research beyond humans? Thank you."

Daray figured that would be her question. She was an enthusiastic woman, and he did not doubt the kind of answer she was looking for.

"Thank you for your kind question, Dr. Mullins. And nice to see you again." He briefly hesitated a moment, looking again for the right words to stay, careful not to overstretch the bounds of his years of work. "I can't say for sure if this work applies to our four-legged friends or not. I'm sure there will be other scientists out there who will put that theory to the test, the door now being open to those wanting to follow in my footsteps. But honestly, I can't see why it wouldn't apply. Humans have ancestral roots in the primate tree, as you all know. We are also animals, after all. So, I have a sneaking suspicion that applying the results of this research to our furry companions wouldn't be that far of a stretch."

Daray could tell the crowd liked that response, whispers and murmurs spreading across the crowd like wildfire. *Who didn't like a happy ending for their furry friends?*

The next to ask a question was one of his students, a bright young mind named Dylan Summers. He never got anything short of an A-minus on any of Horvac's exams throughout the years and could be defined as the gleaming example student Acadia University strives to attract, if you believe that marketing mumbo-jumbo. His question, however, was simple and genuine, straying away from the academic perspective and diving into a more personal aspect.

"Thank you, Professor, for your uplifting words. As we drift off to sleep, we'll all have a lot to think about tonight. I've taken several of your classes throughout the past four years, and from what other students have told me, you've never once taken a vacation from home in the past ten years of study. Now that your research is complete and published to the world, do you think you'll take a few days off to see the world? Maybe get out of dodge for a few weeks? It seems you deserve it."

Daray smiled at the young man, happy that some of his students were attending his lectures after hours. "If there's one thing we can take away from my research," Daray said, looking not only to Dylan but the rest of the crowd as well, "is that there's always more to be learned. Opening one door does not mean there aren't more left to be unlocked. In fact, I'd say the opposite is true, and the results of this research will only lead to more staggering explorations for young minds like yours to discover."

There was a small applause after delivering that response, a few of the other students in the crowd nodding in appreciation of Dr. Horvac's words. Daray had no doubt there would be ongoing experiments to follow his own, but he doubted any of them would have the advantages that he had in this research. But Daray didn't want to think about that right now. This was his time in the sun, and he was going to soak in every drop.

The questions continued for another twenty minutes, some repetitions of older questions, some entirely irrelevant to the speech he just gave. Even if they weren't related, he was just happy to see the public taking an interest in his field of work. It wasn't every day you had the eyes of the average Joe glued onto a field as open-ended as Cognitive Psychology. Of course, this research was no ordinary project. It would resonate with even the least-scientific mind in the room. That was the beauty of his work. There was something in it for everyone, because it related to each and every person.

The runner handed the mic to a lady named Irene O'Connell. Daray knew Irene well. She was wife to the Sheriff and longtime friends with his own wife, Janene. They had Irene and her husband over their place quite a bit, so he was confused as to why she needed to ask a question in such a jam-packed auditorium rather than one of their many household gatherings. But he was happy to answer any question she had for him, no matter the venue.

"Hi, Daray. Let me say that you nearly brought a tear to my eye today. That was some speech." Irene was always so genuine when she spoke. She wore her heart on her sleeve, and Daray had the utmost respect for her. "I have one quick question for you. You mentioned that your research and testing were limited entirely to male children. Why is that? Why not also evaluate us older folk, or even women for that matter? Thanks, deary."

Irene handed the mic back to the runner as Daray prepared his practiced response. This was a touchy subject, so he had made sure to prepare a wholesome, reasonable answer to this question.

"Thanks, Irene. Great question. With the kind of research I do, I needed a mind that was still in the process of developing—a mind without the jagged memories of a long life lived, or a life closer to nature itself. I find that with older folk like myself, it's harder to distinguish between the natural growth of neurological patterns and conditioned memories imprinted on the electrical pathways inside our brains. Working with children provides, for lack of a better term, *a Tabula Rasa*, or a clean slate, if you will. And as for only working with boys, this is simply because I wanted to reduce the number of variables in our research, so I kept our sample size as analogous as possible in biological gender and age. Now, I want to be clear, every test I performed was under the strict consent and supervision of the child's guardian, and I made sure not to overstep any boundaries during any phase of the experimental process. I also changed the names of each subject within the research to protect the identity of those who graciously participated in the experiment."

Daray had nailed his response line-for-line, regurgitating the words he had practiced in front of the mirror every morning for the past few months. Of course, it wasn't entirely true, but the means of data acquisition rarely mattered to the public when results such as this were out for the world to see.

"Excellent question, Irene," he finished, ending his practiced response.

It wasn't until the twenty-nine-minute mark that someone asked him the question he had been patiently waiting for this entire time, and whom better to ask it than the Mayor of Wolfville herself, Jillian Adams. The runner handed Mayor Adams the microphone as she stood to face Daray and the crowd. She was dressed in a sleek grey suit, dawning an Acadian Flag pin on her collar and a pair of clear-framed glasses on her nose. Her hair was long and dark, with hints of grey streaming down the side. If it weren't for her political status, Daray could have mistaken her for a late-blooming model. Daray had never met her in person, but he had voted for her. She was a big supporter of Acadia University and had been an enormous ally in the past as acting liaison between the university body and the town's four-thousand-plus inhabitants.

"Hello, Dr. Horvac," Mayor Adams spoke out, her voice firm and clear, her smile bright and commanding. "Let me say, on behalf of the great town of Wolfville, the impact you leave behind today may be one of the greatest research discoveries of the modern era. You do us proud. I mean that from the bottom of my heart."

The crowd gently applauded, those that voted for her clapping louder than the rest. The election had been close, with Jillian only receiving 44% of the total votes out of the three primary candidates. There were still those who didn't like seeing a woman in a position of power, but those of that generation were thankfully dwindling, along with their dated

39

moral beliefs. Daray shook the thought from his head, focusing back on the Mayor of Wolfville addressing him for all the townsfolk to see. "Dr. Horvac, It seems that we have dabbled around the question that seems most prominent, given the nature of your brilliant work. So let me ask what others may be hesitant to put forth. And forgive me, I'm a politician, not a scientist. But it seems to me, summarizing your speech into a single sentence…and I apologize if I'm reaching—" She paused as if she were reconsidering even asking the question, but curiosity got the better of her, and the well-spoken politician continued her inquiry. "…It seems that you have uncovered irrefutable evidence of the human soul, using nothing more than a few fancy scientific instruments and years of hard work. Am I correct in saying this? Is this the truth that brings a larger crowd than my inauguration speech here this evening?"

Daray smiled; the crowd was so silent you could have heard the wings of a hummingbird flap in the stuffy air. He thought about giving a complicated response, saying the work was much more concentrated than it seemed and that there were still many variables to consider before jumping to concrete conclusions. But he decided to sway away from the generic scientific response, shifting his words to appeal to those less scientifically inclined. He was going to be famous, *after all*, so why not also try and be a little profound along the way and give the people something to quote him by?

This was his time in the sun.

This was to be his lasting legacy.

"Yes," he said, looking directly back at the woman too gorgeous to be a politician. "Through the comprehensive research I have gathered, and the irrefutable results uncovered, it would seem for the first time in recorded history, humankind has quantitative and statistically reputable scientific evidence of a human soul, if you should like to call it that."

Daray could tell everybody like that answered, the whispers and murmurs rising again, bouncing off the concrete walls of the undersized auditorium.

The major continued her closing remarks, happy that she had the final word over a gawking crowd. "Then, may I say that this may be the single greatest discovery of our generation, if not ever, right here in the greatest town on earth?"

Daray was gleaming from ear to ear. He always dreamed of becoming a scientist greatly recognized by his peers, but he never dreamed of the international recognition that would follow his speech today. He tried to remain humble, knowing there was no further need to forcibly amplify the ramifications of his research, the crowd doing that for him just fine.

"I don't know about that," Daray responded modestly, knowing the mayor was most likely correct in her judgment. "But to have proof of a human soul. Well, I think it's the start of something fantastic. Maybe even a new branch of science itself."

And it would be. Daray knew this research would go on to change the lives of everyone it touched, his name to be plastered as the forefather of whatever name would stick with this new branch of research. He knew it would alter the lives of all those lucky enough to understand the implications of his thirteen-long years of work.

Most for the better.

Some for the worse.

But for Daray in his family, fate would have something much more sinister in mind.

The discovery of the soul didn't come without some equal cost.

3

As Daray was delivering his revolutionary speech at Acadia University, a few kilometres away, seventy-two-year-old Debbie Oslo was continuing the back half of her eight-hour shift, driving to the Horvac household to prepare the place for an afterparty celebration for close friends and colleagues of the soon-to-be world-famous scientist. Debbie wasn't used to working such long shifts, having owned the business herself and hiring some young students to run the show for her, but one of her employees was out with the flu, and the other had travelled back to Calgary for the month to help with a sick family member. That left her and her staff quite short-handed, so for the time being, Debbie had decided to jump in on a few of the vacant shifts to help her remaining staff.

The business was a small cleaning company Debbie had formed a few decades ago. Initially, it was just her, driving from house to house in her rusty Dodge Caravan, cleaning the messes of overpaid real-estate agents and car salespeople in homes she could only ever dream of owning. She wasn't salty about it, however. Debbie knew the rarity of owning a semi-successful business in this economy and was proud to boast that she made it on her own, despite her abysmal high-school grades and lackluster desire for further education in a town *literally* designed for the academically inclined. It took many years, but she had gone a long way from working out of the back of her old Caravan, posting ads in the local newspapers, praying she'd have enough work to cover the ever-increasing bills each month. It was tough, but she started to find her groove after a while. Her clientele grew more and more each year, a mix of repeat customers and new ones gathered through word of mouth. She attributed her success more to her charm than anything else. Debbie prided herself in her ability to relate with her clientele, her personality fluctuating and adapting should the need arise, making sure she put on a welcoming smile for each home she entered, always taking care not to disturb the house in any way that may displease the client. She also made sure to name-drop her business every chance she got during a conversation with the clients and always left a business card behind. Eventually, once the company grew larger than she had ever hoped, she hired a third-party developer to build a website that she could easily edit and change to her liking. Then, once her clientele grew beyond what she could handle with her own two hands, she began to hire students from the university. The student-to-job ratio was dreadfully low, so it wasn't hard to find desperate students willing to put in a hard day's work for minimal pay. And if one student didn't work out, there was always another willing to take their place, and so on and so forth. Debbie did well for herself, and she was *damn* proud of that.

But the years seemed to be passing even faster now, and the widowed Debbie Oslo was growing old, arthritis spreading more quickly than anticipated, her eyes losing strength by the day. It wouldn't be too many years before she either sold the business or packed it in altogether—*or kicked the bucket*, she would joke with her two sons living abroad, praying God had left her a good twenty-plus more years before she had to worry about things beyond heaven's veiled curtain.

The Horvac's house was the third and final stop on her agenda today, having visited another household earlier in the day, as well as a small pit-stop at an independently owned daycare which had contracted her for bi-weekly deep cleans.

Typically, Debbie wouldn't have accepted a job so late in the day, having only gotten the call this morning, but from what she understood, both Daray and Janene were heavily tied up with whatever it was he was presenting tonight, their son, Amon, along with them. That left the Horvacs little time to clean before the afterparty began, their home not usually tidy on the best of days. Plus, the Horvacs were regular customers, getting a routine cleaning every month for the past several years. *They also tipped well,* which was a bonus. So, after some consideration, Debbie had decided to take the job (for a slightly higher fee than she would usually charge), knowing her back would surely regret it the following morning.

But that was a problem for tomorrow.

It was about 5:30 pm when she rolled into the drive in her silver Nissan Sentra, a few steps up from her bucket-and-bolts Caravan she had all those years ago. She peered out the window, the sky growing dark as the clouds slowly rolled in, the sun gradually sinking beyond the tree line.

The Horvac house was an older style, somewhere between fifty and sixty years in age. The front door was Burgundy red, and a brick foundation circled the lower level of the home. The upper half was a creamy white, detailed with a dark brown trim running along the edges of the first and second-story windows, closely matching that of the roof and rusted gutters. It wasn't an overly large home, usually taking Debbie anywhere between one-and-two hours to do a head-to-toe scrubbing of the place. *She rarely worked on the entire house anyway.* As messy as the Horvacs could be, they were still a relatively clean family compared to some of the other homes she's conquered. Most of the floors were hardwood, so no carpet cleaner or steamers were required, and the kitchen was small enough that it only took a few minutes to clear out the countertops and give them a decent polish. Usually, Debbie would scrub down the bathroom with some TLC and spend a little time organizing Amon's room, not enough to disturb his organized chaos, but just enough to make his mother content. Besides that, it was the general light scrubbing and dusting across the entire house, followed by a gentle vacuum of the primary two levels and basement. She would perform a quick sweep of every room in the house, *with the exception of Daray's basement office*. One of the contract's stipulates was that she was forbidden to enter his office, which she was perfectly fine with. She got paid either way, and it was one less room she needed to worry about.

Debbie stretched out her arms and cracked her sore knuckles as she prepared to complete her last job of the evening. She swung open the car door, exposing her skin to the crisp autumn air. The snow hadn't fallen yet, but it wouldn't be long before the ground was coated with a blanket of white fluff. She'd be pleased if the snow never fell at all, but that was wishful thinking in Nova Scotia. Debbie lifted the hood of her trunk, pulling out her usual bucket of cleaning supplies, a broom, and a few old rags and dusters. She carried the supplies to the front porch in two trips, setting them on the ground while she scrummaged through her keychain to find the right key. It took a minute or two, Debbie always having about thirty different keys on her at any given time. Some houses had electric locks, which required a punch code for entrance, but the Horvac household was old school, with vintage iron locks on the external doors and even a few on the internal ones as well. Once she found the key, she twisted open the lock and entered, flicking on the light and carrying her supplies over the threshold. She was happy to step out of the cold, the thermostat reading 22 degrees Celsius inside the Horvac home.

As usual, she slipped off her purple coat, placed it on the empty hook on the side wall, tucked on her yellow silicon gloves, and began her ritual cleansing of the Horvac house. Debbie started in the kitchen, sweeping the floors, careful to gather any dust building up around the edges of the counter, and polishing the marble with a special chamois cloth. Once the countertops were good and tidy, she grabbed a Swiffer from her supply box, extending the retractable handle and running it across the tiled floor. The kitchen was small, one of the few rooms in the house other than the primary bathroom with a modern flair, most likely from post-build renovations. The rest of the home had a more classical feeling, with dark wood trim and cream-coloured walls dimly lit by small-hanging chandeliers and a few original wall-mounted lamps.

Once she was finished with the kitchen, she moved on to the living room. Daray had asked Debbie to focus most of the cleaning in that room since most of the after-party guests would be gathering there. Overall, the room seemed clean enough as it was. Debbie could tell that Janene had already completed a few touch-ups of her own. The couch cushions were perched upright and organized in the corners, and the coffee and end tables were wiped clean and vacant any forgotten mugs or crumbs. It even looked like Janene had done a bit of sweeping, because from what Debbie could tell, there wasn't a lick of dust anywhere to be found—until she lifted the grey rug, where a few piles had covertly gathered. She grabbed her Dustbuster and sucked up what was left of the dirt. After that, she quickly wiped down the 52" flatscreen, dusted a few bookshelf shelves, and finished with a few minor organization tidbits to soothe her self-proclaimed OCD.

She checked her watch.

6:36 pm.

It only took her just over an hour to run through the primary two levels of the house, a record time at the Horvac place. The house had been in better shape than she expected, with no significant messes left behind to speak of. Perhaps the Horvacs were just nervous about having company over, taking extra precautions by hiring her for a few hours. It didn't matter the reason, it was an easy paycheck, and she would be done soon enough.

Only the basement remained, which hardly ever took any time to clean. Daray's office was downstairs, which was off limits, leaving only a quick sweep of the tiny storage room, the den—*which was barely ever used*—the bathroom, and the stairwell. Usually, it would only take about twenty minutes to do a full sweep, and she was in no mood to go any longer than that today. Debbie grabbed her bucket, a duster, some spray cleaner, and a few rags and made her way to the basement to finish the job, the old stairs creaking as she descended.

Debbie could feel the temperature gradually shift as she made her way into the basement, the downstairs living space noticeably colder than the rest of the Horvac household. She could practically see the chilly bumps on her skin grow as she stepped off the final stair, her breath starting to become visible in front of her nose. Debbie checked the thermostat; the setting dialled the same as upstairs at 22 degrees.

It certainly wasn't that warm.

Not even close.

She placed her hand next to the electric heaters, the warmth of the hot metal near-scalding to the touch, the heaters clearly working as intended. *Strange,* she thought, wondering how it could be so cold with the heaters working as hard as they were. She figured a window was left open somewhere but wasn't sure where. She circled the basement, checking each room for an open window above the foundation but finding none. *Very strange.* Debbie scanned the room, knowing she should just get back to cleaning and tough it out, but curiosity crept over duty as she searched for the source of any potential air leakage.

She never liked being down here.

For whatever reason, it always felt too dark—*or too musty*, like there wasn't enough circulation in the basement of the older home. The den had been painted dark blue, furnished with worn black leather couches and rickety end tables likely bought from IKEA or Wal-Mart. A 38-inch television was perched on a small black stand holding nothing more than a few old gaming consoles and a Blu-ray DVD player that looked like it hadn't been used in years. Other than that, a few fake plants and some dated paintings, there really wasn't much else to look at in the Horvac basement. The storage room was filled to the ceiling with boxes, and the bathroom was probably only ever used by Daray during long hours in his office. The only thing that really stood out in the dark basement was the entrance to Daray's office. The door was more prominent than any other in the room, built from solid oak and stained a light brown to give that rustic Irish feel, matching absolutely nothing in the rest of the house. White trim surrounded the door, and a brass door handle with two locks guarded the entrance. Normally, Debbie would never enter on account of her contract, but she would hate for her client's electric bill to ramp up due to a forgotten open window on the cool autumn night.

Besides, what they didn't know wouldn't hurt them.

She walked over to the heavy oak door with brass handles, kneeled, despite the warning given by her arthritis, and lowered her fingers to the crack between the bottom of the door and the hardwood floor, where sure enough, she could feel a cool draft seeping through.

"Ah-ha," she said alone in the seclusion of the Horvac basement.

She raised her arm from the ground, reaching for the brass handle, hesitating momentarily. Daray was very stern about her not entering his office, but again, *he wouldn't even know*. She would hop in, close the window, and hop out without anyone ever noticing. Of course, her plan was immediately thwarted when she went to twist the handle, the knob not budging an inch.

Locked.

"Darn."

She tried again, twisting the knob in the opposite direction, but it was useless. The door was sealed shut, and the cold draft could not be stopped.

Or could it?

Debbie strolled over to her bucket, grabbed a dirty old rag from her small pile, and returned to the office door. She placed the grey rag on the floor, stuffing it as tightly as possible between the oak door and the hardwood floor. It wasn't perfect, but she no longer felt the cool draft seeping through. *It would have to do*, she thought, happy to put this distraction behind her and continue with her work.

It was still cold downstairs, but at least this would help bring the room back to a livable temperature save Daray and Janene a few pennies on their next power bill. She doubted it would be warm by the time she finished cleaning, though, and she didn't feel like catching a cold to start the winter months, so she decided to do the rest of the job in her jacket. Heavy cleaning products were no longer needed, so she was okay with slipping on her fancy purple coat for the remainder of her stay.

Debbie continued her session by sweeping the floor around the den, wiping down the TV stand and tables, fluffing the cushions and spraying the fabric with a few squirts of Febreze. She also gave the rug under the coffee table a quick vacuum, rapidly sucking up the loose dirt from corner to corner. Once the den was up to snuff, Debbie made her way to the overfilled storage room, placing the duster down and grabbing a broom from the corner. None of Daray's soon-to-be guests would probably come in here, but she decided to give it a quick sweep, *nonetheless*. It wouldn't take long, and the room looked like it needed some help. Besides, it was that tiny extra mile that gave her the best review on Google, the reviews that often stirred up a few additional clients here and there.

She went to pull the cord for the storage room light, and for a moment, it illuminated the room, along with its boxes, packed Christmas decorations, and undesired dust.

But only for a moment.

After a short minute, as Debbie began sweeping the room, the hanging overhead light tripled in brightness, glowing from a calming yellow to a blinding white; then, with little warning, *the light burst*, glass shattering into a thousand pieces as it plummeted to the concrete floor. Debbie released a short shriek, the mini explosion catching her utterly off-guard as she stood in the cold dark.

"Jesus-Mary," she stammered out, a dim glow shining in from the den.

She released a quiet sigh, looking down at her watch and carefully avoiding the shards of glass scattered across the floor.

6:58 pm.

The job was already taking longer than expected, and Debbie wanted to get out of there and go home for the night. But she couldn't leave glass on the floor for Daray, Janene or Amon to step in. So, with a roll of her eyes, Debbie left the storage room and hopped back upstairs to grab her sneakers, enjoying the warmth for a few seconds longer as her arthritis-filled hands slowly tied her tricky laces. *It wouldn't be long before she'd need Velcro shoes*, she chuckled to herself, looking at her slightly crippled hands. Debbie shook the thought from her head. *Not that old yet.*

After grabbing a plastic bag from the kitchen, stepping lightly so as not to trace any dirt from her shoes across the clean floors, Debbie made her way back to the basement, stepping into the dim light once again.

This time though, as she descended into the dark, she could see her breath evaporating in front of her like steam from the kettle. *She couldn't believe it.* In the time it took her to toss on her shoes, the temperature seemed to have dropped another five degrees at the very least.

"How was that possible?" she thought aloud, reaching the basement floor, and turning toward the storage room. Of course, she only made it a few steps before her question was answered. Just when Debbie thought she couldn't get any colder, a chill raced down her spine like a midnight wind, racing across her shaking bones with vicious haste…because across the dimly lit den was Daray's office, the thick oak door slowly crept open, Debbie's old grey rag resting at the foot of the darkened entrance.

For a moment, Debbie didn't move. The intention to fix the shattered lightbulb in the musty storage room had vanished entirely from her mind, her gaze fixated on the open doorway to Daray's office. The mist of her breath was heavy, evaporating before her nose as she waited for whoever opened the door to step out from the dark.

But no one emerged.

She waited…

And waited…

But she was alone in the growing cold.

Not even the whisper of a mouse could be heard stirring in the reticent basement gloom.

Debbie waited, bag in hand, at the far end of the den, staring over the worn furniture and plastic plants, praying that she was *truly alone*. Debbie considered turning tail and heading upstairs, but her feet were fastened to the floor, and her eyes were locked upon the open entranceway of Daray's forbidden office.

"Hello?"

Silence.

Nothing.

Zilch.

She could hear the hum of the baseboard radiators fighting off the frigid air, failing to overtake the cold so as the temperature plummeted onward.

It somehow felt even colder than it was outside.

It's just in your head, Debbie said, forcing the courage to take a step forward.

It's just in your head.

"Hello?" she spoke out again, met with the same chilled silence as before.

Her brain began to do the only thing it could within the presence of the unexplainable. It started placing reason to confusion.

Maybe she jiggled the door loose when she tried the handle earlier?

Maybe that accidentally opened the door?

Maybe the door was on a tiny slant?

Maybe it was a draft from upstairs?

Or perhaps a cool draft was flowing from a window in the office?

Debbie didn't feel a draft when she grabbed her shoes or coat, but then again, she thought the door was locked, *so what did her old bones know?*

It's nothing, Debbie.

It's nothing.

Debbie Oslo took a reluctant step forward, her unwavering gaze glued to Daray's open office. Then she took another step, this one larger than the last, her fingers shivering in the cold. She slowly crossed the den one dawdling step at a time, making it halfway to the door before stopping once more, her eyes slowly adjusting to the increasing dark. Debbie could barely see into the office, but she could make out the corner of a desk and what looked like a small martini bar with a few glass decanter sets on top. There was zero light emerging from the office, every faint glow emanating from the den's overhead light, which was dim in itself.

Once more, she left a hallowed greeting to the forbidden dark, praying for a familiar or welcoming response. "Hello?"

Zippo.

"All right then," she said to no one but herself. "I'm coming in."

Debbie halted for a few seconds, hesitating to explore the prohibited office. She could just as easily head back upstairs, dash to her car and drive back home.

The job was completed.

All she had to do was leave.

But she couldn't just leave with the office door open. Daray would think she went in. Then he'd surely fire her for breach of contract. And in a town where most advertising was done by word-of-mouth, she would do *anything* to ensure there were never any complaints about her or her business.

So, defying what the chill in her spine warned her, Debbie pushed ahead, stepping over her grey rag on the floor and into the freezing dark of the office. It took a few extra seconds for her eyes to adjust to the darkness, the cold wrapping around her like a blanket. The office was small, not much larger than the storage room. Daray's desk stood in the centre near the back wall, covered in chaotic papers, notes, and a laptop. The floor was a continuation of the living room, and the walls were completely covered with bookshelves. Every wall had a bookshelf on it, Daray's own personal library surrounding every corner of the office. Most shelves had novels and textbooks, a few knick-knacks and ornaments, and a few were filled with office supplies.

But it wasn't what was in the icy room that caused a subtle alarm for Debbie Oslo.

It's what *wasn't* in the room.

There were no windows.

None.

It was completely isolated from the outside world, the glass-framed bookshelves the closest to a window as there was.

Then where was the freezing air flowing from?

Debbie reached for the light switch with her shaking hand, flicking it on, only to be filled with anxious disappointment.

The switch did nothing.

The light was dead, the room enduring the dark.

Debbie flipped it a few more times, wishfully hoping it was a loose connection, but she had no luck. Instead, she reached for her cell phone in her pocket, pulled it out, and used the screen's light to try and illuminate the room. She wasn't technologically inclined, unaware of the 'flashlight' feature on her fancy cellphone, though in such a small room, the screen's light would do, her boney thumb constantly clicking the power button to stop the phone from turning off.

Debbie took another step into the empty office, searching for a hidden window or faulty air-conditioner, anything that could explain the open door and freezing air, but other than the martini bar, wooden desk, green office chair and a lifeless lamp, there was nothing else in the room.

How in God's name did the door swing open then? Debbie thought.

Maybe the floor was slanted, and when she jiggled, it swung open?

Maybe...

More speculation filling the unknown…

Humans were good at that.

Especially when their skin was as tense as polar ice.

Debbie took a deep breath, letting her nerves slowly calm, knowing at the very least that she was alone. She ran her hand through her short grey hair, her other arm holding the phone as a makeshift flashlight. She released a small smile of relief, the anxiety beginning to fade, her heart sinking back to a healthy pace.

"You're going crazy, you old bag," she said to herself in the isolation of Daray's office library.

"You're truly going…"

SLAM.

A deafening noise exploded to her right as Debbie released a howl of a scream echoing almost loud enough for the neighbours to hear.

Almost.

Her heart promptly doubled in tempo, the anxiety racing through her veins as if it were injected by an invisible needle. In a swift motion, she pivoted to identify the origin of the loud sound, the noise still reverberating through her ears as if it weren't totally silent once again.

On the floor behind her was an oversized purple book, lying face up on the hardwood floor. Debbie kneeled and grabbed it, surprised by the weight of the hefty textbook as she lifted it with trembling fingers. The cover read '*Diagnostic and*

Statistical Manual of Mental Disorders - DSM-5.' She had no idea what it was, but its contents didn't matter

How in the hell did this fall from its place on the bookshelf?

Debbie had no idea.

But she didn't care.

She wanted the hell out of this house.

Now.

Debbie lifted the book from the ground, rising and placing it back in its spot on the shelf.

And that's when she felt it.

The crisp breath on the back of her neck, matched with the deteriorating smell of blight rising within the teeny office. It filled her nose like swamp water, drowning her airways with a wretched stench. The distinct, concentrated breeze bounced off her wrinkled skin, her eyes watering with malodor. It wasn't until she turned to run did Debbie witness the source of endless trepidation that had corrupted her so effortlessly.

It lingered before her...

Hovering inches off the ground...

A demon mentioned only in the darkest of church sermons...

Floating within the center of the forbidden office, arm outstretched and jaw snapped from its hinges, dangling from the loose thread of rotting muscle, was what Debbie Oslo could have only described as the Devil.

Debbie could see the creature's mid-ridden tongue waggling back and forth in the dark as drool and rotten blood oozed from the gashes where its jaw should have been, black eyes glaring down upon her behind rotten skin.

Debbie didn't scream.

She had no voice to scream.

She couldn't find the will to scream.

Her breath drew shallow as her heart pounded from within her tensing ribcage.

Debbie could only stare with faith-breaking dread as the broken-jawed woman floated before her, as clear as the mist from her lungs, staring directly into Debbie's immobilized soul. Then, after what felt like the longest three seconds of Debbie's life, fear turned to adrenaline, her instincts overtaking any logic that remained within her forsaken mind. Her feet began to tumble forward before her mind could even conclude that that was the only decision available to her. Debbie turned from the woman floating before her, the rotting stench drowning her shallow-drawing lungs, and ran as fast as she could from Daray's forbidden office.

But she didn't make it very far.

Her bones were tense, and her coordination and arthritis could not overcome her panic.

She scooted about two steps before her right foot caught the corner of the grey rag lying at the entrance of the office door, and Debbie went tumbling down, cracking her head off the edge of the IKEA coffee table and landing on the cold floor with a harsh thud her fragile body could hardly handle.

When she came about, the room was whirling, the smell of rotten stench triggering her eyes to water, her mind slowly wavering back into consciousness. Debbie rolled over onto her back, an egg-like bruise forming on her right temple and a large dribble of blood gushing from her broken nose.

It took a moment for her vision to roll back into focus, but when it did, the only thing she could see was the broken-jawed woman floating above her, bone-exposed arm outstretched, reaching down to Debbie as if to rip out her throat, a single abrasive and coarse word splitting from her rotting throat...

"...Releasssse..."

Debbie stared in horror at the monster towering over her, the demonic spectre closing in as the remaining light seemed to slowly wane.

Running was no longer an option, her head spiralling too fast for Debbie to find her bearings.

And at her age, fighting was never a possibility.

This left one last alternative as she awaited her fate in the freezing dark basement of the Horvac household.

Debbie screamed...

She screamed as if her life depended on it...because she was pretty sure it did...

Her screams drowned out the howls of the demonic creature, Debbie's crying voice hollering louder than she ever thought capable.

And this time, the neighbours would hear her screams....

Every house within three blocks would hear the horrid shrieks of Debbie Oslo, under the menacing gaze of the broken-jawed demon in the depths of Daray Horvac's blackened basement.

Debbie screamed...

...and screamed...

...and   screamed.

4

araydarayay Horvac had almost made it to the refreshment table in the foyer outside the auditorium when an older gentleman stopped him, his hand outstretched to congratulate him on his galvanizing speech. Dr. Horvac recognized the friendly fellow but couldn't pin down how he knew him. The man was much older than he was, easily pushing eighty. His grey hair was almost gone, and liver spots had sprouted across his wrinkled scalp. But despite his age, his handshake was firm, and his voice was strong. Daray could tell the man took good care of himself, and hoped he would be in a similar state when he reached the stranger's age.

"Fantastic talk," the older man spoke, releasing his wrestler's grip on Daray's hand. "I can say that in all my years, I've never witnessed a talk quite as eye-opening as the one you presented here today. Well done, lad."

"Thank you—" Daray hoped the name would come to him, but alas, it never did, so he simply finished off his sentence with, "—sir," forcing a smile.

"I mean it," the man continued, fulling taking advantage of his short time with the scientist of the hour. "The research you've done will truly put our university on the international map. I've never seen such excitement."

That's when it clicked for Daray. The man was an economics professor at Acadia. He'd seen him around a few times, but the psychology department and business school didn't cross paths very often. The buildings were across campus from one another, and the students, except for the generic intro classes, rarely shared the same lectures. Daray was still unsure what his name was, but there was now some context at least.

"Thank you for your kind words," Daray replied, offering the same generic response as he did to the last three people that stopped him on the way to the sandwich and beverage table. "This truly is a marvellous day."

"Just one question for you, son. Before I let you go."

Dammit, Daray thought to himself, his stomach grumbling at the sight of the egg salad sandwiches calling his name a mere few feet away. "Shoot," he said, resisting the urge to move the conversation toward the food.

"Some of your ideas—your methods—I'm no scientist—but they're very unique and quite extraordinary. How did you gain the insight that no one else ever had before? Not many academics can say they've accomplished as much as you, nor have they ever tried to dabble in a field so...*divisive.*"

Daray smiled. As hungry as he was, he would never grow tired of hearing his name spoken with such high praise. It took thirteen years to get here, after all. "Hard work, my friend," he answered plain and simple. "And years of late nights, stressful grant applications, and a few too many bottles of whiskey."

"Right-o," the man said, giving him a light jab in the shoulder. "And it's paid off indeed. Let me shake your hand one last time. For it will be holding the Nobel Prize before long. That I'm sure of. I just hope I'm around long enough to see it."

Daray extended his hand again, realizing the economics professor was still somewhat out of touch with the scientific world. As great as Daray's results were, finding a hint of proof of what some may call the human soul, there was no Nobel Prize in Psychology. Maybe this could classify under physiology & medicine, but he doubted it. Rarely did the prize cross fields. But the gesture was lovely, and the concluding handshake meant he was one step closer to the hors d'oeuvres.

"Thank you," he said politely, and the economics professor went on his merry way.

Dr. Horvac was able to reach the concessions table without any more interruptions, doing his best not to make eye contact with the crowd of hundreds gathering around him for concluding words and discussion. He was pretty sure every professor at the university had attended the talk, not to mention some of the other staff, the dean, and a few students here and there. On top of that, the mayor was making her presence known, walking from group to group, shaking their hands as if it were *her* lecture they had attended, not Daray's. It didn't bother him too much that she was using his revolutionary presentation to gain a political edge—*maybe a little*, but the more attention and people of stature bringing notice to his speech, the better. But that didn't matter right now. At the moment, the only thing that mattered was the gaping hole in his grumbling stomach.

Daray grabbed a paper plate from the table, filling it with the first bits of food that crossed his path. He smacked on a few wedges of various sandwiches, a chocolate brownie, some scones, a shortbread cookie, and even a few carrot sticks to balance the sugar. He topped it off by pouring a warm cup of coffee into a cardboard cup, capping it with the plastic lids sitting nearby. Then, without turning around to risk drawing the attention of another gracious spectator, he hammered down the snacks, stuffing his face with the brownie, then the sandwiches, then whatever else was within arm's reach. He washed it down with a taste of coffee, then took a few large breaths to calm his nerves. The food dropped in his stomach like a rock, but it was well worth it. He felt his strength flowing back, his mind slowly lifting back into focus. *What a day*, he thought to himself, listening to the inharmonious chatter of hundreds echoing throughout the foyer.

Every single soul in the room was there for Daray.

To watch his talk.

It was a surreal feeling.

Daray had been so busy conversing with every person he came across that he barely had the opportunity to fully enjoy the significance of the day for himself, realizing what it would mean for his family and career. So much had been sacrificed to get to where he was today. So much hard work, perseverance, and late nights. *But it was all worth it.* Every member of the busy crowd told him so. And he believed it as well.

It was all worth it.

It was worth it.

He could only soak in the overwhelming self-gratitude for a few minutes before he felt a light tap at the back of his right shoulder. Daray turned around, half-expecting to see another audience member looking to shake his hand in congratulations, but was presently surprised by the familiar face hovering before him. It was his wife, Janene, and their son, Amon standing next to her.

Janene had long, dirty-blonde hair with a few gentle grey streaks running down the sides. Her eyes were hazel, and her skin was smooth, appearing younger than she otherwise was. She wore sleek black dress pants and a red turtleneck, matching her lipstick and tiny pin-drop earrings. They had been together for about thirteen years, starting to date not long after the incident with his supervisor—*not that he ever shared that incident with anyone. Not even his own family.* Janene had recently been on the rebound from a short-lasting headache of a marriage, and Daray was fresh out of his postdoc position, accepted as a part-time professor at Acadia University under special circumstances, given the fact his supervisor was no longer around to support the remainder of his research. Their meeting wasn't anything overly special. A friend of Daray's suggested they go on a blind date. At the time, Daray was barely leaving the house, and Janene was hesitant to date another man, given her horrible track record of short-fused partners and poor life choices.

But Daray was different.

Janene realized that on their very first dinner date at Rosie's restaurant. Her previous husband was verbally abusive, never striking her but breaking her down mentally day by day, which was somehow worse. It was more than she could handle—*and less than she deserved*—so after a few months of slowly severing the bonds between them—*secretly opening another bank account, building up a case for the court in her defence, finding another place to live*—Janene finally cut ties, moving from the South Shore and landing a job as a full-time tutor at the University. Then, after finishing her education degree on the side, she found work as a permanent teacher at Horton High-school. It wasn't long before she moved into Daray's home, where they would slowly build a life together, getting married within the year, faster than most people their age. And Daray loved her ever since, raising Amon together and living the white-picket-fence lifestyle they always wanted. And she was still just as beautiful as the day they met, standing before him by the refreshment table with stunning elegance. Some days he didn't think he deserved such a woman, but he was blessed with one every day.

"Hello," he said, his face half-stuffed with scones, his words muffled by the food in his mouth.

"Hello, *man of the hour*," she mocked, kissing him on the cheek and a giving him a hug to boot. "Am I now married to a famous scientist?" she continued, smiling with her sparkling-white teeth.

"Weren't you always?" Daray retorted sarcastically, swallowing the last bit of pastry and washing it away with the remainder of his coffee in the tiny cardboard cup.

"You killed it up there! It was fabulous. They loved you!" Janene gave him another quick kiss, this time on the lips.

"I screwed up a few lines," Daray contested humbly.

"No one noticed. Not after showcasing your work. Did you talk with the mayor?"

"I sure did." The mayor was attractive for a politician, but she didn't have a dime on his wife. If there was a God above, He was indeed looking out for Dr. Daray Horvac. *For now.*

"Amon, did you have something to say to your father?"

Amon was standing behind her, eyes glued on the cell phone *Santa* had given him the previous Christmas. He was tall for his age, one of the tallest in his grade eight class. Despite his parent's efforts to put him in nice dress clothes for Daray's big day, he was still showcasing baggy jeans, a brown American Eagle Hoodie and skateboard shoes—*not that he knew how to skate.* Amon lifted his brown eyes from the device, glancing up at Daray, and released a half-hearted "Nice job."

Daray knew that Amon didn't truly understand the magnificence of his work at such a young age. He would someday, but for now, the most important thing to that kid was texting his friends about some menial stuff they would forget within a few hours. Amon also didn't realize what a huge inspiration he was to Daray. Everything Daray did, was to ensure a solid future for his wife and son. That's what he told himself during the long hours locked away in his office conducting and polishing his research. And with the fame that was to follow today's incredible speech, he felt that he had achieved that certainty of lifelong security—*for both himself and his family.* With the publishing of his jam-packed research paper thirteen years in the making, Daray had catapulted himself to the top of the scientific community, putting his name next to those like John Anderson or Albert Bandura. Of course, their research areas were focused on slightly different concepts than his, but to the public eye, their fields were similar enough to be placed in the same boat.

"Thank you, son," Daray responded, knowing the boy barely heard a thing above the distraction of his cell phone, Amon's eyes locked solely on his touch screen. Daray lifted his focus back to his wife, who, unlike his distracted son, was exclusively focused on her husband.

"How much longer does this thing usually run?" Janene asked, not overly in a hurry to go home but certainly not opposed to the idea of laying in the silence of her own warm bed.

"Usually, it lasts about an hour, maybe thirty minutes more. But this one might go a bit longer. You know how it is."

"Well, you enjoy every moment of your big day. And when you come home, I'll be waiting for you in you-know-where wearing you-know-what," she winked, smiling like a queen, looking like a princess.

"Mom—" Amon's eyes were plastered on the screen, but his ears rarely missed a beat. Janene covered his ears, Amon shaking his mother away, his face shifting slightly redder. He was a teenager now, after all.

"Don't forget about the afterparty," Daray reminded her, remembering they had invited over a few close friends to celebrate his big day.

"Shoot, I almost forgot. Debbie should be finishing up soon if she isn't done already."

"And the snacks and drinks?"

"All in the fridge, ready to go.

"Great. Thank you."

"Anything for the man of the hour," Janene chuckled.

"Oh, be gone with yea…"

Janene was about to turn away when she flipped back to face Daray one last time. "Oh, by the way, Daniel is apparently looking for you. I got a text from Irene."

Daniel was the sheriff of Wolfville and a close friend to Daray and Janene for the past decade. He wasn't the one that set them up on their blind date, but he was part of that immediate friend group. Irene was his wife, working with Janene at the high school as the guidance counsellor.

"What does he want?"

"Not sure. But keep an eye out for him, will you?"

"Will do."

Janene left Daray with one final kiss, Amon giving a half-hearted goodbye as they turned to leave.

What a day it was, Daray thought to himself as he watched his wife and son vanish into the crowd. *It was all worth it.*

Since Janene had left, Daray had shaken the hands of about fifteen different people. Half of which he'd already forgotten, each saying the same thing, *more or less. "Great job,"* or *"Best talk I've ever seen."* It's not that Daray didn't love the compliments, but the time was nearing 7:30 pm, and the crowd had barely begun to disperse. There must have been another hundred people to shake hands with and thank for coming out. His throat was sore, and a headache was starting to form above his left eyebrow—most likely from the ten cups of coffee he indulged in to get through this day unscathed. He would need a few more cups if he were to survive their afterparty, not caring what it might do to his sleep schedule. He doubted sleep would be an issue after the relentless madness of the day, the exhaustion starting to creep back in as the previous coffee's effects began to fade. Daray could have curled up on the dirty floor and taken a nap. It was about a 50/50 he'd get through the rest of the night. Fortunately, fate had something else in mind for Daray that would take him far away from the crowd's praise and toss him into a whirlwind of chaos.

As he was shaking the hand of a younger man he'd already forgotten the name of, Daniel popped over, interrupting the group's conversation and nodding for Daray to follow him. It was weird to see Daniel wearing a dress shirt and formal pants. Generally, if not dawning his sheriff's uniform, it was jeans and long-sleeved shirts for Sheriff O'Connell. When he put in an effort, he looked sharp, like a marginally more rugged Han Solo, with significantly less charm. But Daray could tell by the look on his face that he wasn't coming over to give a friendly '*hello*' like he would before a Sunday afternoon barbecue.

His face was too stern for that.

Too serious.

Something was up.

"A word?" Daniel asked, his voice as stern as his gaze. Daray nodded, tearing himself away after giving a few quick apologetic farewells to the small group he was in.

"What's going on?" Daray asked.

"Not here. Follow me."

Daniel led them outside through the glass doors of the science hall foyer and out into the cool evening winds of the November night. The sky was especially dark tonight, the stars blocked out by the wavering clouds, a faint orange glow from the town's lights emanating in the sky. The wind was cold on Daray's face, blowing in from the Bay of Fundy, cutting like a knife as raindrops dribbled from above.

"Daniel, what's going on?"

"Sorry, bud," Daniel responded, turning around to face his friend. "But I have some unfortunate news for you."

"What?"

"I got a call from some of the boys at the station. It looks like someone may have broken into your house and given your cleaning lady quite the scare."

"Fuck." Daray felt a rush of blood on his face. Of all the *God-damn* nights there were for someone to break into his house, it was *this* night—*practically the biggest night of his life*. Of course, his public talk *had* been posted across the town for everyone to see. Everyone knew *exactly* where he'd be tonight, leaving the perfect opportunity for someone to break into his home. He knew it might be possible to receive some backlash from the public due to the nature of his work. Not everyone liked the idea of science intermingling with that which we knew little about, threatening people's beliefs and preconceived notions toward the more spiritual realm. Humans often have an instinctive ability to fill that which we don't understand with stories and theories with little basis or evidence if any at all. And when science *did* come knocking on the doors of curiosity, well...people didn't like that all too much. A fact Daray was well aware of and had mentally prepared himself for, should he ever meet any unruly or upset individuals.

Daray took a second to collect his thoughts, thinking about what an intruder might be doing inside his home. They didn't have many valuables, and all his money was locked up at the bank or digital. His office door was sealed shut, and unless the intruder had some heavy machinery, he knew there was no chance they would ever get to his research. Still, Daray didn't like the idea of anyone inside his home; it left a queasy feeling inside his stomach, the invasion of the same place his wife and son slept at night, where he conducted most of his work, where he had laid his hat the past thirteen-plus years. He took a breath, processing Daniel's information, looking for the appropriate response given the news.

"Is Debbie all right?" Daray asked, looking for a humane reply first. Life was worth much more than any valuables an intruder might take, and Debbie had been very kind to their family for many years. He prayed nothing bad happened to her on account of his own research—*even if it was indirect and unforeseeable.*

"She's fine from what I hear. Banged her head pretty good, though."

"Did the robber attack her?"

"Not sure. All I know is that your house was broken into. I need to talk to my boys to learn more."

"Right." Daray thought of the high-ticket items a robber could steal. Janene wasn't much for jewelry, and the one diamond they did have was on her ring finger. There wasn't much else besides a couple of cheap necklaces and earrings. Maybe the television could be sold at a pawn shop, but that wasn't worth too much either. There was a cheap guitar he never played, and perhaps some of Janene's grandmother's chinaware was worth something, but other than that and a few electronics, there wasn't much else worth a robber's time. Of course, they couldn't have known that until they broke in.

"Does my wife know?" Daray asked, wondering where they were in the crowd.

"Not yet. Irene is looking for Janene now. Didn't want to tell her over text."

"Good call."

"Once she finds her and Amon, she'll give them a ride back to the house. What's the play here, Daray? I can look after it for you, search the house for any damage or signs of theft while you stay here and finish your night. What do you say?"

Daray considered his proposal a moment. He thought about staying behind and letting Daniel take over the investigation, but he was getting tired enough as it was, and the guests were already beginning to dwindle from the main foyer. Daray had been giving and receiving handshakes for what seemed like forever, and his throat was dry from constantly trying to keep up with the conversation. It's not that he didn't appreciate the overwhelming admiration people had for his work; it's just that he could only take so many compliments before his mind became dazed by it. Plus, he didn't like the idea of police officers going through his home while he wasn't there, even if they were under Daniel's chain of command. Daray was a private person, his business his own, that philosophy extending the same to his personal belongings and livelihood, Debbie the rare exception in favour of his wife's wishes.

"No, that's okay, Daniel. But I appreciate the offer," Daray responded. "What you *could* do for me, though, is find the department head, Gregory Dunlop, and let him know what happened. He'll give some closing remarks on my behalf. I'm sure he'll love that."

"You sure?" Daniel jousted back, the cool wind rushing over their exposed ears. "It's no big deal. Today is your day, Daray. It's your call."

"Yeah, I'm sure. I do appreciate it, in any case. But I'm ready to go home now, and this is a good excuse to cancel the afterparty. I don't think I would have made it otherwise."

"Anytime. There are a few cruisers at your place now. They'll be expecting you when you arrive. We'll find Janene and Amon and let them know as well, send them right your way."

"Thanks, Daniel. Appreciate it."

"Of course."

Once Daniel disappeared back into the crowd, Daray turned and made his way in the opposite direction, heading down the hill toward the parking lot attached to the athletic complex. It didn't take him long to find his car, parked in the closest non-handicapped spot to the Auditorium. He had arrived long before any of the guests or spectators, the parking lot completely barren earlier in the day. His drive home would be a little faster than average. It wasn't far, but he hated the thought of people rooting through his house without him there.

Were they even allowed inside?

Did a burglary give them the right to enter without express permission from the owner?

Daray had no idea how the law worked in these cases.

It didn't matter.

He just wanted to be back.

He just wanted to be *sure*.

After a brief four-minute car ride, Daray pulled onto his street, facing the chaos and anarchy that awaited him outside his home. His headlights plowed through the darkness as he crept up the blackened pavement, not bothering to pay attention to the many potholes that snuck up in the dark.

In front of his home, blue and red lights flashed harmoniously throughout the night, shimmering off the windows and doors of every other house on the block as if to shout to the entire sub-division that there was some sort of commotion happening at the Horvac household.

Which there was.

Parked along the curb were three cop cars, each surrounded by officers in bright yellow high-vis jackets and matching uniforms. It was too dark to see if Daray recognized any of the officers, although he most likely met a few of them during Daniel's semi-annual summer barbeques. There must have been five or six officers within sight, each carrying a flashlight and walking over his lawn as if the intruder was hiding between the blades of grass. Daray could see that his front door was open, slightly invigorating him for two reasons.

73

One, it was cold, which meant his home would be flooded with the autumn air, and *two*, it meant there had been officers in his house without his consent. *They better not have started to search the place,* he thought to himself as he brought his car within a hundred yards of his driveway. He hated the idea of strangers going through his things, even if they were officers of the law.

A city ambulance was parked in his driveway in what would generally be his usual spot. Its emergency lights were shut off, and its back door was wide open. He could see a lady sitting inside, sheltered from the weather and dark. She had a silver blanket wrapped around her body, and a paramedic was speaking to her, his hand resting on her shoulder as if he were consoling her about something. Daray recognized the blanket-wrapped lady as Debbie, his monthly cleaning lady. He felt a breath of relief, seeing Debbie without any threatening injuries. If she had been attacked, that would at least explain why there were so many officers present at the scene.

As Daray pulled up in front of his property, an officer dawning a bright yellow coat with orange stripes sauntered in front of his car, motioning for Daray to slow down. Daray did so, rolling down his window to the cool air outside. The officer walked over to the driver's side door, leaning down and looking into the cab with his flashlight shining bright in Horvac's face. Daray didn't recognize him. He was younger, no more than a few years fresh from the graduation stage at the academy, which probably explained why he was on traffic duty so late into the evening, pulling the shift none of the tenured officers would ever do.

"Hello, sir," he said with wavering authority. "I'm going to have to ask you to go around the block. There's been a break-in."

"I'm Daray Horvac..." he said calmly, waiting for the officer's response. Daray could tell the young cop had not clued

74

in, his eyes searching for the connection. Daray added a little more to help his cause along. "...the owner of the house? Sheriff O'Connell said you'd be expecting me."

"Ah!" The officer's rookie brain finally clicked in. "Right. Sorry, sir. If you could pull up to the curb, I'll let Murphy know you're here."

Daray nodded, pulling his car ahead and off to the side. *Murphy.* That *was* a name he recognized. He had talked to Murphy on several occasions over a few bottles of suds at Daniel's parties. Daray didn't know him too well, not having an opinion of him one way or the other. He must have been the senior officer taking charge of the scene—*at least on this account.*

Popping out of his car, Daray turned to face the house, a faint drizzle coating the cool, humid air. He crossed the street toward his home, the red and blue lights painting the siding on his house, spreading across the night and into the abyss. Murphy greeted him at the threshold of his driveway, a mere ten feet from where Debbie sat in the back of the ambulance, shivering profusely under the silver blanket.

"Daray," the officer said, extending his hand for the greeting. Dr. Horvac extended his in return, adding to what must have been his thousandth handshake of the day.

"Officer."

"Did O'Connell already fill you in on what was happening? He said he was talking with yea' already." The officer was studying Daray's face for whatever reason. It made Horvac feel uncomfortable, even though he had no reason to feel as such.

"A bit. Apparently someone broke into my home. Did they take anything?"

"Not sure," the officer responded. "We haven't done a thorough search yet, just a quick sweep to ensure the intruder was gone."

"And they were?"

"Yes. Long gone by now. Searched every room."

"Any idea who they were?"

"No," Murphy responded, disappointed. "But we'll do our best to find them."

"I have no doubt," Daray uttered back, his attention half locked between Murphy standing before him and Debbie sitting in the ambulance, her eyes as far from closed as they could humanly be. One of the paramedics was beginning to tend to a medium-sized gash on her forehead, rubbing it with some disinfectant and diluting it with a wet cloth.

"She hasn't said much," Murphy said, snapping Daray back to full attention. "Not much that makes sense, anyway. She bumped her head pretty good."

"She was *attacked*?" Daray questioned.

"Don't think so. She said she fell on her own accord. That's the only information I've gotten from her that makes sense. But by the looks of it, she could have a serious concussion. She seems confused."

"How do you mean?"

Murphy hesitated, as if he had disclosed more information than he had intended. He looked away for a moment, searching for the right thing to say, then continued with his calculated words. "I talked with her a bit. But I don't think her mind was in the right place. She's probably still regaining a few of her senses. I've seen it before. A dramatic situation will do wonders to anyone unfortunate enough to find themselves victim to one."

"So, she's in shock?"

"That's one word for it," Murphy responded. "She's certainly a bit perturbed. But that's enough about her. When she's right, we'll get a better description of the intruder. For now, I want to move on to what we *can* do. So far, the boys only quickly swept through your home, making sure the intruder was gone. But I'd like them to do a more thorough sweep and look for any items that may be stolen or broken—*with your permission, of course.*"

Daray looked over to the police officers walking around his house looking for clues, footprints, or anything that might give the boys in blue a lead. He was fine with them staying outside, but Daray was a private man and resented the idea of letting a bunch of people he didn't or barely knew root through his personal belongings. Besides, how would they even know what was missing? Only the Horvacs could identify that.

"Officer, with respect, I think I'd prefer to do that part of the investigation myself if that's *okay*?"

Murphy was clearly confused. He was practically already giving commands for his men to enter. "I'd like a professional to do it, sir. It's your house, so you get the final say, but I think it would help us track down the person who did this if you let us run through it first. Won't take longer than an hour."

"I understand, officer. But I've made my decision, and I thank you very much for your help. I've had an exhausting day, so I'd like to turn in. I'll let you know if anything is missing or out of place."

There was an awkward hesitation between them, and the dragging seconds seemed to hold onto the night like static electricity. Then, after the pause, Murphy continued.

"Well, it's your house. You do what you think is best." His voice was clearly hinting disappointment, maybe a splash of frustration.

"Thank you, Murphy. I appreciate the understanding."

"I'll be in touch with more details about the case. For now, all I can suggest is to lock your doors and have a look for any belongings that might be missing. Give me a call should there be anything worth noting."

"Will do," Daray replied, nodding to the officer as a final closing remark to their brief conversation.

The two men split apart, Daray making his way toward his front door, Murphy recalling his officers into a small huddle, like a quarterback to the offensive line. Daray looked around to his neighbours, where he could see a few spying eyes peering through from behind half-drawn curtains. They must have known what was happening, probably interviewed by a few officers to see if they saw anything. Daray wondered how many neighbours the police had questioned already. It didn't matter—*their home was safe, and the intruder was gone.*

Daray also wondered how Janene would react. She was usually fairly calm and collected, but having a stranger break into their home might leave an uneasy taste in her mouth. There was no feeling more intrusive than having a stranger pry through their personal belongings. Of course, the only thing that mattered was that they were safe.

Amon was safe.

Janene was safe.

Stolen goods could be replaced, but people were of a unique mould. Especially his family. There was no one like them in the entire world. Very few could put up with his long hours alone in the basement, researching and studying what had never truly been understood before. They had made many sacrifices for him to get here today. He owed them the world, and now that his work was finally over, he hoped to spend a little more time with them and a little less time locked away in his basement. He would talk with Janene once she arrived. For now, he wanted to get inside quickly and make sure everything was in order.

Unfortunately, Daray only made it to about five yards away from his threshold when he felt a weak grip grasp his left shoulder. When he turned, he was surprised to see Debbie Oslo standing before him in the misty rain, a bandage wrapped around her head and a gleam in her eye like none he'd ever seen. Her skin looked almost pale white, and her face held a permanent state of shock, as if the intruder were still standing before her, ready to strike.

"Debbie..." Daray said, unable to stammer out any more words at the startled sight of his cleaning lady, who usually was such a gentle and caring person.

"Stay away," she muttered, as if there wasn't a hint of life left in her frazzled voice, her frightened eyes locked in on Daray's. "It waits. It waits. It waits!"

"I'm...sorry...?" Daray said, unsure how to respond, Debbie's grasp growing tighter and firmer around Daray's arm, her chewed nails nearly breaking the flesh.

"I saw her," she whispered in a droning voice as if she didn't want anyone else to hear. "With my own eyes, I saw her. Pure evil. I swear it to be true."

The lady standing in front of Daray barely resembled that of Debbie Oslo. She was usually so joyful, so welcoming. She was the kind of woman who would bake cookies for the local church or go out of her way to make a stranger feel welcome in her community. She wasn't rich, and she wasn't young, but she was undoubtedly an admirable lady, one Daray and Janene spoke highly of when recommending her services to other potential clientele. But there were no shades of Debbie Oslo behind the cold eyes of the lady standing before him, a bandage wrapped around her head, blood dripping from under the bind.

"Saw...who?" Daray said, doing his best not to flinch under Debbie's claw-like grasp

"The devil. A woman. *Rotting. Floating. Freezing. I swear it to be true.* Stay away!"

Daray flashed back to the night at his supervisor's home thirteen years ago.

He had witnessed evil before...

...stared it directly in the face...

...and it had been a woman.

But that was thirteen years ago, and he still wasn't sure exactly what he had seen that fateful night. Debbie had clearly banged her head, as shown by the Loonie-sized bump growing above her brow and the blood continuing to trickle. Daray didn't answer. He just watched as Debbie continued to murmur to herself, her eyes never locking from Daray's, the crazed look on her face only growing wilder under the tightening grasp of her boney fingers.

"*...I swear it. I swear it. I swear it. I swear it. I swear it. I swear it. I swear it. I swear it. I swear it. I swear it. I swear it. I swear it...*"

Her eyes began to drift from focus, looking directly through him as if he weren't even there—as if he was simply a figment of her disturbed imagination.

"Debbie?" he said, lifting her hand away from his arm before she punctured the skin with her nails.

There was no response.

Her droning whispers echo through him like jagged daggers.

"*...I swear it. I swear it. I swear it...*"

A paramedic rushed up behind her, grabbing her like he had just found a lost child in the depths of a busy shopping centre. "I'm so sorry about this. She's had quite a shock. Isn't quite herself."

"That's okay," Daray gulped. "I understand." Daray was more than happy to let the paramedic guide Debbie away.

He didn't know what she saw and didn't want to think about it. He hated seeing Debbie like that, but in a weird way was also thankful it was her that had been here rather than Janene or Amon.

He watched as the paramedic caressingly steered Debbie away from Daray and back toward the ambulance one baby-step at a time. She wasn't herself, Daray thought, watching her feebly make her way toward the EMS truck. It was strange to see her like this, a woman who typically carried herself like a proud oak, walking like a broken stump. Daray felt a headache slowly building up around his eye, the day clearly taking a toll on his mental state. The mind was designed only to withstand so much, whether it be positive or negative, and Daray had had an extreme taste of both throughout the day.

As Debbie disappeared into the ambulance, Daray turned away from the disturbed woman, making his way back home, away from the bright emergency lights and dwindling commotion. He hopped up his tiny threshold and stepped into the darkness of his home, closing his door on the world behind him, ready to face whatever '*evil*' it was that might be waiting for him in his home.

Of course, he didn't believe in such nonsense.

He knew there was nothing waiting for him in the shadows.

At least that's the lie he told himself.

And belief hardly cared for the truth when fear was involved.

5

Janene Horvac pulled into her driveway just as the last cop car pulled out. Amon sat in the passenger seat, staring at the Dodge Charger with red and blue lights and police emblems. The officers gave a light wave, then drove down the street and out of sight. Daray's car was parked alongside the curb, void of its driver. She had tried texting him a few times already, as well as an attempt at a call, but he didn't answer. He rarely answered his phone. Daray, as advanced as a scientist as he was, was *terrible* with technology, not because he didn't know how to use it, but because he was absent-minded half the time, thinking about his research, his projects, or whatever else distracted that overloaded brain of his. Daray was a busy man, self-inflicted, *perhaps*, but busy all the same.

Janene stopped in their driveway, pulling up the emergency brake and unsnapping her seatbelt, Amon doing the same. The windshield wipers halted, raindrops taking their place on the glass, distorting her view of their home. She could see that the living room lights were on, so Daray must have been inside. Irene told her that he'd be home, waiting for her when she arrived. She was a little frustrated that they had told her husband before her, but that feeling had almost completely evaporated, replaced with worry that someone had broken into their home.

Their safe space.

Their home.

Janene had moved in with Daray a little over twelve years ago, not long after they met. Daray had owned the home for some time beforehand and had been insistent on not leaving the place that, as he quoted, "had been the perfect place to conduct his research." She didn't really understand. She barely ever understood his work or why he was so infatuated with keeping it so private and isolated. They had many fights over the years over reasons related to his studies and the amount of time he spent researching alone late into the night. They never went on vacations, and he would spend countless hours locked away in his office, never speaking of the specificities of his studies. There was so much more to life than academics and theory, yet Daray seemed to have little interest in anything else.

But Janene still loved him.

A workaholic husband was far better than the previous headache she had been married to. Daray may have spent many long nights in the office, but at least he was never out until 2:00 am, coming home reeking of booze and perfume, blaming Janene for things she never did or never understood. Daray may not have been perfect, but at least he was there for them. He cared for Janene, he cared for Amon, and he provided for them as a husband should. *So what* if Daray missed a few of Amon's hockey games here and there? It was far better than finding him at the hospital after a drunk night of driving—car smashed, memory vacant. *So what* if they lived in a house far below what they could afford? It was far better than watching him gamble her paycheck away, putting two weeks' work on black, only to lose it on the first spin.

Daray wasn't perfect, but he was hers.

That was enough.

That was enough for Janene.

Janene shook the thought of her previous husband from her head, grabbing the car-door handle and making her way out into the cold. The night's air was splitting, a signal that the darkest nights of winter weren't too far off. It wouldn't be long before their yellow lawn was covered in a blanket of thick ice and snow, matching that of every other property across the country. *Oh, the joys of living in Canada.*

"Come on, Amon," she said to her son, who was still looking at his phone in the passenger seat. "Let's go find your father and figure out what's going on."

In the typical fashion of their thirteen-year-old, he didn't respond. He simply hopped out of the car, eyes glued to his cell phone, and made his way to their house alongside his mother. Janene could see the muddy footprints across their lawn left behind by the investigating officers, now starting to freeze as the temperature slowly dropped into the night. She certainly wasn't pleased with the sight of dozens of footprints scattered across her lawn, but then again, someone *did* break into their home. It was a small price to pay for safety and security.

Stepping in through the front door of their house, Janene had a quick look around the illuminated entranceway; no sign of her husband in sight. She smoothly slid off her coat, tossing it on one of the hooks below the oversized mirror, Amon doing the same.

"Daray?" she called out to the abyss that was their home. It seemed that every light in the house was on, both upstairs and downstairs, but no response was heard. Janene waited a few seconds, listening carefully, slightly nervous, slightly worried. There was nothing but the hum of the lights. It was an uneasy feeling, yet she couldn't pin down why. She knew her home was safe, yet, something felt off—like it had been tainted in some way—like it was no longer *her* home but a violation of what used to be hers.

"Daray?" she called out again, louder, dragging out the syllables of his name like a song. Again, there was no response.

"Want me to go find him?" Amon gestured, looking away from his cell phone as he sensed the worry in his mother's tone. He was a kind boy, sometimes distracted like his father, but an intelligent, compassionate teenager. And although he wouldn't like to admit it, he *was* sensitive. Maybe that's what lent a hand to compassion.

"No," Janene said firmly. "Why don't you stay with me, just until we know where your father is." A mother's instincts were strong, and she always knew what was best for her child. In this case, her instincts told her that her son should not leave her sight for no other reason than an uneasy feeling sitting in the depths of her heart. "Thanks, though," she said, forcing a transparent smile. "Why don't we go find him together?"

Amon nodded, following alongside Janene, his cell phone holstered in his pocket.

It only took a few seconds to clear the main level. Every light was on, but Daray was nowhere to be seen.

"Daray!" Janene shouted out again. This time, a response was given. Janene heard a bump echoing from the basement, like a door slamming shut.

"I swear to God if you're working…" Janene muttered under her breath, too quiet for Amon's receptive ears. "Daray?" she yelled out again, facing the stairs into the illuminated basement below.

"Yes dear, I'll be right there," her husband finally responded from out of sight, his voice carrying nearly inaudibly from what was surely his office.

Janene felt a soft sense of relief flow over her, nearly striking out the persistent uneasiness.

Nearly.

"What are you doing?" she hollered from the top of the stairs, Amon standing behind her.

There was a pause, and for a moment, she thought he didn't hear her, but after a few seconds, Daray shouted back, this time a little louder and less muffled. "I'm just...making sure everything is in order."

Janene could now hear her husband's footsteps echoing off the cold basement floor, followed by the gentle slam of his office door. Only a few more seconds passed before she saw his shadow appear at the bottom of the stairs before the solid silhouette of Daray himself, standing face-up at the base of the steps.

"Hi, honey. Sorry, I was distracted downstairs."

Typical, Janene thought to herself. "What were you doing?" she repeated herself as if she didn't believe him the first time.

Daray began climbing the stairs, still wearing his formal clothes from the presentation he had given a few hours ago. "Just making sure the intruder didn't take anything important."

"And did they?"

"Not that I could see. I checked the house from top to bottom, and from what I could tell, everything was as it should be. The office door was open, which is strange, but nothing was taken or touched. You should go through your belongings, nonetheless. It's possible I missed something. You too, Amon."

"Is she all right?" Janene said, referring to Debbie, a tone of worry hinting across her voice.

Daray paused a moment, not overly sure how to answer. "More or less," he said. "She's a little shaken up and has a bump on her head from falling. But other than that, I think she'll be fine. Debbie's a tough lady. Takes more than a little intruder to knock her off her feet." He didn't mention the state of her mind. Some things were best left unsaid.

Janene nodded. She didn't know Debbie personally, but from every short encounter she had with her, she always got the feeling that their cleaning lady was a strong, independent woman with a rough past. Janene had no idea if that was true, but that was the vibe she got, and her instincts were rarely wrong.

"What did the police have to say?"

"Not much," Daray responded. "They checked the place over and the surrounding areas, with plans on interviewing Debbie once she's feeling better." Daray also left out the part about not allowing them to investigate the house. He may have liked his privacy, but knew Janene might not see it that way. Again, some things are better left unsaid.

"Did they find any clues? Or figure out how the intruder broke in?"

"Not that I'm aware. They said they'd get back to me once they know more and that we should be safe."

"Should be?"

"We're safe."

Janene was wary. If they didn't know how they broke in, who was to stop them from breaking in again? From what she could see, there was no patrol car standing guard outside.

"Maybe we can give Daniel a call? See if there's anything else he can do for us?"

"We're fine, Janene. It was probably just some young gun looking for a few things to pawn off for a few bucks. Nothing more."

"I'd feel better if we at least..."

"We're fine," Daray responded more sternly than he intended. He lowered his temper a bit, taking a breath and trying not to start anything he didn't want to finish. "I'll put a baseball bat next to the bed just in case and check all the windows and doors before we sleep. Sound good?"

"Fine," Janene said, conceding to her husband, "I just want to feel safe in our own home."

"I know. We are safe. I promise," Daray said, unsure of his own words but speaking them nonetheless. "We're safe."

Janene heard the words, and although she had no reason to feel otherwise, every instinct in her soul told her otherwise. A gentle whisper echoed at the forefront of her mind, like a breeze before a hurricane that told her Daray was wrong, that they weren't safe, and that there was some unknown danger lurking in their home, a danger she couldn't pin down to anything but an uncomfortable feeling settling within. It's rare that humans truly listen to their instincts over the convenience of misinformation around them.

But no one could have guessed the truth.

No one would ever have imagined what truly awaited the Horvac family.

Only Daray, of course.

Daray knew.

He   just   chose   not   to   believe   it.

6

Janene had made the executive decision to order pizza that night. Originally, they were going to order dinner with a few couples they had invited over for an afterparty, along with enjoying some snacks and white wine Janene had tucked away in the fridge, but the break-in had toppled those plans. It was perhaps the one good outcome from someone breaking into your house. Janene was far beyond tired, as were Daray and Amon. After the endless chatter from Daray's big presentation, Janene would have been perfectly content never to see another face again. Even the weeks leading up to the big lecture had been busy. There had been a constant buzz around the house since the announcement that Daray would release his work to the public. It had been a long-awaited publication that had captured the eye of every scientist around the world, the public, the locals, the students, and everything in between. It was a topic no scientist had ever even come close to scraping the surface of—*nor dared to try*. The idea of quantitatively measuring the human soul was simply something that still held no scientific merit until tonight. And Janene's husband had worked tirelessly for many years to polish his work, to ensure there were no loopholes, loose ends, and no angle from which anyone could draw any doubt. It was a near-flawless and perfect analysis, precisely applying the scientific method, providing clear and concrete statistical evidence within the bounds of certain probability, all avenues of evidence pointing to the same, irrefutable conclusion.

So they say, anyway.

Janene was no scientist.

These are all the things that had been told to her over and over the past few weeks by the lucky few that had sneak peeks of Daray's work, or inside information straight from Daray himself.

Anyone that knew anything about Daray's line of work had talked about it like it was some kind of second coming of Christ, that it would revolutionize the way humankind looked at themselves when they woke up in the morning, and that it would send a ripple so large through the rigid pillars of science and religion that even they would crumble.

But again, Janene was no scientist.

Janene was a teacher, and she was good at it.

But she was also a wife.

Daray's wife.

And for the longest time, that seemed to be all she was in the eyes of all those around her. Every conversation she had in the past few days leading up to the conference had been the same, every conversation prefaced with, "*You must be so proud of your husband...*"

You must be so happy for him...

You're Daray's wife...

Daray's wife...

Daray's wife...

Daray's shadow....

Janene was *absolutely* proud of her husband. There was no doubt about that. He had done what no other person in history had been able to do, and he had done it all while helping support Amon and herself. Of course, that sort of dedication didn't come without a cost, a gentle toll on the family that she had gradually become numb to over time.

The long nights at the University...

The overnight sessions he spent downstairs in his office, locked away behind his computer...

All of Amon's practices, recitals, and other life events that he missed...

It was a perspective only *"Daray's wife"* could comprehend, but again, what was a missed soccer practice compared to proving the human soul to be quantitively real?

What was a half-empty bed compared to all the minds Daray's work would put to ease?

What was a forgotten, tinfoil-covered supper left in the fridge compared to research that would last for generations?

It had been an exhausting many years, *but they had made it.*

They had finally made it.

And Janene had looked forward to what was promised to follow. She looked forward to finally having Daray back in their lives, back in their regular daily routines.

They would go on vacations...maybe see Rome, or Greece, as she's always wanted.

They would have game nights, and maybe Daray would make supper now and then rather than ordering takeout on nights when Janene had been running behind at work.

They would go for treks through the forest—maybe finally hike Cape Split together.

They would finally be a family...

But of course, there was still a little further to go before they could ultimately have the family time Daray had promised them. There were many conferences to be had, video calls to be made, events to speak at, and magazines to talk with. The research had been completed, but there was still the exertion of sharing it with the world, and all the world would want to have their little sliver of Daray, questioning him, praising him, and even ridiculing him if they're with those religions nuts that would rather see the world stand still than witness any bit of progress within humanity.

Yes, the academic journey had yet to be completed. There were still going to be many instances of being called *"Daray's wife,"* and probably a few more missed practices along the line, but at least the end of the tunnel was within reach, rather than being a long road capped with unknown darkness.

The end was near.

And Janene was thankful for that.

Janene loved her husband, and the end was near.

"Janene?" a voice bounced around the back of Janene's mind as she drifted within her thoughts.

"Janene," it repeated as she snapped back to reality, realizing her husband had been calling her name, her thoughts momentarily clogging her perception.

"Yes, dear?" she said, forcing a smile as she sat in their family room, Amon sitting next to her, playing games on his Gameboy as usual.

"Where did you go?" Daray said. Janene had no idea how long he had been standing in the doorway. He had already switched over to his pyjamas as the hour grew late. Any plans for after-conference wine and Hors d'oeuvres among friends had been postponed, and Janene was more than thankful for that. It had been a long day, and it was simply nice to sit at home, even if an intruder had recently been within their walls, even if their space felt tainted and corrupted. It felt like there had...

"Janene?" Daray said again, a little louder, a little firmer.

"Sorry," she responded, forcing her thoughts onto more present things. "Just thinking about the intruder, that's all."

"It's okay," Daray responded, content with her answer. "The pizza will be here any minute. Could you listen for the door? I'm just going to run downstairs to double-check that everything is in order."

"Sure," Janene answered. "Are we paying cash or by card?"

"Cash. I left some on the table by the door." Daray gestured toward a small pile of tens and fives sitting on the table. It's funny, there had been an intruder in their house, but from what Janene could tell, not a single thing had been stolen. In fact, barely a drawer had been opened, their entire house as they had left it before making their way to the conference. You would think someone going through the trouble of breaking into their home with the intent to steal something would at least sift through all the drawers, looking for cash, jewelry, or anything else that could hold value at a pawn shop. But not a thing had been taken. Not even the obvious stuff, like her single pair of diamond earrings left on her dresser-top or the jar of toonies and loonies sitting on the kitchen counter, which must have held over $150 in value by now.

"Thanks," Janene said, sitting silently on the couch, wondering what Daray could possibly be checking out in his office this late at night after his big speech.

"Oh, and I thought about what you said," Daray continued. "I called Daniel, and they're going to put an extra cruiser on patrol around the neighbourhood all night, looking for anything suspicious."

"That's great news," she said earnestly. It was an uneasy feeling to have a stranger know break-into the house. It left behind a nasty, odourless scent everywhere you went, something one could only really understand if it happened to them.

"I'll be downstairs," Daray said, disappearing, his footsteps fading.

Janene looked over at Amon, sitting beside her on the couch, his face lit up with the bright light of his Gameboy, inches from his eyes. She didn't know if it was *actually* a

Gameboy, or something else entirely. Janene had no idea what the electronic gaming devices were called anymore. They were Gameboys in her day, so that's what she would always call them, regardless of the brand or make. Her son was deep into whatever game he was playing, not seeming bothered by tonight's events—*water off a duck's back*. His focus was entirely sunk into his videogame, looking the same as on any other typical night. Amon looked older and older every day, transitioning slowly into the teenager he was. Janene knew it wouldn't be long before he was gone, living in some distant town, always a phone call's distance away, visiting on long weekends and holidays a few times a year. There were only about five-or-so years left before he'd be flying the nest. If they were lucky, he would stay home and attend Acadia University, but it was still too early to tell what path he would travel. For now, all she could do was enjoy the time they had left, watching his hockey practices and games, enjoying their thirty-minute screen-free conversations at supper time. And it was important to her that Amon's father find the time to spend with their son. The research would always be there, but the time they had with Amon was waning. Time somehow seemed to march onward faster than ever before. It was a solemn and sobering thought that Janene did her best to push to the back of her mind.

"How are you doing, Amon?"

"Good," he answered with acute automation.

"Just good?" she pushed.

"Yup," he responded again, his eyes never leaving the screen.

"Can you put that down and talk to me for a second?" There was no response. Sometimes she wished she had never given that thing to him. He spent as much time behind the screen of that Gameboy as Daray did behind his laptop. *Maybe that's where he got it from.* "Amon…" she said sternly.

Amon tapped the screen, pausing his game and looking up at his mother. "What do you want to talk about?" he answered, a slight hint of sarcasm lingering in his voice. Janene was used to it. She had learned to brush it off like a bug on a windshield.

"I want to know your thoughts…about tonight…about the break-in."

"I don't have any," he replied, refusing to give a full or well-constructed answer.

"It doesn't bother you that someone broke into our home? Went through our stuff?"

"Should it?" he answered, his tone monotone and unamused of the conversation. "They didn't take anything, did they? No one besides Debbie got hurt, and father said she'd be okay."

"No," Janene answered. "But it could have been worse. Doesn't that bother you."

"But it wasn't worse," Amon retorted.

"Then why do you think they broke in?"

"I don't know. Maybe they saw Debbie and got scared before they took anything."

"Maybe…"

"Why do you think they broke in?" Amon cut in, the Gameboy resting next to him.

"Not sure," Janene answered. "Maybe they were mad about Daray's work. They did say the intruder had been in the basement. But maybe you're right as well. We won't know until they find them."

"*If* they find him," Amon snarkily corrected.

There was a long silence between them, Amon clearly wanting to return to his game but experienced enough to wait until given the green light from his mother. Janene wanted to push the conversation further. It was a rare moment that she had his full and undivided attention, and she didn't enjoy the idea of letting her thoughts retake control. They seemed to drift to darker subjects, the break-in leaving an uncomfortable feeling in her head. But a knock at the door had broken her train of thought, along with the conversation with her son. It wasn't a loud knock, no louder than one would expect, but it was still enough to stir a quiet gasp from Janene, her tense body startled at even the slightest unexplained noise right now. Of course, it only took a split-second of conscious reasoning for her to realize it was the Pizza Delivery driver waiting outside under the light of the streetlamps and absent moon.

"I got it," Janene said to Amon as she hopped up from the living room couch and grabbed the cash from the end table, Amon diving straight back into his game the second their conversation had ended. She looked out their peephole before opening the door to double-check it was indeed whom she expected on the other side. A teenager only a few years older than Amon waited in the rain, holding two square boxes, acne running across his entire face.

Janene opened the door, accepted the pizza, paid the young delivery boy along with a generous tip, and closed the door again, all within the short span of twenty seconds. She had no intention of conversing with a stranger, even if it was an awkward pizza delivery driver barely old enough to hop behind the wheel. Janene wanted to shut out the world. The day's commotion had been sufficient enough to last her a lifetime.

The pizza was good enough. It filled the void of her stomach, and the grease provided a necessary comfort, helping settle the anxious feeling that had grown within her grumbling stomach. Amon had taken a few slices to his room, shutting the door behind him for the night. Daray was still downstairs, and Janene knew better than to call down for him. He would be up when he was ready and didn't like to be disturbed when he was in his office. Daray was never mean or rude about being interrupted but had always been very adamant that he did not like to be distracted. So rather than bothering her husband, Janene texted him, knowing Daray would check his phone at his leisure and come upstairs when he was finished.

But Janene didn't enjoy being alone.

It was dark, and every tiny sound and creak the old house managed to stir up caused her trickling apprehension and unwarranted concern. It felt like every little thing was there to set her off—*her mental stability was wound tighter than a grandfather clock.*

She needed to relax, even if it meant forcing herself to do so. Simply scrolling on her phone wasn't enough. Every second article talked of war, crime, or something else negative about the world. It wasn't a good place to be to invoke calmness. She would have to do that herself, with her own means of doing so. And there was only one thing that could genuinely calm and relax Janene to the point where she might be able to sleep tonight.

And that thing was a nice, warm bubble bath.

Janene twisted the silver faucet counter-clockwise, cutting off the flow of water and watching the last few drops dribble into the warm-soapy bath below, the small jacuzzi tub filled to the brim. She dropped her hand in the water, swirling it around, letting the water's resistance squeeze between her opened fingers—*a bit warm, but near perfect*, she thought, as her clothes tumbled off her naked shoulders.

She looked at herself in the steamy mirror, the damp condensation blocking a clear view of her aging skin. Janene stood in the absolute silence of their upstairs bathroom, admiring herself with acute judgement, wondering where the last twenty years had slipped away and what the next twenty would do to her once-perfect skin. The steam on the mirror was a grace to her already wary mind.

Janene drew her locked gaze away from the mirror. *I'm beautiful as I am,* she told herself, unconvinced, turning her attention toward the bath. She dipped her toes in first, feeling the embracing warmth seep up her submerged leg and into the rest of her body. Already she could feel a sense of relaxation and familiarity kicking in. This is *my* home, she whispered silently, *and I am safe.*

She lowered her other foot in, letting the hot, steamy water slowly spread across her legs. Standing still a moment in the candle-lit aroma of their tiny bathroom, she closed her eyes, feeling the almost-still water swish around her polished toes, tired feet, and stiff bones. Then, as she slowly adjusted to the change in temperature, she calmly lowered herself, letting the water advance across her entire body, like sinking in a lull of welcoming quicksand.

First, her sore hips dropped below the surface, then her breasts, floating for a moment, then too, sinking from the cool air to the warm, soapy liquid. Then with a final grunt, her bum touched the ceramic basin, and she lowered her entire body into the suds, the tops of her shoulders barely skimming the surface.

Janene kept her eyes firmly closed, allowing the water to caress every inch of her skin. These precious moments of relaxation were *desperately* needed. Behind her, a single candle flickered, illuminating against the wavering dark as Janene soaked in silence. Somewhere outside, a neighbour's dog barked profusely, but she forced it from her mind. Nothing was going to ruin her precious minutes alone in the dark.

It was in these moments of absolute solitude that Janene could serenely think about whatever her mind decided was worth musing. Today—*for instance*—had been a great day if one ignored the break-in that capped it all off. Daray had finally released that which he had been working on for so long, another step closer to the Horvacs eventually becoming a functional family again. Janene got to watch a crowd of hundreds applaud her husband as he helplessly smiled on stage in front of the admiration of his peers and friends. Janene let her body sink further into the soapy suds, forcing images of the intruder from her mind, keeping her thoughts on more positive and meditative reflections. She had so much to be thankful for.

She worked a lovely job with amazing colleagues and outstanding students at the school.

She had a roof over her head and food in her belly.

Her son, Amon, was growing up to be a fantastic, thoughtful young man, and her husband was at the peak of his career, putting their shared last name at the forefront of science.

Janene was thankful.

Janene allowed her mind to fade, focusing solely on the warmth of the water, the gentle fizzing of soapy bubbles, the dancing flicker of the glowing candlelight, and the peacefulness of solitude within her private bathroom.

Seconds turned to minutes…

…ten minutes…

…twenty minutes…

…thirty minutes of blissful, uninterrupted isolation, her mind balancing on the edge of dreams, her headache nothing more than a fading memory.

Another few minutes passed before Janene opened her eyes to the dark, the radiance of the *sandalwood* candlelight flickering off the charcoal Merola tile, the alluring aroma encapsulating the entire bathroom. It was nice not to be disturbed. All Janene wanted after a busy day was peace, solitude, and relaxation. Daray was somewhere downstairs, most likely responding to emails or editing his presentation. Amon would also be in his usual spot, playing video games with his friends in his bedroom, enjoying his own relaxation from the hustle and bustle of publication day. They were a good family, typical in some ways, even if Daray was distracted most of the time. But even a family needed alone time. *Especially after a day like today.*

She wondered if the police would ever find the person who broke in. Debbie had seen them face-to-face, and that woman practically knew every single person in the town. If there was ever a person to have as an eyewitness, Janene was glad it was their contracted cleaner. She just hoped Debbie would be okay. Even a woman as strong-willed as Debbie Oslo must be disturbed after being attacked by a stranger, alone, unprovoked. Janene shook the image from her thoughts.

This was her time to relax, not to think or worry about such things.

She could figure out the details later.

For now, she just wanted to unwind.

Another ten minutes had passed, the candle still burning strong, Janene soaking like a raisin in warm waters, careful not to let her mind sink to unwanted places. The soap suds had almost all disappeared, her naked body distorted in the ripples of the bathwater as she swished her hand back and forth across the surface, extending her time in the tub as long as she could. The smell of sandalwood filled the humid air, seeping into her nose at the precise frequency of smell needed to let her mind drift aimlessly once again. She thought of her wedding day, just under twelve long years ago, Daray and Janene quickly hopping into the bonds of marriage after only fourteen months of knowing one another. It didn't matter how long they had been together. Janene knew he was the one, a far stretch from her previous mistakes. There was no more worrying about *'disappointing'* her partner or wondering where he was at 2:00 am, watching him stumble through the front door, having spent the day's pay on liquor and cigarettes. *Those days were long behind her.* Daray was a man of respect, of honour, and that was something Janene was more than happy to lunge herself into. *Sure,* he had his flaws. He spent countless unattended hours in his basement office, they never went on vacation, and whenever she brought up the idea of upgrading to a house or expanding their family, he would push the idea aside, stating that they were happy as they were, and needed not to search for greener grass.

This would frustrate her, *of course,* but in the end, she was content with their life as it was, the alternative being locked away with a boozer in an apartment a fifth the size, raising Amon to be another asshole just like so many before Daray.

Instead, Amon had a future.

He laughed.

He loved.

And more importantly, her son knew nothing of the hardships that could have been if she had stayed with her previous partner.

He was young now, perhaps still too young, but someday she'd sit him down and talk about the past, how things could have been, and how all it takes to enjoy your life is just a little bit of perspective. That conversation was over the head of a thirteen-year-old, and one that could wait a few more seasons.

Janene shook away the thoughts again from her mind. It was amazing how your memories could flow when left unattended, drifting like a log in the river, free to go in whatever direction the rapids wished. She hated that her mind sometimes chose to drift toward negative thoughts, but then again, she was always able to overcome them, something that took years of practice, meditation, therapy, and a great many bubble baths.

The water was begging to grow slightly cooler, and she knew her time in the tub was coming to an end. She was okay with that. Janene was growing tired, the events of the day a whirlwind of a ride, her mind ready to hit the hay. This day had held—*so far this year*—both the worst and best moments she could account for. *The worst* was an intruder thrusting themselves into their home. The *best* was seeing Daray finally share his remarkable discoveries with the world, cementing his place in scientific history and putting a cap on what had taken ninety percent of his attention these past years. It was a rollercoaster of a day, and in direct consequence, she found her mind racing from one thought to another, unable to pin one down with finality, always moving on to the subsequent reflection, then the next—*and the next. Maybe a little more meditation exercise is needed,* Janene thought to herself, recognizing the inability to control what should belong to her.

Maybe another day.

In a last-ditch effort, as a final part of her bathtub routine, taking a large breath, Janene slowly slipped deeper and deeper into the warm water, lowering her chin beneath the surface, then her nose, her eyes, and the rest of her head. Her naked body was warm, submerged, and utterly silent beneath the soapy water.

Her eyes remained closed as she let her body soak, as though she were adrift in the cosmos, lightyears away from all the memories that made her whole. She felt her arms floating in the saltless water, then sinking to the bottom as if an invisible force had pulled them under. She imagined what it would be like to stay like this forever. Not in a suicidal way, just...*peaceful*...without obstructive thoughts prying their way through unwanted memories. *Alone* and in complete solitude, Janene enjoyed her time below the water's surface, staying submerged for as long as she could hold her breath, her long greying hair wavering in the self-contained currents.

And it was peaceful. And it was solitude. And it was hers.

But all things good in this world, like all things evil, come to an end with intertwining balance. She felt it first—*the water*—slowly dropping in temperature at the touch of her skin, the gentle odour of rotten eggs drifting through the tub like toxic waste dumped into a still pond. Initially, Janene thought nothing of it, a simple trick of the mind, but then cold shifted to a freeze, the smell rapidly growing more rancid by the second. Then suddenly, as if a winter storm had overtaken the autumn warmth of her private bathroom, Janene felt the water's temperature profusely drop, a frigid and inexorable chill overtaking her body as if she were submerged in a frozen lake beneath the icy curtain of night. The feeling came so quickly, *so suddenly*, that all thoughts in her mind plummeted to a frosty halt...

...and the first thing Janene saw when she opened her eyes beneath the icy depths of the fetid water was a single pair of rotten black eyes glaring back at her from above the ripples—the rancid, decaying face of a disintegrating woman glaring down, her jaw broken and snapped, her face deplorable to ranges a human mind could barely comprehend. The near-frozen water gripped Janene's body like a vice, holding her below the surface as she struggled to escape, gasping for breath, fighting the hypothermic urge to black out under the gaze of rotten flesh. Janene screamed but produced no sound, her lungs filling with ice-numbing bathwater, overtaking her like a waterfall down her throat. She tried to yell for Daray, gulping in another swig of soapy, frigid water, then Amon's name, calling for her son beneath the icy surface in a final plea for help. It was no use. It was like something had seized her, pressing down on her chest, forcing her under as she desperately grasped for air.

Janene felt the water trickle into her lungs, her vision beginning to blacken and numb, her body engulfed in the tingly sensation of her nerves fighting to survive, barren black eyes glaring from above the ripples under the flicker of dying candlelight.

Janene screamed — but was heard by none...
Janene thrashed — but seemed to connect with nothing...
Janene panicked — but it would do her no good...

Then finally, with a violent act of hopeless defiance, Janene gripped her hands on the edge of the tub like a steel clamp and hauled herself from beneath the water, straining every muscle and every nerve as she desperately broke the tension of the surface, gasping for air as water and soap splashed across the Merola tiles. She coughed and spit, choked and breathed, but when her blurred vision finally rushed back into focus...*there was nothing...Janene was alone...the water was warm...*

The candle flickered vacant shadows across the darkened bathroom as she shook, naked and afraid, in the isolation of her private bathroom.

Janene had never felt so scared in her entire life.
Janene Horvac had never felt so forlorn.

7

Daray was alone, sitting in the quiet seclusion of his basement office.

Janene was just beginning to run the bathtub.

Amon was hanging out in his room, eating pizza, and playing online games with friends.

Both his family members left to their own devices, Daray two floors beneath them, thinking silently to himself.

If someone were to open Daray's office door, they would have seen him sitting in his leather chair staring blankly toward his bookshelf, his eyes seldom blinking, his body as rigid as stone. He was content to sit alone in his windowless room, his family otherwise preoccupied, not around to distract or disturb him, not that they would. Janene and Amon knew better than to bother Daray while he was in his office. Over the years, he had made it clear that he did not like to be disturbed. It was his one and only rule, never to be broken. If they wanted his attention, they could text him, but no one was allowed to open his office door. No one was allowed to come in and disrupt his process.

But Daray wasn't currently working.

He wasn't responding to emails.

He wasn't grading reports, editing his research, sorting through his papers, or doing anything remotely resembling what he'd typically be doing within the secluded confines of his tiny basement office. Daray was sitting in his black leather chair, blankly staring toward the bookshelf, whiskey glass in hand, letting his thoughts run wild across his mind. For about thirty minutes, Daray simply sat in the dark, sipping thirty-year-old malt whiskey, pondering the events of the day, his foot tapping silently on the hardwood floor.

On the wall, a single clock ticked onward.

Tic...

Toc...

His computer was off, and his emails were of no pressing concern to him.

Tic...

Toc...

His phone had been placed on silent, the countless texts and missed calls to congratulate his successful conference put on hold.

Tic...

Toc...

If someone had been there to ask Daray what it was that was consuming his thoughts, he would have told them some story about his research—*or that he was tired*—or that he was silently running through his presentation, taking mental notes, and considering how he could make it better.

But those would be white lies.

His research was of little importance to him right now, which, for those that knew Daray well, would be a shocking statement to make. Anyone that knew Daray could tell you that his research was the defining characteristic of his daily life.

When he was home, he'd be working in his study.

When he lay in bed, he'd be thinking about his day's work.

When he was at work, he'd be thinking about what proceeding steps he needed to perform when he got back home.

Tic...

Toc...

But right now, in the darkness of his solitary office, research rested far from his anxious mind.

Right now, only one image pressed its way to the forefront of his thoughts.

Right now, only one moment in his life seemed to stand out from the rest.

And that was what happened thirteen years ago, in the basement of his supervisor's home, a baby's shrieking cry echoing in the dark, the mangled corpse of Allan Springs laying on the floor, Daray's shuddering body staring mindlessly at the vile creature that had inflicted such suffering.

Tic...

Toc...

He remembered the rotting skin—her torn clothes barely covering the bits of skin that had begun peeling away...

Tic...

Toc...

...her jaw snapped and broken, dangling by the threadlike strands of muscle and skin that remained...

Tic...

Toc...

...her whole self seemingly levitating off the bloodied floor, her blackened feet plastered with dirt and muck...

Tic...

Toc...

It had been thirteen years since that fateful night, thirteen years since Daray's life had been changed forever. He had managed to put it behind him, burying those memories in the innermost chasms of his mind, tucking them away in the darkest corner he could find. It had been thirteen years, and despite his best efforts, there wasn't a single day where Daray hadn't thought about those horrors...about the two simple words the spectre had spoken to him before disappearing into thin air...

Tic...

Toc...

That creature had shown him the truth of the world, the veiled curtain behind which humankind was not meant to see. He had witnessed something no other had ever seen before, and he had taken advantage of that, despite years of sleepless nights, of waking up at night in a fit of sweat and screams, explaining to Janene that it was only a bad dream, rather than ever divulging the reality he had experienced.

She did not need to know of such things.

She did not need to know the demon of his past.

And for thirteen years, that demon had remained at bay, unstirred, unsullied, but never forgotten.

For thirteen years, Daray was able to conduct his research within the quiet confines of his office, never disturbed by what lurked beyond, never bothered by the creature that had left his supervisor mangled and dead, left behind as an unsolved mystery to the local police, and all those who investigated thereafter.

After thirteen years, Daray was only just beginning to accept that he may be in the clear, that his demon had been put to rest, and that he had nothing to worry about.

But he was wrong...

He was absolutely, definitively...wrong.

Tic...

Toc...

He had heard Debbie's description—Daray knew what she had experienced. He had listened to the words she had used to describe the supposed 'intruder' that had broken into their home and stolen nothing.

...rotting...

...floating...

...freezing...

Daray had used all these words himself, describing the demon of his past. He had experienced the mephitic odour of rotten eggs and sulphur haunting the air that had dropped several degrees within seconds. He had seen the peeling skin, the exposed skull, the filthy clothes, the cracked and dry toenails floating above the dust...

He had seen it all thirteen years ago...

Tic...

Toc...

Despite his best efforts, there was nothing Daray could do to erase those images from his mind. He could visualize the bones of his supervisor splitting and pushing their way out from under his skin—*Allan's head popping like an apple in a vice.*

Those were images one did not forget...

Those were images that never vanished...

And if what Debbie had seen was true, then his worst fears had been reimagined...*she was back.* If what Debbie saw was real, then Daray had much more to be worried about than the delivery of his speech and the approval of colleagues from around the world. If what Debbie saw was real, then Janene, Amon, and himself were in danger.

Real Danger.

Tic...

Toc...

But it wasn't that simple—*it never was.* Daray could not so easily abandon all that which he had earned and attained. He had just spent the last thirteen gruelling years working to achieve everything he had so recently accomplished. He had spent countless nights and endless days exploring that which had never been explored, studying that which had never been studied, and sharing that which had never been understood before.   Daray   had   given   up vacations...friendships...hobbies...game   nights...local shows...concerts...trivia nights...hot summer days...Christmas mornings...weddings...and countless other life events just for a *shot* at achieving greatness. He had given up thirteen years of his life simply for the chance to do what no other scientist had ever done in the history of humankind.

And he had done it.

The sacrifices he had made had finally paid off...

The long, lonely nights had not been for nothing...

The time Daray had spent away from his personal life had been entirely and utterly worth it...

Tic...

Toc...

He had uncovered what no other person or scientist had ever done...

He had witnessed what had never been seen...

He had gone further than any researcher or self-proclaimed guru had ever gone before...

Daray had uncovered the reality of the soul, revealing truths beyond the moments of life's inevitable passing. He was going to be named one of the most outstanding scientists of their generation, if not of all time. His name would be with the likes of Albert Einstein, Richard Feynman, Marie Curie, Charles Darwin, Galileo Galilei, Isaac Newton, and Rosalind Franklin.

His name would be one that would be remembered long past the veil of death, which he had partially and *not-so-coincidentally* opened to the world. The name 'Daray Horvac' would be written on the forefront of every textbook and manuscript for decades and centuries—all because he spent thirteen long years neglecting that which mattered to his own life, in sacrifice for what would matter to all those that came after.

Tic...

Toc...

Daray was not ready to flee from that reality so easily.

He was not ready to surrender what he had worked so tirelessly to attain.

And he was not ready to let a murderous creature decide the fate of his name.

So, *for now*, Daray decided within the secluded darkness of his office that his family would stay put. They did not need to know the demon of his past or what danger they may or may not be in. It was a risk Daray was willing to take and one he was sure they would understand, given the weight of his research and the impact it would have on the world, its religions, and its perspective on the question that had remained so elusive for endless generations. *What happens to us after we die?*

Tic…

Toc…

It had been thirteen years since that fateful night.

What were another few days…

What were another few weeks…

He didn't even know what that creature wanted…

They would be fine.

They *had* to be fine.

Daray's legacy depended on it.

The future of their family depended on it.

…Tic…

…Toc…

…Tic…

…Toc…

…Tic…

…Toc.

8

I t was almost *2:00 am* when Amon decided it was finally time to get ready for bed. His mother had gone straight to sleep after her bath, and Daray had slipped off to bed a few hours later. Amon had heard his father's footsteps creaking in the hallway just before midnight, the boards of the old home rarely silent under his father's heavy frame.

It was like clockwork.

Janene would always head to bed first—*alone*—leaving a few lights on in the hallway.

Then after an hour or so, Daray would make his way upstairs from his office, tip-toeing through the house and flicking off all the lights, doing his best not to wake Janene, regularly failing to do so in his late-hour trek to bed.

Then later—*usually much later*—Amon would finally drift away as well.

Tonight was no different.

Amon heard his father carefully creep through the hallway at about ten to midnight, the floorboards playing their usual song, the door of his parent's bedroom gently squeaking as it closed, the sounds of their old home audible through Amon's paper-thin walls.

There would often be countless nights when Amon would get home from school and never see his father. Amon spent most of his time in his bedroom, and Daray spent most of his time in the office, the two of them rarely crossing paths throughout their regular routines. The most common place they would spend time together was the kitchen, where Amon would often run into Daray, who would be grabbing his usual tinfoil-covered plate and a beer before making his way back to his basement office. Sometimes they would have family dinners under the stark command of Janene, but that was few and far between, less so more recently as publication day approached.

It had been the same for as long as he could remember, their family routine seldom changing over the years, everything nearly the same as the day he was born. If someone were outside looking in, they would never be able to tell the difference between an average family and the Horvacs. Daray got home from work just like every other father did. He provided a steady income for the family, supplying Amon with almost anything he asked for—*within reason*. He always had the most modern gaming console, brand-named clothes, full-course suppers, and most other things you'd expect the son of a university professor to have. And his mother was as *textbook* as they came. Daray was often busy, so Janene would cook most meals, take him to hockey in the winter and soccer in the summer, drive him to school if he missed the bus, take him to Jeremy's or Carl's place on weekends, and always make sure he had a packed lunch before heading off to school. Of course, that was what the outside world saw, and seldom did they have reason to look further than what was expected of a white-suburban family whose income was high above the salary threshold of some of his other friends and their families. Amon wasn't *stupid*. He understood that he was privileged and hated when some of his friends called him out on it. He hated that they assumed he had a *perfect* life, because only Amon knew how far from perfect it truly was.

Most of his friends had fathers that would cheer for them in the stands.

Amon didn't.

Most of his friends had parents that didn't argue or bicker every second day about the sharing of household responsibilities.

Amon didn't.

Most of his friends had been to places all over the globe.

Jeremy had been to Mexico.

Carl had been to Scotland.

Sarah had even been to South Africa.

But Amon hadn't been anywhere further than Toronto, and that was for a school-organized trip that included almost everyone he currently hung around with after school. He had no stories of fantastic beaches, historic castles, or diverse cultures. All his stories had already been experienced by all those around him.

And it's not that Amon wasn't grateful for his life.

He understood the harsh conditions some kids grew up in.

He'd heard stories of abusive fathers or absent mothers.

He knew there were kids who worked in sweatshops and barely made it beyond the age of twelve without holding a gun in their hands.

Amon wasn't naïve.

He was a smart kid, often the top in his class, constantly getting full marks on tests and assignments, always completing his homework on time and rarely missing any school days.

But how many Christmases had there been where Daray skipped out halfway through gift opening to make sure his numbers were up to date? How many gold, silver, and bronze medals had he told his father about after the fact, without his father being there to witness it in person? It had been years of this, and Amon was accustomed to it. He was numb to the fact that his father would instead put his research over his son.

Amon didn't hate him.

He understood why his father worked so hard. He knew the importance of his work, as Janene had explained to him many times before as means of justification for his long hours away from the family. *How could he hate his father?* His titanium work ethic was all Amon had ever known.

It's how he was raised.

But it was getting too late to think about such things. Amon was tired, and there was school in the morning. It had been a long day, and Amon was finally ready for bed. He rested his PlayStation controller on the desk beside him, flicked off the television, and quietly made his way to the bathroom to clean up. The hour was late, so Amon knew to be as quiet as a mouse, putting into practice the same late-night technique his father had unsuccessfully executed, tiptoeing down the hallway and stepping into the bathroom, softly closing the door behind him.

He brushed his teeth, splashed a little water on his face, put on some acne cream that his mother had gotten him to try and combat the impending puberty, and once all that was said and done, Amon finally made his way off to bed.

Amon's bedroom wasn't overly large. Their house was old and small, and despite his mother's best efforts to try and relocate them to a larger home, Daray had successfully deflected all his mother's attempts, the Horvac family staying put in the same home they had been in for Amon's entire life. His room matched the design and feel of the rest of their house. It was barely big enough to hold his double bed, computer chair, desk, and dresser. He also had a tiny closet that could fit about thirty hanging sweaters from side to side and some pull-out drawers built into the frame of his bed. Outside of those few spaces, there was very little square footage that Amon had to himself, but it was still his own space, and for that, he was thankful. He spent most of his time on the computer or PlayStation anyway. If he wasn't doing that, he was most likely scrolling on his iPhone in bed, watching late-night links and videos his friends sent him, or just mindlessly bouncing from one form of social media to the next.

The room was small, *but it was his.*

And that was enough for Amon.

It wasn't long after he hopped into bed before he felt his eyelids beginning to droop, his phone nearly falling on his face a few times. He looked at the clock in the top right corner of his phone. *2:23 am.* It was late, even for him, and he would have to get up in five hours to get ready for school. He knew he would be tired in class, but there were seldom days where he wasn't exhausted—tomorrow would be no different. So, on that note, Amon plugged in his phone, tucked himself comfortably into the blankets, and slowly drifted off to sleep…

…Amon had no idea where his consciousness ended, and his dreams began. They sort of just melted together, one jug spilling into the next. Tonight, his dreams were all over the place. Sometimes they would be long, drawn-out adventures with wild turns and impossible directions. But tonight, each dream dripped into the next as fast as one could blink…

…One moment, he was venturing through vast mountains, pursued by something through the winding woods, the night too dark for him to see what it was, Amon only knowing that he was being hunted and had to run…

…then he was in a hockey game, *only* his entire team hadn't shown up, and he was left to play all positions in the championship game by himself. His father was the coach, and his mother was the goaltender for the other team—not wearing a helmet and yelling at him to shoot the puck, but Amon not wanting to on account of his mother's missing head protection...

...then he was on a plane—only the plane wasn't in the sky, but treading across the vast ocean waves, skipping like a stone as Amon sat amongst strangers in a window seat, trying his best not to vomit...

...then he was at school...

...then he was at home...

...then he was back in the jungle, running once again from the darkness. He could hear something calling his name from somewhere in the forest, never revealing itself, always watching from under the concealed cover of thick woods. The voice had a deep grumble, sounding like something between a lion's roar and a man's conversation. It quietly called out his name, growing louder with each rumble..."*Amon, Amon, Amon*"...The forest around him seemed to grow thicker, his breath quick and shallow. There was something after him, but Amon's eyes couldn't cut through the shadow of darkness. The trees seemed to be closing in on him, all while in the background, a heavy grumble called for him from the deep—"*Amon, Amon, Amon*"—He was searching frantically, his eyes rapidly darting back and forth, the forest thickening all around Amon inch by inch, his body barely able to move as the trees and branches cut across his path, squeezing him tightly, holding him firm as the moonlight slowly ceased to exist...and somewhere nearby, a dark grumble called out his name...

..."*Amon, Amon, Amon,*" The voice was growing louder, the trees squeezing tighter...

..."*Amon, Amon, Amon,*" Something jumped from the brush, and the last thing Amon saw was a set of jaws crunching down on his skull through the thick of the vine...

...then he was awake.

Amon's eyes darted open, and he was back in his bedroom, lying in the center of his double bed, a thin dew of sweat covering his body, the blankets wrapped tightly around him as if he had coiled them while he slept. It took a minute for his heart to slow back to a healthy pace, his breathing following the same path. The stress of the dream slowly faded away, and Amon could ease his mind back to the land of the conscious, the memory of the deep grumble already dissolving from his thoughts.

He tossed the covers to his feet, allowing the cooler bedroom air to chill him down to a more comfortable temperature, the sweat on his body dripping away. He rolled to his side and stared up toward the only window in his room, the sun's light far from breaching the sanctity of night, the hum of the crickets remaining loud and harmonious. Flicking on his iPhone momentarily, he could see it was only half-past-four in the morning...he had only been asleep a couple of hours, even though it felt like he had been out for some time.

Amon waited until the entire dream had faded from his mind before trying to fall back to sleep, letting the deep grumble echoing in his mind slowly fade and dissolve from memory. He closed his eyes and tried to doze off...but sleep seemed more elusive than it had been only a couple of hours earlier.

He tossed...

He turned...

He wrapped himself tightly in the blankets, then after a few minutes, he tossed them to his feet once again, repeating several times as he tried to get comfortable, but no matter what Amon tried, he couldn't seem to slow down his mind to the point where sleep could arrive. He wasn't one to let a nightmare scare him, but the unwanted adrenaline seemed to have other plans for the night, and Amon couldn't fight that extra bit of energy away.

So, after a hesitant thought, Amon decided it might be best to try and walk off the overflowing energy by getting a glass of water from the kitchen. Whenever he couldn't sleep, he always found it helpful to do a *mini*-reset, as if he were going to bed all over again, rather than trying to fall back to sleep in the place where he had awoken. Amon hopped out of bed, his bare feet pressing against the cool hardwood floor, his head adjusting to suddenly being vertical. Then once the dreariness had passed, Amon made his way out of the bedroom, tip-toed across the hallway—careful to avoid the spots he knew were most likely to creak—and made his way downstairs to the kitchen.

He didn't notice that the basement light was on upon first passing. Amon walked by the basement stairs, oblivious to the dim shine that gloomed from below, and made his way to the cupboard, grabbing a small mug with the words 'Acadia Staff' painted on the side in blue and red font. He filled it up from the tap and took a swig of the water, feeling his dry throat thank him for the late night drink. It only took a few gulps, Amon downing the glass in its entirety, the remnants of his nightmare already fading away, his mind already starting to feel better.

His heart rate had dropped back to normal.
His breathing was as desired.

And he could feel the clutches of sleep beginning to trickle its way back in. The reset was working, and Amon was starting to feel tired again.

After one last quick swig of water, Amon placed the glass in the sink where his mom would find it in the morning and made his way back toward his bedroom. But the dim shine illuminating from the basement would not go unnoticed a second time. Amon stopped at the top of the basement stairs, staring down at the gentle glow as he rubbed his eyes to adjust. *It was strange for the light to be on,* he thought. *Was Daray still working?* He didn't think so, having heard his father go to bed around midnight. Daray seldom left the light on, always getting after Amon for forgetting to flick off the kitchen or bathroom lights when he went to bed late at night. But the past twenty-four hours were unlike any other, and it didn't seem unreasonable for Daray to forget something so small and unnoticeable. *Still,* Amon had just awoken from a nightmare, and earlier in the night, there had been a stranger within their home, so it also seemed reasonable for him to feel a little uneasy at the sight of something slightly off from the regular, even if it was something as simple as a light on in the basement.

Perhaps it was the nightmare…

Perhaps it was the grogginess…

Perhaps it was the recent break-in…

Or perhaps a mix of all three, but for whatever reason, the sight of the basement light glowing downstairs left an uneasy feeling deep within, even if it was only a very minuscule and unwarranted response to such a trivial and conventional mistake.

Everyone had asked him how he felt about an intruder breaking into their home…his mom…his dad…his friends…they all seemed to want to know how the break-in had impacted Amon. And he gave them the same exact answer every time. *"It doesn't bother me."* And it was the truth. He didn't know why, but it didn't feel like the home was 'tainted,' ' unsafe,' or any different than it had been before. They have had many strangers in their home over the years…cleaners, professors, students…and to Amon, the intruder seemed no different. It wasn't like he was still inside, hiding somewhere within their tiny house. The police had cleared their home, leaving no real cause for continued concern.

But for some reason, staring at the light in the basement, Amon felt a slightly apprehensive knot in his stomach. He knew it was irrational to feel that way, but he felt it anyway, the same way you feel uncomfortable standing on the balcony of a tall building. You knew you were safe, but you still felt slightly *on edge*.

The Police had cleared the entire house, right?
Of course they did.

Amon tried to shake those thoughts away. He knew there was nothing to be afraid of. He knew there was nothing down there, and he had gotten over his fear of the basement many years ago. That was a fear for children, not teenagers. He was old now, more mature, with little time for childish worries such as this. He could have left the light on, but that was something kid did, not adults—*so on that note*, Amon made the mature decision and made his way downstairs to turn off the light, just as his father had reminded him countless times.

Almost every stair creaked on the way down, but he was far enough away from his parents' room that they wouldn't hear. Their walls were thin, but they weren't *that* thin. As he reached the basement, he saw that one of the table lamps had been left on, not the overhead light, which would seem more reasonable for Daray to forget, not that Amon put any logic to that thought.

The thirteen-year-old Amon scanned the basement, and everything seemed to be in order, everything in its usual place as he had known it would be. Amon could see into every room from where he stood, the small basement not overly large or overwhelming in size. The bathroom was empty, the dim light of the night peeking through the tiny window near the ceiling. His father's oversized office door was closed shut, most likely locked as it always was, and the storeroom was as dark as a cave deep underground, not a speck of light peeking through. Apparently, Debbie had broken one of the bulbs in the storeroom, and the chain-pulled light fixture had not yet been replaced.

Yet—despite everything being in order—Amon's unwarranted anxiety remained as he stood alone in the basement, cool air pressing against his skin.

He didn't know if it was his fading nightmare, the intruder, or just the numbness left behind by lack of sleep, but for some reason, Amon couldn't shake that feeling that something was out of place. It wasn't overwhelming, and he didn't feel scared or frightened, just slightly off-kilter, as if he was operating at 98% rather than his full potential.

It's okay, he silently told himself.

It's just the exhaustion.

It doesn't bother me.

Turn off the light and go to bed.

Amon brushed his anxiety aside and made his way toward the lamp, reaching under the shade and twisting the knob, the basement turning pitch-black the second he switched it off. It took a moment for his eyes to adjust, Amon holding still until he could at least see where he was standing. The moon must have already set, because not a lick of light was sneaking in through the tiny basement window, Amon barely able to see the hand in front of his face.

He could feel his stomach tightening, the anxiety creeping back in, slowly crawling back to the forefront of his mind as his eyes did their best to adjust to the darkness surrounding him.

You're fine, Amon said as the silhouette of the room slowly drifted back into focus.

You're alone, and you're fine.

They cleared the house earlier.

It doesn't bother me.

"*It doesn't bother me,*" he accidentally whispered aloud to himself.

After a few more seconds, Amon could finally see where the basement ended and the stairs began. It was still difficult to see, but he knew the basement well enough to get around, and he wanted nothing more than to be out of the basement and back in the safety of his bed. He slowly made his way across the room, dodging the coffee table and armchair as he waded through the dark, and reaching the stairs. Amon turned to do one final scan around the basement, a final ease-of-mind check to make sure everything was as it should be, validating that his anxiety was truly unwarranted.

And it was.

He was fine.

It didn't bother him.

The bathroom was asleep, the living space was quiet, the office door was resting shut, and the storeroom was…

…Amon stared into the pitch-black storeroom from the bottom of the staircase, his motionless body facing the overwhelming darkness. He could see the frame of the door, but that was about it. The veil of night's shadow shrouded anything that rested beyond the threshold.

He had no reason to stare…

He had no reason to wait there as long as he did at the bottom of the stairs, gazing into their darkened storeroom—but he stared anyway—not letting it bother him—not letting the darkness claim victory over his unwarranted anxiety…

For what must have been fifteen long and drawn-out seconds, Amon waited in the basement, staring into the storeroom, not moving a muscle…not even drawing a breath…

…*he just waited*—*It didn't bother him*

...and waited—the police had cleared the house after the break-in...

...and waited—there's nothing staring at you from within the storeroom...

...there's nothing...

...nothing...

When Amon finally decided it was time to leave the seclusion of the basement, he did not walk up the stairs—*Amon sprinted.*

He sprinted as if something were behind him, pursuing him up the stairwell, always one step behind, chasing him from the dark.

Amon did not care that every step was twice as loud as it should have been, nor did he care about the heavy creaks of the old wooden staircase. He just wanted to be out of the basement and back in the snuggled comfort of his bed.

He wanted nothing more in this entire world than to be back in his room.

And he was willing to sprint up the stairs to get there.

Upon reaching the top of the stairs, he did not turn and take one final glimpse into the basement, for he feared what he might see, *not that there was anything to be seen.* It was just his mind playing tricks on him, after all.

Upon reaching his bedroom, he did not stop to take one final glance down the hallway. He slammed his door and tucked his body into the familiarity of his room.

Upon reaching his bed, he did not turn to look at the closed bedroom door. He tossed the covers over his head and planted his face directly into his sheets, forcing his eyes closed and praying sleep would return so he could escape the night.

Only one thought raced through his head before he finally dazed off to sleep upon the rising of the morning sun…only one thought that struggled with him as he did his best to fend off the nightmares and unwarranted anxieties…

It didn't bother him.

It didn't bother him.

It didn't bother him.

Amon didn't see the square photograph of a woman in a blue dress resting on his pillow.

He would not find the photograph until the knotted fear inside his stomach had run its course.

He would only find the photograph once the shadows of night had finally disappeared.

He would not find that photograph until morning's light had finally arrived.

·9

etting out of bed was a milestone for Janene that proved more complex today than most mornings. Sleep had barely arrived throughout the night. In fact, Janene wasn't overly sure if rest had come at all. She had spent most of the time laying on her back, staring at the ceiling, watching the shadows of the dawn slowly shift to daylight as her mind raced around in unplaceable circles.

The thought of the intruder kept her awake.

The creaks of the old house kept her awake.

Amon slamming his door around 4:30 am kept her awake.

And her anxiety-caused dream in the bathtub had kept her awake.

Everything seemed to be working against Janene—*but life goes on*—she had children to teach and classes to conduct.

Most mornings were the same. She'd hop out of bed, sludge her way to the bathroom, brush her teeth, comb her hair, dab a gentle amount of makeup on her slightly aged skin, toss on some school-appropriate clothes, and make her way downstairs to greet the coffee machine with a smile—but she would need more than one coffee to survive the day, most likely several if she planned on getting through it *alive*.

Glancing out the window, Janene could see the police cruiser resting on the curb, two cops inside, patrolling the area, making their presence known. She would have to thank Daniel for sending over the patrol or perhaps bring them some dessert or flowers as a token of her appreciation. They had known Daniel and his wife Irene for many years now, and Janene knew they would not think it necessary to give them any gifts, but it still seemed proper, given light of recent events.

Daray was already out of bed and down in his office. He had received a few dozen emails from the other side of the globe as he slept, and knowing that he was bound to get a few dozen more as the day went on, he thought he'd get a head start on responding to as many as he could. Janene had felt her husband toss and turn throughout the night as well, wondering if it was the intruder that disturbed his slumber, or the excitement of forthcoming attention from the scientific world that kept him up. Whatever it was, she never got the chance to ask. He was out of bed and downstairs before Janene even had the opportunity to get her housecoat on, barely speaking two sentences to each other before parting for the day.

Janene was okay with that; she wasn't sure if she could yet hold a conversation, the grogginess in her mind still lingering, the coffee not yet batting away the dark clouds. She popped a bagel in the toaster, then stood mindlessly for the next ninety seconds, gazing down at the bagel as it warmed, no thoughts crossing her mind, no plans unfolding for the day. Her mind was blank, her reflections locked within the ethereal abyss of the tranquil void.

Somewhere upstairs, Janene could hear the shower running, Amon likely up and about. She wondered how her son slept, knowing he was at least up early in the morning on account of his slamming door. The intruder didn't seem to bother him as it bothered her. She seemed to be the only one in the house that was even a little bit perturbed by the events of yesterday, which was one of the many thoughts that crossed her mind during the night as she stared up at the ceiling's shadows as if she were a character in Plato's *Allegory of the Cave*.

Janene hadn't even noticed that the bagel had popped, the loud release of the toaster a distant sound to her absent mind. Only when she looked down did she see that her breakfast was ready, not knowing how long it had been sitting there before she realized. She grabbed some strawberry cream cheese and slathered it as thickly as possible over the toasted cinnamon bagel. *It was going to be one of those days,* she thought to herself, slowly biting away at her half-hearted meal.

After another ten minutes, Amon finally made his appearance in the kitchen, wearing his usual blue jeans and baggy black sweater, his hood resting over his head, and his eyes locked on his phone. His breakfast of choice was a bowl of Honey-Oat Cheerios mixed with Almond Milk, along with a few slices of cheese and a small glass of orange juice. He sat silently at the kitchen table, Janene joining him in the early morning hours. Breakfast was one of the few times of day she could enjoy a few minutes alone with her son, without the hustle-bustle of the day or the hum of the television in the background. Every day she found it harder and harder to communicate with Amon. It wasn't that they didn't get along or that there was any resentment between them—*they actually had a lot in common.*

Their distaste for baseball…

Their love of limited-series HBO and Netflix specials…

Their constant loathing of the old house…

The constant seclusion away from Amon's father…

Amon and Janene had many similarities; she just found that as Amon got older, it became harder and harder to start conversations with him, more difficult to draw parallels and make her son laugh. But he was growing into a young man, and she knew this was the natural process of raising a son. This was the price a mother paid, a price she was slowly beginning to understand as her son grew more independent. She didn't loathe it or regret any of the space that had grown between them. She understood what it was to be a thirteen-year-old boy.

She had been young once, too, even if it seemed a lifetime ago. And there were still those moments between them that will be remembered, those one reflects upon when times seemed harsh or dull. She loved her son, and nothing in this entire world could ever change that. She loved Daray too, but each love was separate, and no love could match a mother's love for her son. That much she knew to be true. More than anything in this world, she knew that to be true.

Janene once read that other cultures had different words for love, and various meanings. The love one has for a son is different from that for a friend, a husband, a movie, or a pet. Love is a universal word, often thrown around too easily and freely. It made sense to break it into various subcategories, each form of love given its respective phrase or terminology. Of course, that was all Janene remembered, never having researched it further. It was a neat thought, and that was that.

"How did you sleep?" she asked her son, sitting across from her at the small round kitchen table.

"Good," he said, a lie, but a white lie. Amon had slept like garbage, tossing and turning for the remainder of the night, the deep grumble returning to call his name within the darkened forest of his dreams until his alarm had finally rescued him from his tilted slumber.

"I thought I heard you up in the night?" Janene pushed.

"Went to get a glass of water."

"Ah," she said, silence returning between them. The clock on the microwave read 7:46 am. She would have to leave soon. Classes began at 8:40 am sharp.

"Do you have any plans today?" she asked, looking to continue the conversation.

"I was planning on hanging out with Jeremy after school," he answered. "If that's alright?"

"I don't see why not," she replied. "Just don't stay out too late, and text me where you are if you can."

"I will, mom," he assured, sipping his orange juice as Janene did the same with her coffee, almost nearing the bottom, still desiring more.

"Mom…" Amon said, now looking up from his phone and making rare eye contact with Janene.

"Yes?"

"I wasn't going to mention…" Amon trailed off as if he were looking for words to speak.

"Mention what?" Janene asked.

"…well…"

Janene could tell that Amon was hesitant to speak, which meant that whatever he was planning on telling her bothered him to some degree. That much, a mother could tell.

"…It's probably nothing…" he continued, finally revealing his cards, "…but I found this on my blanket this morning. I must have missed it last night, but it was beside my pillow on the edge of my bed."

Amon reached down and pulled out a creased piece of paper from his pocket, handing it across the table to Janene. The paper was thick, more like cardboard than paper, the stiffness resembling a playing card. It only took Janene a moment to realize what she held in her hands.

It wasn't paper; it was a *photograph*—a polaroid, to be precise.

She unfolded the small square, revealing the image that hid inside. The photograph was faded and discoloured like it had been sitting under the weight of direct sunlight for several seasons, the once vibrant hues now washed and worn, and there were what looked to be tiny bits of mud and dirt splattered across the square image, the edges damaged by water, the photograph in dire condition. Janene had to focus her eyes to discern the picture; the details difficult to grasp with all the damage, but after a moment, she could make out the underlying features.

The photograph was of a younger woman wearing a long blue dress. She stood next to a swing set, holding the chain with her right hand, smiling brightly toward the camera. Her hair was black and long, clean, and well-maintained. It was hard to tell, but her eyes were blue and gorgeous, matching her well-fitted dress around her skinny body. *Although*, it wasn't skinny everywhere. Janene scraped away a bit of the mud with her fingernail, revealing an unmistakable bulge on her stomach, her dress wrapped tightly around her protruding belly. The woman in the photograph was pregnant. She looked about seven or eight months along, if not more, although it was difficult to discern with all the sunspots. The photograph had been taken on a day of overcast and clouds, and a thick forest lingered in the backdrop behind the pregnant woman in the blue dress. Whomever the woman was in the image—she looked happy and healthy, the person behind the camera likely a husband or friend, although that was just guesswork at this point.

Janene studied the image for a few more seconds, then flipped it around to the back side, where an equal amount of mud and dirt-stained the white cardboard-like material. She brushed it aside with her thumb, the initials 'M.M.' written on the bottom right-hand side in faded black ink. She flipped the small polaroid photo over a few more times, studying every detail, ensuring there was nothing that she missed. Then after a few more moments, she looked back to her son, puzzled and confused.

"This was in your room?" she asked first, not yet drawing any conclusions or connecting any dots.

"Yup," Amon answered. "On the edge of my sheets."

"Did someone give it to you at school or something?" Janene pressed.

"No one gave it to me. I just found it this morning," Amon repeated.

Janene looked at the woman in the photograph, her faded smile staring back toward her. She didn't recognize the woman nor knew what the initials 'M.M.' could be referring to—*although most likely a name of some sort.*

"Could it have fallen out of your bag?" Janene asked.

"I left my bag in the living room."

"Then where did it come from?" Janene pushed.

"I don't know," he answered truthfully. Janene knew Amon wasn't lying to her, he had no reason to be, and there was a slight hint of concern in his voice that, once again, a mother could always pick out. "It wasn't there yesterday morning."

Several theories bounced across Janene's mind, each without merit or logic, each thought simply spurring from nowhere as she stared down at the pregnant woman in the blue dress.

Someone must have slipped it into Amon's pocket...but who? He must have forgotten that someone gave it to him...but why? It must have been there for a while...but she had just cleaned his sheets the night prior?

None of her theories seemed to have any weight to them. She thought about who could have put it there, and the list of potential candidates was relatively short.

Daray never went into Amon's room. He sarcastically deemed it the 'Devil's Dumping Ground' due to the state of chaos Amon perpetually left it in.

Janene obviously hadn't left it there; she had never seen the photograph in her life.

Amon hadn't known about the photograph; otherwise, why would he bring it up now?

She considered it possible that one of Amon's friends had left it there, either unintentionally or as a prank, but they hadn't been over in a few days, and Amon would have noticed if it were there yesterday or any day prior.

None of those options seemed reasonable, leaving an uncomfortable notion that something unexplainable was left behind in her son's room. Now her mind drifted to the alternatives she didn't like, but as the old proverb says, when you have eliminated all which is impossible, then whatever remains, however improbable, must be the truth. That was a quote Janene had used annually in one of her English lessons at school, combing over the works of Arthur Conan Doyle, although she never expected to be applying it to her *own* mystery. *Sherlock would have figured this out in a manner of seconds...*

Janene began working on her *own* process of elimination, trimming the possibilities down to three potential options, however improbable, based on the information her groggy mind was able to process on a minuscule amount of sleep. Each option was undesirable—*yet*—they held enough merit that they remained potential candidates to explain the appearance of the mysterious photograph.

Option one—a police officer could have left it behind when conducting their initial search of the house after the intruder broke in. It seemed unlikely and very irresponsible if that were the case, but it wasn't out of the question. At the very least, it would be an easy lead to follow up on and one that would easily explain why a stranger was in her son's room.

Option two—Debbie Oslo could have left it behind when preparing the house for their cancelled afterparty following Daray's big reveal of his research. Debbie was one of the few people that would ever have reason to step into Amon's room, and although Amon had explicitly requested that Debbie not clean his space, she might have done so anyhow, being the ever-caring woman that she was.

Option three—the person who had broken into their home had left it behind. Janene detested this possibility. She hated the idea that a stranger had uninvitedly entered her son's room, sifting through his things, leaving behind his wretched stench, disturbing one of the few spaces Amon could call his own. *No*...this option was not a welcoming thought for Janene's early-morning mind, nor was it one she intended to share with her son. That space was his, and his alone, and she had no intention of disturbing the peace for Amon.

Three improbable options. Three avenues of research.

Janene never enjoyed leaving any stone unturned, and the idea of an unknown variable invading her own son's personal space made this stone even more unpleasant. If it had been her own space, she may have been able to brush it aside, tossing the photograph away and never looking back—but it wasn't her room...it was her *son's* room, and that was something she could not simply let slip to the shadows of her mind.

"Mom?" Amon asked, the gears of Janene's mind spinning rapidly. "Where do you think it came from?"

"I'm not sure," she answered, not revealing any ideas she was concocting. "But I'll have a little look around. I'm sure there's a perfectly reasonable explanation." That last statement was more for her ease of mind than her son's. Still, she could tell that the idea of something unknown making its way to his room the day after someone broke into their house also made Amon feel off-kilter, and that was enough to make Janene want to dig for the truth behind the photograph—*if not for her, then for her son.*

Maybe she was overthinking. It was just a photograph, after all. But then, why did she feel so unsettled? She wasn't sure and loathed that sensation, especially when her son was involved.

"Thanks, Mom," he answered, carrying over his dishes and dropping them into the metal sink with a gentle clank. "Ready to go?"

"Ready when you are," she said. Janene would drive Amon to school this morning. It wasn't far, but it was in the opposite direction of her own, and rush-hour traffic on the road to New Minas was killer this time of day, so it was worth leaving just a little earlier.

Janene didn't bother going downstairs to say goodbye to Daray. She knew he didn't like to be disturbed, *and frankly*, she didn't feel like it, so she sent a single text that read, 'We're off. Have a good day, dear. Don't forget about us when you're famous!'

Daray wouldn't read that for another hour or so. Janene knew that. She had grown accustomed to it. She also didn't mention that she'd be home a little later than usual. Once the school bell had rung, and classes were over, Janene planned on heading to Debbie's place to begin her investigation on the mysterious faded photograph. Today was going to be a long day.

Today was going to be a long day for *everyone*.

10

For the past several hours, Daray had been doing nothing but responding to emails, taking calls, and answering text messages. Ninety percent of every message he received, regardless of the medium, was overwhelmingly positive, all acting as a distraction on recent events, drawing his attention away from the darkness that gloomed at the back of his mind.

Hundreds of supporters were endlessly congratulating him on his mounting success, proving that his paper had reached the ears and eyes of almost everyone within the scientific community. It was even beginning to trickle into the hands of the public. However, it would be a little while before the average joe could understand the scientific nuances of his technical report.

Most branches of science and scientists could be broken up into two parts. There were those that studied theory, spending most of their time behind their computer, plugging in simulations based on previously understood and verified theories, searching for answers by simply using the power of their minds—*and perhaps a little computing power to boot.* Physicists would run extravagant Monte Carlo simulations, modelling everything from the interactions of particles to the bending of space and time. It took a specific type of person to fall into the realm of deep theory, as it could be a lonelier and more monotonous route, spending every waking hour running and re-running equations and testing hypotheses, knowing that they wouldn't be thoroughly tested or vetoed for years beyond publication, sometimes decades or even longer.

And that relates to the second branch of science, the experimental side. This branch focused more on theories that had already been published; the minds behind this branch of science focused on proving either correct or incorrect concepts within the bounds of statistical certainties rather than trying to come up with new theories of their own. Of course, Daray would be ostracized if he ever used the words *'prove'* or *'correct'* when referring to the verification of scientific theories. That's something most people never understood. Science was never about proving or disproving a hypothesis. It was about evaluating a theory to its absolute limits from every angle and vector it could be attacked from. It was about verifying with as much statistical certainty as possible the bounds in which a theory broke down and the limits in which a hypothesis could be extended. That's what experimental scientists did. They pushed theories to their absolute limits, bending and squeezing every ounce of information they could muster with each test, making sure there was no variable or uncertainty left unturned that couldn't be verified.

With Daray's work, though, his type of science didn't fall under either category. It fell in the middle, somewhere between theory and experimentation. His field was incredibly fresh, and Daray was sure that if his work expanded in the way he expected, he would indeed be considered the forefather of his branch of science, whatever they may call it in the future.

The study of the soul…

The study of the limits beyond human consciousness…

The study of what happens after we 'pass on…'

His branch of science was so new that there was no distinction between the sects of theory and experimentation. His branch of science was so small that they needed to go hand-in-hand, which made his work so exciting, so impressive, and so crucial for the growth of his field. There were undoubtedly already those that had studied these concepts in the past, but they had yet to achieve what Daray had been able to accomplish. None had ever broken the barriers as he had. He had laid the groundwork of theory, spending the first couple of years building up enough written documentation and calculable derivations before he was ready to move on to the testing phase. He then spent most of the past thirteen years experimenting and assessing his theory, unfolding it from whatever angle he could think of, evaluating the bounds of his equations and derivations, adjusting his calculations if the statistical bounds didn't line up, doing his best to avoid any biases or naïve perspectives. He then spent the final year making sure all of his work was air-tight, constantly and feverishly safeguarding that there was no reason to doubt his work and no reason ever to question any of the methods or techniques he had used to achieve his goal.

Of course, Daray could only put so much into his publications.

Some details were better left undisturbed, rather than putting a magnifying glass to each step along the way. He understood it wasn't the purest way to achieve results, but he was confident enough in his research that he knew there would be no reason to be concerned at the time of publication.

And publication day had most certainly arrived.

Here he was, sitting alone in his office as he had done so many times before, basking in the glory of thirteen years of hard work and sacrifices, watching the endless praise from known and unknown colleagues continually roll in.

His inbox had exceeded hundreds of emails.

His phone had constantly been ringing ever since waking up in the morning.

There was more praise than he could have ever envisioned, not that he thought his work wasn't important; he just lacked the imagination to visualize the level of admiration he had been receiving.

One German scientist had applauded his work, asking him to be the head speaker at a conference in Berlin a few months from now.

Another American mathematician had emailed him, telling him he was already sharing Daray's work amongst anyone willing to listen.

A Dutch biologist and old friend had messaged him, telling Daray he had never seen anything to the likes of his work before.

And an English physicist had sent a short email that read:

Dr. Daray Horvac,

The work you have so rigorously completed will prove unparallel to anything we are expected to witness within countless generations. Your research has inspired me, as I'm sure it has for thousands of others. I have no doubt there will be talks of a Nobel Prize in the years to come. You deserve every bit of praise that flies your way, and I'm sure there will be an ample amount.
Congratulations, and I look forward to seeing you at future conferences around the globe.

Sincerely,
Carl A. Loxley, Ph.D., Ph.D.

Daray had read that email a half-dozen times already. It almost didn't feel real, his name being mentioned in the same context as the Nobel Prize. He knew it was possible, but he had chalked it up to a pipe dream rather than a possible reality.

And he knew of Dr. Loxley. He was a well-respected physicist in the community, studying the intricacies of Dark Matter and Dark Energy, as well as taking a stab at Baryon Asymmetry on the side. For him to mention the possibility of a *Nobel Prize*— there was bound to be weight to that statement and perhaps some sway when it came down to choosing the laureates. Dr. Loxley would also know that there was no Nobel Prize for Daray's branch of research, but there was always the hope of it getting considered under the physiology & medicine category, *even if it was a fool's hope*. There was the far-fetched possibility that he could be considered for a *Nobel Peace Prize* if his research was used to help combat years of needless religious wars and philosophical squalls, not that Daray even wanted to think about that right now. That was a conversation for another day.

Of course, not every response had been positive. He had indeed gotten a few that slammed his research, telling him that he dabbled in things not meant to be explored by the realm of humankind. A few devout religious nuts had also weighed in on his study, one of them an archbishop from the U.S.A, telling Daray he had no business meddling with the providence of God. Daray pushed those comments aside. Anyone foolish enough to let God into the discussion of science rarely deserved a say. Some would disagree with him, but he had no patients for God. He had seen true evil, and God had not intervened. God had not explained the mysteries of what happened thirteen years ago. Only science could uncover those secrets— *That*, Daray knew with unwavering certainty. Daray brushed away anything negative that came his way. He would not let the likes of lesser men and women ruin such a long-awaited day. This was his day, and he would enjoy every last second of his colossal accomplishment.

There was *nothing* that could ruin his time in the spotlight.

Daray was so lost in the flood of positivity that he had forgotten entirely about yesterday's events, his supposed bright future the only concept within his tunnel-visioned mind. It was a mistake he would soon regret, but what was fate to get in the way of a man oblivious to his peril?

11

ebbie Oslo sat in the center of her living room, every
light on within her tiny one-bedroom apartment. An
old black-and-white western film was playing on the
television, but Debbie hardly noticed. The radio in the
background talked of sports and local news, but Debbie didn't
hear a word. Debbie hadn't moved since she was driven home
late last night by the police, the foolish and naïve officers. They
had been utterly oblivious to the truth she had warned them
about...about what she saw lingering in the dark of the Horvac
basement.

Debbie's phone had rung several times—clients and
missed appointments failing to get ahold of her. She didn't
care. Her job meant nothing to her now. Debbie hadn't moved
from her rocking chair since the moment she got home late at
night, nor did she ever release her grip on the family bible
resting firmly on her lap, the cover tattered and worn, the
pages heavily used and studied.

*Debbie Oslo's stomach growled, but she had no intention of
eating...*

*Debbie Oslo's bowels grumbled, but she would hold as long
as possible...*

*Debbie Oslo's scrambled mind raced and twisted from
within, but she had no intention of calling for help...*

Debbie also was afraid, for fear was all she knew...

She was afraid for the Horvacs...

She was afraid for Daray, for Amon, for Janene...

Debbie Oslo was simply afraid, and no one would
again recognize her for the sweet, commanding, considerate

woman she was. That woman died last night, replaced by the shell of dread she was now.

Debbie Oslo was afraid...
Debbie Oslo was afraid...

12

I t had been a long, crawling day at work for Janene Horvac. Every minute seemed twice as long as it should have been, each lesson dragging on longer than she had ever remembered. She had spent the day teaching her class lessons based on geography, maps, terrain, and how different cultures are affected by their surroundings around the world. She talked of how the Inuit people of Canada historically adapted to their surroundings and how that impacted the evolution of their day-to-day life, asking the students how their views may differ from ours, yet how each viewpoint can also co-exist alongside each other, exploring what complications may arise as each culture evolves together. It had been a long and in-depth discussion, asking her students to write several small essays on the subject to be handed in next week.

By the end of the day, Janene was long past tired, her four cups of coffee seemingly not doing the trick, her thoughts swollen with the image of the woman in the photograph found in Amon's room. She did her best to give herself some breaks throughout the day, asking the students to perform some self-readings and locking herself in her classroom at lunchtime to avoid the hustle and bustle in the overly narrow hallways. Janene knew if she had spent any time in the break room among her colleagues during lunch, she would have been hounded about the news of her husband's research, which was already spreading within their small town like wildfire, the impact of his work making its mark known amongst the locals, his research at the forefront of today's local newspaper—*not that many read the newspaper anymore.*

"You must be so proud of him," Rachel said when she walked past her in the hallway early this morning.

"He'll be famous soon," Cindy had told her when she went to refill her coffee cup during a short break between classes.

"You must be getting a lot of attention," Paula had asked as she watched the last of her students make their way to the busses.

Janene had been bombarded with countless questions throughout the day, and although she held no ill will toward her fellow teachers—all of them curious as to what the events of his publication would unfold—she had simply wished for an hour of peace, a moment where Janene could rest her head and be-gone with anything related to Daray or his research. For what seemed to be the entire year, she no longer seemed to be identified as Janene Horvac, but instead, 'Daray's wife,' *and she was not a fan of being referred to in such ways.* And most of the other teachers didn't even know about the last night's break-in. Her friend, Sheriff Daniel O'Connell, had kept everything hushed and silent even after Daray made an early exit from his conference and cancelled the afterparty. The other teachers kept asking about Daray's work, looking for details and the 10-second cliff notes on her husband's thirteen years of complex and time-consuming research.

But Janene was never spiteful.

She was undoubtedly proud of her husband's accomplishments, even if it meant she would be standing forever in his shadow. It was a harsh contrast, comparing the revolutionary work Daray had completed to the cultural lessons she had given her students. She knew her work was important, and that was enough for her. It just didn't seem to be enough for everyone else.

Janene was relieved when the final bell rang, marking the end of a long day of classes and lessons. Usually, Janene would have stayed behind, marking the daily quizzes she handed out to her students, scanning through any mounting homework or reports, and grading everything from grammar to logic, but Janene had other plans after the school bell. The quizzes and tests weren't going anywhere, and she had questions that needed answering.

She *needed* to know where the photograph of the pregnant lady in the blue dress had come from. So, *on that note,* Janene packed up her bag, slipped on her coat, and made her way out of the building, strategically taking the back exit to avoid any unwanted conversations with colleagues or students still lingering in the halls.

She was able to take a long, tranquil breath the moment her car door slammed as she rested her head against the headrest, taking a small moment to herself before heading out.

She had made it. She had survived a day of exhaustion and relentless questioning.

She idled in the parking lot a moment, enjoying her seclusion, enjoying her peaceful and rare alone time as the children slowly piled onto the busses at the front of the school.

It was only when Cindy Lawless appeared on the steps outside the school did Janene finally decided to shift the car into drive and make haste. Cindy was the kind of person that, if she saw Janene sitting in her car, would walk over to try and say goodbye, a simple *'goodbye'* transitioning into another ten minutes of fluffed conversation. Janene had no interest in gossiping about celebrities, her husband, or anything else for that matter. She just wanted to put this workday to rest, and with the gentle roll of her tires, she did, and she was off.

It was only just after *3:00 pm* by the time Janene had made it onto the main road, which was still early enough that traffic had not yet become bumper-to-bumper on the main drag between Wolfville and New Minas, between the University town and the shopping hub of the Nova Scotia Valley. Debbie didn't reside far away—nothing was *that* far in this tiny town. She lived in a small apartment building up the hill beyond Acadia University. Janene had gotten the address to her apartment from the yellow-pages application on her phone, truly showing her age by using such an app. It only took eleven minutes to get from the school to where Debbie lived, including a few red lights along the way. Janene had tried calling her a few times throughout the day but had never received an answer, all her calls going directly to voicemail.

Janene pulled into the parking lot of Debbie's apartment building, parked in the nearest non-handicapped spot by the main entrance, and turned her car off. Debbie's building was probably fifty or sixty years old by the looks of it. Janene hadn't lived in an apartment building for nearly thirteen years. Upon looking at Debbie's building, she was delighted to live where she did, even if it was only a tiny home relative to their take-home salaries.

The apartment's walls were concrete, the old-fashioned and callus style not getting any favours from the passing of time. Most of the balconies were small, barely large enough for two Adirondack chairs, a thin black railing the only thing between safety and falling, and from what Janene could tell, most of the windows were decorated with blankets or shower curtains rather than the usual drapes, one window even covered up by cardboard and duct tape. It was undoubtedly an older building for those less fortunate than herself, but a roof over one's head is better than sleeping in the rain, and for Debbie, she had called this place home for many years, and home was home, no matter where one lived, or in what condition.

Though Janene did not come here to judge. Janene came here for answers.

She took out the photograph from her pocket, unfolding the old polaroid square and glancing down at the image, the pregnant woman in the blue dress smiling back at her, sunspots and dried muck splattered across the picture. She hoped Debbie could explain the photo because she didn't like the idea of alternative explanations for the photograph's mysterious appearance.

Janene made her way to the front entrance, entering the first set of doors and searching for Debbie Oslo's name on the building's intercom system, needing only a second to find it on the directory console. Debbie Oslo's name was next to apartment number *0215*, the dashboard covered with a faint graffiti mark left behind long ago. Janene pressed the dirty silver button next to *0215*, the loud sound of a buzzer emanating from the speakers with a frizzled pop.

There was no answer. Janene waited a few more seconds, then tried again, the buzzer singing its loud song once again. *And again, there was no answer.*

Janene was worried that Debbie might be out at work or away from home at the very least. It seemed apparent, but Janene hadn't even considered the possibility that Debbie may still be working or that at *3:20 pm*, Debbie wouldn't even be home. *Of course she's at work,* Janene thought to herself, disheartened that she had driven all this way for nothing. *At least it would explain why she never answered her phone.* She tried the buzzer several times, but no responses were returned. Janene was about to leave, her visit a failure, when a young man no older than twenty exited the building, pushing the cracked glass door just far enough that Janene could grab it before it swung shut. Debbie wasn't answering the buzzer, but knocking on her door was at least worth a shot. *She had come this far.*

Janene made her way to the second level, navigating her way up the narrow stairwell—the tile on each stair cracked and faded, the railing not worth touching unless one wanted to go home with some virus. *For such a clean lady, she sure lived in a dirty building,* Janene thought to herself, following the signs toward unit *0215.*

Debbie's apartment had been at the very end of a dimly-lit hallway, a small decorative cross displayed on her door directly under the numbers indicating it was indeed her unit.

Upon a second's hesitation, Janene reached her hand and tapped lightly on the door.

Again, there was no answer.

But Janene could hear the loud hum of what sounded like a television echoing through the thin wooden door, the echoes of televised gunshots and screams vibrating through the wood loud enough for her to hear.

She knocked again, this time a little louder, with more intent. And this time, she got an answer, two simple words from what Janene immediately recognized as Debbie Oslo's voice.

"Be gone!"

"Debbie?" Janene answered, surprised at the tone of her cleaner's voice. "Debbie, may I come in? I need to speak with you."

"Be gone!" Debbie repeated back, her voice harsh, her words harsher still. It had utterly thrown Janene back. Debbie was undoubtedly upfront, but Janene had never known her to be rude or unpleasant. She was always a strong and independent woman, happy to go the extra mile in anything

she did—*as if Debbie had something to prove*—as if every little thing she did was a reflection upon herself.

"Debbie, please. It's me, Janene. Janene Horvac."

This time, there was no harsh response.

Janene could hear a gentle rustle from beyond the veil of the door decorated with a religious cross, the sound of footsteps approaching from the other side, followed by the clink of several locks and the turn of the round metal handle. The door opened a crack, and Debbie peeked through, her one-eye scanning up and down Janene's body as if she had never seen Janene in her entire life—as if she was a complete stranger rather than a long-time acquaintance.

"It's me, Janene," she repeated, the photograph held firmly in her hands.

Debbie didn't respond. She just stared through the crack of the door—*her one-eyed gaze locked upon Janene.*

"I wanted to see how you were doing," Janene lied, trying her best to break down whatever barriers stood between them, sensing something was wrong with Debbie Oslo.

"I'm fine. *Leave,*" Debbie said, finally breaking her silence, her voice cracked and low, her watching eye still locked upon Janene as if she were inspecting or scrutinizing her.

Janene couldn't tell.

Without warning, Debbie went to slam the door shut, but without hesitation or intent, Janene pressed her hand firmly against it, blocking the lock from latching. *This was unlike Janene,* but she needed answers and wasn't leaving until she got something out of this visit. She could tell Debbie didn't like that, their cleaning lady releasing a low grumble, like the pestered growl of a frustrated animal.

"Please," Janene asked, the desperation evident in her voice. "I won't be long. I promise. I found something in our house and just wanted to ask you about it. That's all; then I'll be on my way. *I swear.*"

Janene didn't know what was wrong with Debbie. She knew she had been shaken by yesterday's events but had clearly underestimated the extent to which Debbie had been disturbed. The lady was *not* herself. That much was clearly evident.

Debbie eased her strength against the hidden side of the door for a moment, her one eye connecting with Janene, possibly signalling that she was at least willing to listen to what Janene had to say. There was an awkward silence, the moment dragging on longer than Janene would have liked, a thin tension building between them like an invisible force. Janene was only able to see a narrow strip of light seeping across Debbie's worn face, the crack of the door only ajar an inch or so.

Debbie was the first to cut the silence, her voice hushed and crazed, absent any of the welcoming tones she usually held. "*You saw it?*" Debbie asked.

"Saw what?" Janene answered, unsure what it was she was asking.

"The Devil," Debbie returned as Janene began to feel increasingly uncomfortable by the second.

Every ounce of her soul told her to walk down that narrow hallway, hop in her car, drive home and never return. But again, Janene would only be leaving here with an answer to her question. The answers she sought were not only for her sake but for her son's, and that was enough for her to brush aside the distraught mannerisms of the disturbed woman before her.

"I saw this," Janene said, revealing the photograph to Debbie, elusively dodging any conversation about *the devil.*

"Amon found it on his bed. I need to know if you left it there last night before...*you know*...the intruder."

Debbie didn't answer.

Debbie stared at the photograph through the crack of her door, her one-eye wide, her breathing shallow and coarse, whispering silently to herself something Janene couldn't quite make out. Her words were quiet and repetitive, her lips moving ever-so-slightly, her eye never leaving the photograph as if she were studying it—as if she were investigating every square inch of the faded polaroid.

"Debbie...?" Janene said, the silence and tension rising again. Janene observed as the door gradually swung open, revealing a woman in a disastrous state. It became clear to Janene the dire circumstances that Debbie Oslo was in as she caught sight of her in full view.

...her face—worn and fatigued, as if she had been awake the entire night. A thin trickle of blood had dried on her forehead, the stitches ripped and torn as if she had scratched at them with her dirty fingernails.

...her clothes—they looked like her typical work clothes. *Had she never changed after yesterday? Surely her clothes had been soaked from the rain last night?*

...*her stench*—Janene could smell her the second Debbie opened the door, the heavy mildew-like stench rising from her unwashed body, the body odour resembling that of recent roadkill.

...and posture—hunched and feeble, as if she hadn't eaten or moved in hours, Debbie looking decades older than she truly was, her dingy hair appearing much greyer than usual.

Janene was appalled at the sight of Debbie, who was usually such a proud and well-manicured woman, one that would never let herself get to as she was, not even in the private comfort of her own home.

Whatever had happened to her in their basement, it had indeed done a number—Debbie no longer resembled the woman she was, but a pale shade of the woman that once was.

Janene listened as Debbie's maniacal whisper slowly began to crescendo, her voice a monotonous monologue to herself, her hands clinching an old leather bible to her chest as she spoke with zealotic intent. *"Put on the whole armour of God, that ye may be able to stand against the wiles of the devil..."* Debbie continued to talk manically, stepping slowly over the threshold toward Janene, pushing the boundaries of proximity typical in any normal conversation. But this was no ordinary conversation. Janene was unsure if Debbie even knew who she was—the lady who was usually so welcoming and happy appeared entirely lost, bordering delirium.

"...For we wrestle not against flesh and blood, but against principalities, against powers, against the rulers of the darkness of this world, against spiritual wickedness in high places..."
Debbie took another step forward, and Janene could smell her breath reeking in the air, a foul odour rising from the same sweaty cleaners' clothes she had worn the day before. Debbie continued to speak, not *to* Janene, but *through* her, a distraught expression of fear and exhaustion amplifying with each crazed sentence. *"...so the great dragon was cast out, that serpent of old, called the Devil and Satan, who deceives the whole world; he was cast to the earth, and his angels were cast out with him..."*

"Debbie?" Janene croaked out, stepping slowly back as Debbie advanced, the brown leather bible never leaving the clenches of her white-knuckled grasp.

"...be watchful. Your adversary, the devil, prowls around like a roaring lion, seeking someone to devour..."

Janene was not conversant enough in the ways of the bible to know which sections or verses Debbie spoke. Still, she did not doubt that it was indeed the Bible Debbie recited with insanity upon her lips, a fevered look upon her dark-circled eyes.

"Debbie, you're scaring me," Janene pleaded, backing up as far as she could, her back pressed firmly against the wall, the overhead lights dim and spent—Debbie creeping forward one distraught step at a time.

"...people will seek death and will not find it. They will long to die, but death will flee from them..."

Debbie was no longer recognizable from her usual self, the bible-reciting lunatic before her replacing the sweet lady entirely, only the shell of herself remaining in the wake of looming insanity. Her whispers slowly transitioned to staggering screams, wide eyes swaying side to side as if she barely knew where she was, her tongue waging back and forth as vile spit sprayed from behind yellowed teeth.

"...And this shall be the plague with which the Lord will strike all the peoples that wage war against Jerusalem: their flesh will rot while they are still standing on their feet, their eyes will rot in their sockets, and their tongues will rot in their mouths."

"I'm going to leave now..." Janene spoke, abandoning her mission to uncover the truth behind the photograph, which was still tightly grasped between her trembling fingers. "Sorry to have disturbed you." Anyone could have noticed her voice's insincerity, as Janene wanted nothing more than to be rid of this nightmare and out of this decrepit building.

Debbie reached out, dropping her leather bible to the floor, grasping onto Janene's jacket with both hands, holding her firmly to the wall, mindlessly hollering into her face as spit and phlegm spurted into Janene's face.

"...*give no opportunity to the devil... give no opportunity to the devil...*" Debbie began to repeat herself—over and over, Debbie Oslo muttered the same nonsensical words, her foul breath and fetid stench lingering in the dim, narrow hallway as she shook Janene with the strength of her haunted muscles.

"You're hurting me," Janene pleaded truthfully, Debbie's grimy nails pinching into her skin through the delicate fabric of her jacket.

"...*give no opportunity to the devil... give no opportunity to the devil...*" Debbie continued, no sense to her blathering tongue, the demented look in her eye never ceasing.

Finally, Janene was able to break free, twisting out of Debbie's clenching grasp, her shoulder accidentally connecting with Debbie's nose, forcing the lady back and allowing Janene to flee.

She never looked back, and she never slowed her pace. The second she was free, Janene briskly retreated down the hallway toward the stairwell, never turning to see Debbie standing manically in the hallway, trickles of blood dripping from her nostril, biblical phrases pouring from her unwanted and nonsensical sermon.

"...*Submit yourselves therefore to God. Resist the devil, and he will flee from you...*" Debbie's words bounced around the empty hallway, spinning in Janene's mind as she broke toward the stairwell, finally escaping Debbie's twisted vision. As Janene fled down the stairs into the main entrance, she heard the final words of insanity echo from behind, a final farewell from a woman Janene know-longer recognized and would never seek out again...

"...*This kind cannot be driven out by anything but prayer...*"

Then finally, with a distantly fervent scream...

"...*Pray Janene...pray...pray...or run.*"

13

araay had only left his office once throughout the day, and that was to get a slice of pizza left over from the night before. Other than that, the blooming scientist had spent the entire day behind his computer, answering emails, phone calls, texts, forums, and any other form of media where his name had popped up, and during this entire time, he held a metaphorical smile brimming from ear to ear, the overwhelmingly positive response to his years of work acting as justification enough for the hardships and long nights endured throughout the gruelling endeavour. *It was all worth it,* he told himself repeatedly, justifying every missed birthday, anniversary, homecoming, and all the other pleasures he denied himself—and by association, his family.

He leaned back in the comfort of his black leather chair, watching as additional emails continued to roll in, more and more doctors and scientists praising his work, a deep and fulfilled joy bubbling up inside him, every review positive, every comment a reflection of his granular attention to detail and commitment to science.

"It was all worth it," he would keep on telling himself, sitting alone in the basement of his house, his phone constantly vibrating on his desk.

But as the clock slowly crept passed *4:00 pm.* Daray decided it was finally time to take a short break from his computer. He had lost count of how many emails he had answered, but it must have been approaching nearly one hundred. His knuckles were starting to grow sore, and his vision felt like it was going cross-eyed. Daray was used to long hours in the office, but this constant stream of responses was starting to take its toll, *even for him*. Usually, he would sit back and allow himself time to think while his laptop ran extensive simulations, but today was an endless continuation of one digital exchange after the next, with little time in between to breathe or think. He *needed* a break. He had spent enough time in his office for now. Besides, Janene should be home soon, and he wanted to share all the good news with his wife.

He felt he had neglected her the past few months leading up to the final publication and grand reveal. Almost every night had been spent in the basement or at the university. Daray would have liked to take a vacation, considering he hadn't been on one in over thirteen years, but he also knew there would be no time for that any time soon. There were conferences to prepare for, lectures to conduct, and many other responsibilities that came with a publication such as this. That was the price to pay for becoming famous, he thought to himself, standing up from his chair, his shirt practically sticking to the black leather it had been pressed against for several hours.

"It was all worth it," he thought softly to himself.

As he walked toward his closed office door, he noticed a faint cloud from his breath appearing before him, disappearing quickly as it dispersed in the stale air. Daray had been so caught up in his work that he had hardly recognized how cold it was in the basement, his breath indicative of the dropping autumn temperature. He didn't remember seeing his breath earlier when answering emails, but then again, he was so focused on sounding sensible and knowledgeable that he wouldn't have noticed an elephant if it had been standing in the corner of the room. He walked over to the thermostat in his office and was surprised to see that it read 20 degrees Celcius. He turned it up a little higher before exiting his office, knowing he'd most likely be back in about an hour once he felt refreshed and ready to respond to the next batch of emails.

Daray thought about what he might do to relax as he exited the office, locking the door behind him in a typical fashion. He considered playing a little online chess on his phone, a favourite past-time of his, even if he only held a *1,300* ranking in blitz-chess, constantly getting beat by those that practiced and studied the openings, unlike himself. But then again, he had already experienced enough screen time today and figured it might do him a little good to stay off technology for a while. He also considered grabbing a shower but figured that might do him more good later on tonight as a way to close out the day right before bed. He also considered making supper, a surprise for Janene and Amon as a small token of his appreciation for their understanding these past few months, but then again, he was tired already, and the idea of slaving away in the kitchen didn't overly appeal to him at the moment. Daray could order the food instead, from somewhere like Joe's Restaurant or Paddy's Pub, and get it delivered. That would have the same impact and save him the time and embarrassment of trying to cook dinner himself. He craved something greasy, like potato skins or a burger that would fill him up on the spot, along with a side of some fries and gravy or a large plate of crispy onion rings. All that sounded delicious to him right now, and although they had ordered pizza only the day before, he didn't see why they couldn't order out again. It had been a long week for all of them, especially considering the unexpected intrusion last night, so he was sure Janene would be okay with not having to cook tonight as she typically would.

Daray slowly trudged out of the basement and toward the stairs, his stiff bones cracking and aching, the past thirteen years of sitting in an office chair doing no favours for his spine.

It was all worth it, he joked to himself, grabbing the railing and yanking his slightly overweight body up the steps.

It was only when he reached about halfway up the stairs did Daray first hear the soft whisper of his name gently caressing his ear, as if a soothing breeze had picked up from inside the house, carrying his name along with it.

"Darraaayyyy ..." murmured the breeze, Daray halting in his tracks on the stairs, silence returning within his empty home.

Daray felt his grip tighten on the railing, but after only a few moments of silence, he brushed off the invisible wind's whisper to his exhausted imagination. It had been a long day, after all, and he had read his name a thousand times across countless emails. It had been a many long weeks, and there was no reason to think....

"Darraaayyyy ..." the hallow waft repeated itself, not a lick of wind on his face, but the chilling voice arising all the same.

Images of thirteen years ago immediately popped into his mind, images of Allan dropping to the ground like a sack of eggshells—images of the demonic women floating inches above the ground in the forsaken basement.

He shook those images from his mind. There was no reason to think such thoughts. Such gruesome reflections would do him no good anymore. He closed his mind to the whispering wind, ignoring it as best he could, pretending it was a trick of his weary brain, praying it would simply go away and leave such a perfect day untainted.

It wouldn't...It would only get worse.

"Darraaayyyy ..." it muttered once more, now with the haunting voice of a woman, stretching across his house and mind, the unsolicited call of his name originating from

seemingly everywhere, the source of the whisper hidden within obscured shadows.

Despite his best efforts, he could not brush away the sound of the woman's chilling voice, her raspy tone bleeding from the walls, the ceiling, the stairs, and every other direction Daray thought to cower.

"*Darraaayyyy …*" The voice was callous, cold, and coarse, the thin tone of his name no longer able to be ignored. *Fate did not like to be ignored.*

"Go away!" Daray called out to the invisible force around him, the temperature within the stairwell growing noticeably colder with each passing second, the air in front of his nose swelling and swirling with each breath in a milky, vaporous cloud.

"*Darraaayyyy …*" the voice called out again, louder, no longer a whisper, echoing as if it had been spoken from behind him.

He spun around rapidly, the stairwell absent of anyone but himself. Whatever was calling his name remained hidden from sight, its cold presence the only hint that Daray was no longer alone.

"Go away," Daray shouted, his grip squeezing the railing like one might hold the handle of a winding roller coaster, his teeth beginning to chatter, his breath growing thicker and colder.

"*Darraaayyyy …*" repeated the relentlessly callous voice, calling out his name more and more frequently, louder with each passing phrase.

"*Darraaayyyy… Darraaayyyy … Darraaayyyy …*"

"I did what you asked!" Daray finally screamed, submitting to the voice wrapping around him like a snake. "I did…I did…I did…" If there were anyone there to see Daray's face, they would have seen nothing but fear and despair. He no

163

longer looked like the confident scientist one might see giving the speech of a century, but that of a little boy about to wet his bed at the sight of a *twisted boeman* lurking within the darkness of his bedroom closet.

"Please..." Daray pleaded to the shadows, no one around to witness his cries, no one around to witness his cowardice. "...I did what you asked...leave me be...leave me be..."

He struggled to speak, the air reflecting that of an artic frost rather than an autumn chill, fear choking his ability to form coherent sentences.

"*Please...Please...Please...*" Daray repeated, his parroted response all he could muster amongst his fear, the images of Allan firmly within his mind, as if he were laying in front of him—as if it had happened only moments ago, rather than thirteen years prior.

Then there was a pause. Shuttering silence.

Daray's sobs the only sound amongst the freezing cold.

Daray slowly gathered himself, his muscles tense as ice, his lungs absorbed by the everlasting chill that lingered around him. For a moment—and one cannot begin to fathom how short that moment was—but for a moment, Daray thought he might be in the clear, he thought he might be safe, he might be okay, that it was all a cruel trick originating from his mind...*but that moment fled faster than it had ever arrived.*

Three simple words broke the evocative silence as Daray stood alone within the stairwell of the only home he had known for a decade and a half...

...*Three simple words would make anyone in Daray's position shutter in the isolated darkness...*

...*Three simple words that would bounce around within Daray's petrified mind, as if those words now owned him, his thoughts no longer his own to enjoy, but the afterthought of the fear that consumed him...*

...Three drawn-out words were spoken with coarse ferocity from the invisible darkness that lurked around him, devouring the icy space in which Daray breathed...

"......Itttt......wassssn't......enoughhh......"

The precise second the last syllable had been so hauntedly spoken, a series of endless bangs and crashes exploded from somewhere upstairs. Large thuds and booms echoed across the entire house, the sound of shattered glass and ripping fabric all Daray could hear from his petrified stance on the stairs, a tinkle of piss leaking into his boxers as he hopelessly awaited the same fate as his supervisor. It sounded like an eruption had burst within the confines of his home, the debris and rubble blasting in all directions.

With all the strength he could muster, Daray forced himself up the remaining stairs toward the main level just as the final crash bellowed throughout the house, and although he missed the entirety of the chaotic commotion, he knew upon the sight of his living room, that the worst had only just begun...

...Every chair, sofa, and table had been crushed to bits, slivers of wood and metal scattered across the room...

...Every piece of fabric had been torn to pieces, ripped apart and shredded as threads of cloth and cotton danced around the room like ash...

...Every lamp, every bulb, every screen, and every vase had been bashed to bits, razorlike fragments of glass covering the floor in its entirety...

...Everything in the room had been entirely destroyed, as if a stampede had barged through their living room, leaving nothing untouched, a whirlwind of disaster forcing its way across the Horvac household.

...Everything had been completely and utterly demolished—everything but one, small, decorative mirror, left perfectly untouched on the wall as if a category five tornado hadn't just barged across their living room.

But there was a reason for that—an apparent, obvious reason left behind by the demonic creature that Daray had not seen for thirteen serene years—and that reason was left in the form of a single word, written in what appeared to be mud and dirt with jagged lettering across the entire four-foot by four-foot decorative mirror. Daray spoke the word aloud, his boxers damp, every muscle in his body shivering and trembling in the wake of the demon's relentless rage...

"...RELEASE..."

He knew what the word meant....
Daray knew precisely what it was referring to...
It meant the destruction of thirteen years of hard work...
The end of his chances at winning a Nobel Prize...
The end of his fandom and legacy...
The end of everything he had worked so hard to achieve...
The end of his life as he knew it...
It meant all the sacrifices were for nothing...
It meant Janene's sacrifices were for nothing...

He could not have that—it would destroy her—It would ruin them...it would tear their family to shreds...

As if right on cue, Daray looked through the front window, somehow still intact, and caught a glimpse of his wife slowly pulling into the driveway, her car quietly rolling to a stop just next to his own.

He had to act...he had to act now...or it would have all been for nothing...

Daray didn't think, nor did he consider how he would explain any of what had just happened. He could only try and hide the warning painted in mud that lingered on the decorative mirror. He only had a few seconds before she was inside, so he had to be quick.

Daray lunged over the broken furniture, not noticing that bits of glass forced their way into his sock feet, not concerned that a large sliver of what used to be a lightbulb had forced itself half an inch into his heel. Daray sprinted across the room, and with the force of his bare hand, he smashed the mirror with all his might, watching it shatter to pieces and fall to the floor, the mud-written message along with it. Then with haste, Daray grabbed as many pieces of glass as he could and rushed them to the garbage bin, forcing them to the bottom, tossing a few more bits of splintered wood and torn fabric atop the glass, hiding as much of the message as he could manage, covering up the demon's presence to the best of his ability within the timeframe he had.

His feet burned...his head throbbed...but he would not let thirteen years of work go to waste. He would not surrender everything he had only so recently achieved. *It had all been worth it.*

It   had   to   be   worth   it...

14

Janene had already hit her limit on what she could handle in a single week. In fact, she had already hit her limit on what she could handle in a single day. So, when she walked into her house and saw the unrelenting mayhem that had unfolded in her own living room, one could understand why she immediately burst into a fit of uncontrollable tears, screaming and crying without any restraint, holding nothing back and collapsing to the floor at the sight of her ruined home.

Daray had rushed over to her, holding her tightly, his bloodied feet and hands staining her jacket, which already had a few small rips from where Debbie had grabbed it when she held Janene against the wall less than sixty minutes prior.

Janene didn't speak. She didn't even try to draw words. She rested on her knees, sobbing beyond control, the weight of the past few days collapsing on her shoulders, pinning every emotion she had to the floor as Daray did his best to comfort his wreck of a wife.

She looked up at her home, shattered in its entirety, every little detail she had so meticulously put together battered and broken, every piece of IKEA furniture in shambles, every painting she had bought from local artists torn to shreds, every vase that had been handed down from her grandmother smashed and broken.

She wanted to ask why…

She wanted to ask how…

But all she could muster was her overwhelming cries, every thought blocked by tears and rage, every question clogged by sorrow and despair. Daray held her tight, stroking his fingers delicately through her fine hair, rubbing her back with small, soothing strokes. Then finally, once the tears had all been used up, and once the frog in her throat slowly began dissipating, Janene spoke all she could, her red, watery eyes staring into Daray's. "...How?" she asked, as that was all she could force from behind the brittle tremble of her lips.

There was a pause in Daray's response as he helped her to her feet. He wanted to find a place for her to sit, but there was nowhere, so he held her close, ensuring that she didn't stumble once again and was strong enough to stand on her own. Only after that did he finally respond, enough time having passed for him to calculate a believable answer.

"I saw him," he said firmly. "I didn't get a good look, but I saw him" Daray's voice was forcibly confident; his hands were bloody.

"Saw who? Who...did *this*..." Janene asked, her sentences beginning to finally take shape, the tears slowly dripping to an end across her cheek.

"The intruder," he said quickly, without hesitation.

"You were here?" Janene answered—the second question Daray needed to come up with a lie for.

"I..." Daray took a moment, Janene waiting for his answer. "I was in my office, but I had my headphones on. I didn't hear anything until the very end."

"In your office..." Janene responded, trailing off. *Of course, he was in his office. He was always in his fucking office.* She fought away the urge to fight. He wasn't responsible for the damage to their house, *even if he had been in the house the entire time.* He was *okay*, and that was all that mattered.

"I swear," Daray continued. "I heard a thump when I took my headphones off. He must have heard me coming upstairs because he fled just as I got to the living room. He took off out the back. I tried chasing after him, but my feet…"

Janene looked down in horror at the sight of his feet, visible tracks of blood pressed against the floorboards, shards of glass embedded through his punctured skin.

"Daray…" she said, once again unable to break words.

"I'm okay," he said. "It's not as bad as it looks. I promise," he lied again. He was *actually* in a lot of pain, but now was not the time to show any weakness. His story needed to be rock-solid. There was no room for mistakes. *It was all going to be worth it.*

"Who was he?" she asked, looking back up at her husband, the sight of his blood making her squeamish.

"I don't know. I didn't see his face," Daray answered, building upon his off-the-cuff explanation for the chaos within his home. He didn't care how much danger they were in. He would figure a way out of this. He would make sure Janene and Amon were safe, along with his legacy.

"Why would someone do this…" Janene continued, the sight of her living room too much to bear, the distress within her home too much to witness. "What did we do to deserve this?"

"*Nothing*," Daray responded quickly, "We did nothing wrong." *I did nothing wrong.*
"Just some maniac, that's all," Daray pulled out his cell phone from his pocket, slowly releasing Janene from his comforting hold now that she seemed stable enough to stand on her own. "I'm going to give Daniel a call, get him to pop in. Don't you worry. We'll get this all sorted out."

"What do I do?" Janene asked, her mind lost to the chaos of the scene before her. "How do we explain this to Amon?" she thought of her son coming home and seeing the wreck of their living room.

How could he ever feel safe here?

How could their son ever feel at peace in a place where things like this could happen?

"Amon's a strong-minded boy," Daray said honestly as he searched for their friend Daniel in his contacts and clicked the green call button.

Janene watched as Daray disappeared into the other room, trying to figure out what to do next, trying to pull together the shambled events of the past day.

Someone was tormenting them, breaking into their home, destroying everything for no reason...

The photograph's appearance remained a mystery...

Debbie had gone entirely insane...

Daray's work was blowing up at an international level...

And Janene was exhausted beyond belief, both mentally and physically...

Janene walked around the living room, keeping her shoes on as shards of glass, splinters of wood, and chunks of metal constantly crunched under her soles. Their couch had been split into a dozen pieces, the screen of their television was smashed and destroyed, their end tables looked as if an anvil had been dropped on them from the sky, and every single one of her plants had been ripped up and demolished, loose soil scattered across her floor. Janene bent down and picked up what had once been a family photo, the three of them smiling at the camera. Amon had only been about six years old in that picture. The frame had been broken, the glass missing, the photo ripped and torn, and Daray's head was absent from the photograph.

With each step across the room, the crunch of glass and personal belongings echoed beneath her feet. *How did Daray not hear any of this—even through his headphones?* It didn't make any sense, but neither did anything for the past twenty-four hours.

Janene's entire world seemed to have been flipped upside down from the moment Daray published that paper. Part of her wished he had never released that work, or at least had waited until after they had some time to relax, perhaps even a family vacation like he had promised. But the other parts of her told her that was selfish. Daray had worked hard. He deserved to share his efforts with the world. She just could never have imagined it would be this hard so soon.

These events must be connected.

Someone was furious about what he proposed in his publication, and this maniac was taking it out on Janene and Daray and Amon.

That was the only conclusion that made sense.

Everyone liked the Horvac family. Daray's students liked him. The parents of all Janene's students liked her, and Amon never had too much difficulty making friends at school or in sports. *Why else would someone target them if not for Daray's work? And who?*

Daray appeared again from around the corner, sliding his phone back into his pocket. "Daniel is on his way," he said. "Irene too. They're going to give us a hand."

"Can we start cleaning?" Janene asked, "Or are they going to...you know...investigate and stuff?"

"Not much need for investigation," Daray answered, looking around at the mess of their living room. "The guy was wearing gloves and carrying a crowbar, so there won't be any fingerprints."

"I thought you said you didn't get a good look at him?"

"I didn't see his face," Daray corrected. "But I saw at least that, not much else."

"And you didn't recognize who it was?" Janene asked.

"No. Not even a guess." Daray looked down at the blood oozing from his feet and the trail he was leaving behind as he walked around the floor. "I'm going to wash up and ensure this doesn't get infected. Why don't you find a place to rest? I'll help you clean this mess once I'm done."

"I want to start now," Janene answered. "I can't leave this place like this. What if Amon gets home? I don't want it to scare him."

"He'll be fine," Daray said.

"I want to start now," Janene said firmly, her words final.

"Okay...*Okay*...if it makes you feel better," Daray conceded, turning to go upstairs to the washroom. "I'll be down in a minute."

Once Daray closed the bathroom door, he nearly collapsed to the floor himself, his breathing immediately becoming shallow, as if a category-five panic attack had charged through the gates of his soul. He had done his best to hide his fear from Janene, hide the absolute terror that filled up inside of him, and hide the truth of what truly happened here tonight.

There was no intruder.

There was no manmade destruction as he would have led them to believe.

This was the work of something he had no explanation for, something much more powerful than what his research ever could have predicted.

And he was scared. Daray was nearly as frightened as he was that fateful night thirteen years ago in the basement of his supervisor's home. It was the type of terror one could only experience when tied to the tracks of a railroad, the rumble of an approaching train drawing near. Daray was scared, but he had to do everything he could to hide it from Janene and Daniel.

He would not let the creature win.

He could not.

This was his house, research, life, and legacy, and he would not let it be dismantled by any demon of this life or the next.

Daray switched on the tap, splashing warm water on his face, doing his best to shake away the tremble that remained deep within his core. He then placed his feet gently in the bathtub, rinsing them with the extendable shower head he had bought from IKEA several years ago. Each drop of water stung, a few tiny shards of glass popping out of his skin, several deep lacerations still oozing blood. On a typical day, he would have gone to the hospital for further inspection and cleaning, but there was no leaving the house—*not for this*. He couldn't leave Janene, Daniel or Irene here alone, not with that *thing* still lurking about, lingering in the shadows.

No.

He needed to be here to figure out a way through this.

He needed to protect Janene and Amon.

He needed to preserve his research.

He needed to safeguard his legacy.

It would all be worth it.

Janene had already cleaned up most of the glass by the time Daniel and Irene had arrived, two garbage bags already filled to the brim, a third one underway as she began to tackle the soil and smaller bits. She'd leave the heavy pieces to Daniel and Daray. The more significant bits could be tossed to the side of the curb to be dealt with later.

"My word..." Irene said immediately upon stepping into the Horvac household, hands covering her face and nose as if she were hiding a yawn while praying simultaneously.

"Jesus, Janene," Daniel said, continuing his wife's sentiment as he walked behind her, staring at the chaos. "Daray told me it was bad...*but this*...are you *okay*?"

"I'm fine," Janene responded. "Just a little shaken up." She swept up the soil that had once been potted under her English Ivy plant, gathered as many bits of dirt, roots, and other pieces of the plant as she could and tossed it into the trash bag with one heavy thud.

"Here, let me help," Irene said, grabbing a second broom that Janene had left lying against the demolished couch.

"Thank you," Janene said earnestly. "There are more garbage bags in the pantry. And leave your shoes on."

"Any idea who might have done this?" Daniel asked, pulling out his notepad and jotting down a few scribbles. "Anyone that has it out for you? Anything that I can go off would be helpful."

"That's just it," Janene said, taking a short pause from sweeping. "There's no one I can think of. I don't know anyone that hates us enough to do something like this?"

Daniel continued to jot down a few more notes, looking around the room with the eye of a detective rather than a friend. He knelt at the shattered couch, rubbing his hand along the fabric and frame, picking away a few pieces of splintered wood. He then made his way over to the television, observing the smashed-in screen and cracked plastic, writing down more notes on his pad. Janene watched as Daniel seemed to do this around every piece of wrecked furniture, pushing around pieces of fabric with his feet, poking and prodding at anything Janene or Irene had not yet cleaned up.

Irene proved immediately helpful, grabbing all the bits of cotton from the shredded couch pillows and stuffing them into the garbage bag, carefully and meticulously hunting down every piece of shattered glass between the cracks of her floorboards and sweeping them up into the bag. Janene was glad they were here. This was not a job that would be easy for just one person.

After about ten minutes, Daniel seemed to finish his initial observation, standing out of the chaotic mess and taking a few final pictures with his cell phone.

"Anything of note?" Janene asked, taking a small break and stretching her back, always watching where she stepped, careful not to press any remaining shards of glass into the hardwood floor with the soles of her shoes.

"It's strange," Daniel said, taking a few more pictures as he spoke. "Daray said he had a crowbar, but I don't see any indents or damage that would fit the description of someone swinging such a weapon." He pointed down toward the chesterfield, observing how the legs had been dismantled with force. "It's as if four large men yanked each leg of the couch in each direction—as if it had been pulled apart from either end. And the picture frames have no noticeable impact point, as if the glass shattered evenly, rather than from a single point of contact." He then walked over to the television, pointing at the screen. "See here," he said, calling Janene to come over and look. "If someone hit this with a crowbar, there would be an impact point, every crack travelling outward from where it was struck. But the screen is simply shattered, with an even distribution of cracks and holes throughout. *Seems odd.*"

"Maybe he just pushed it down," Janene said, picking the broom back up and cleaning.

"Maybe," Daniel said, scratching his head. "Anyway, let me give you a hand. Will Daray be down soon?"

"I'm on my way," Daray hollered from upstairs, the stairs creaking as he descended to the main level.

"Ah, there's the man of the hour. Good to see you." Daniel outstretched his arm as Daray entered the living, grabbing his friend's hand with a quick shake.

"Thanks for coming, Daniel," Daray said, releasing his grip and forcing a smile. "We appreciate it."

"You guys have been…" Daniel paused, looking for the appropriate word. "…busy," he said, failing to find the right one.

"That's one way of looking at it," Daray jested, looking down at the mess before them. "Before I start, I'm going to have a beer to calm the nerves. Does anyone want anything?"

"I'll take one," replied Daniel.

"I'm good," said Irene.

"I'll take a glass of water," Janene answered.

"Great, I'll be right back," Daray said, lightly limping off toward the kitchen, returning with two Alexander Keiths and a glass of filtered water. "Now…let's clean this mess up."

With the four of them picking away at the disaster within the Horvac living room, it only took about an hour and a half to be rid of the mess, leaving a near-empty room as a replacement for the once-furnished living space. Every couch, every chair, every plant, every electronic, and every decoration had been ripped apart or destroyed in one way or another, not a single thing left behind, not a single thing left intact. The echoes of their voices bounced around in the eerily empty room, all remnants of the bombshell that had exploded in their living room either sitting in one of the twelves garbage bags or resting out by the curb where Daray and Daniel had left it for heavy-garbage pick-up.

Janene scanned the room, wondering how they could start anew, wondering how any of this could have happened. There had been a patrol outside when the incident occurred, Daniel had told them, but they didn't see anyone fitting Daray's description exit or leave the premises. *They hadn't seen anyone at all.* Daniel had been furious at the officers, handing them an earful, questioning how they could be, as Daniel put it, *so incredibly stupid as to have let something like this happen.* Of course, Janene knew it wasn't the officer's fault. The perpetrator had gone through much trouble to inflict as much pain as he could on the Horvacs, and the officers outside only amounted to a few sets of eyes, leaving more blind spots than not where someone could easily break into their home. Janene thought she had left the back door unlocked, but apparently, it was open since there were no other signs of a break-in from what Daniel could tell. He had checked every window and every door, the back entrance the only possible point of entry where the police had no direct visual. The neighbours hadn't seen anyone either, a few of them not home at the time of the incident, and the rest were within their own homes, oblivious to the events happening in their neighbourhoods. It would have been easy enough for anyone to hop the fence in the backyard and creep in undetected, which was Daniel's running theory. There was only one home within the vicinity that had any cameras or security systems, but the lens of the security camera was blocked by the threshold of the owner's porch, not intended for anyone's home other than their own. With no security footage, witnesses, or leads, they were still miles away from catching whoever was causing the Horvac constant headaches.

Janene was just thankful no one was hurt. She was concerned for Daray and worried for herself, but most of all, she was afraid for Amon. Their son was only thirteen, and as tough as he acted, she was still worried about the toll it would have on him. No one ever prepared for such an incident, let alone a young teenager such as himself.

The four of them were sitting in the empty living room on some kitchen chairs they had dragged over, now some of the only pieces of furniture remaining in their living room. Daray was already on his fourth beer. Irene and Janene each shared a glass of white wine, and Daniel was still nursing his first Keith's, sweat stains covering his grey undershirt from all the heavy lifting.

"Thank you for all your help today," Janene said, finishing the last sip of wine, her head throbbing, her eyes exhausted.

"Of course," Irene answered, forcing a smile. Irene was one of Janene's closest friends, having met her through Daray many years ago. They had been through a lot together. She was there when her mother passed away, she was there for almost all of Amon's birthday parties, and she was always available to be counted on when it mattered most—*today included.* Janene was thankful to have Irene in her life. She was always a blessing, even on the darkest days. "You would do the same for us."

"Hopefully, this never happens to you," Janene spoke, her voice bouncing around in the vacant room.

"With all the guns I keep in my house," Daniel boasted loudly as if someone in the other room was listening, "They'd be stupid to try." He finished his last sip of beer, placing the glass gently on the floor next to his chair. "Have you ever considered getting your unrestricted or restricted licence?" he asked Daray, who was sucking back his fourth Keith's, preparing for another.

"Not one for guns," Daray answered. "Even now. Never liked the idea of having them in the house…" he pondered for a moment, then finished his thought, "...but I think I'm starting to see the appeal."

"If you ever want to hop in on a lesson or get registered, I can squeeze you in with some of the squad and get you on the fast track."

"Thanks, but no thanks," Daray answered his friend. "I'll keep a bat beside the bed, however. I don't need a gun."

That was a lie.

Daray actually owned a gun. He had bought one just under thirteen years ago to try and calm some unrelenting anxiety, knowing it would most likely be useless, but getting it all the same, feeling slightly better that he had a means of protection in his possession. But that was a secret best kept from anyone other than himself.

"Suit yourself," Daniel answered, standing up from the kitchen chair, releasing an extensive stretch as his arms reached up into the sky. "Well, Irene. Shall we get going?"

"I suppose so," she answered, then turned to Janene and Daray. "I'm so sorry for what happened. Things will be okay. You'll see."

"I certainly hope so," Janene answered, standing up as everyone did the same. "Thank you again for all your help. You have no idea how much we appreciate it."

"Anytime," Daniel answered, making his way toward the front door. "I'll make sure to get an official report to you right away so you can start making insurance claims. I'll also get my best boys on the case. I'm truly sorry the patrol let this happen."

"Don't be too hard on them," Daray responded, showing them to the door, relieved there were no more *incidents* while they were here. "It was my fault; I should have heard what was going on."

"It was no one's fault," Irene interjected, slowly following her husband toward the door. "I'm just glad you're both all right. Amon too."

"Yes, thank you," Janene answered. "He should be home shortly anyway. I texted him and told him what had happened. Jeremy's parents are going to drive him home tonight, so we don't have to go get him."

"Good, good," Daniel said, opening the front door. "Well, we best be off. Call me if you need anything else."

As the O'Connells left the Horvac household, Janene's mind finally clicked, baffled that she had forgotten to ask him after all this time, the events of the day indeed taking their toll, her exhausted mind struggling to put two-and-two together.

"Wait, before you go…" Janene reached into her pocket, pulling out the small polaroid photograph that had been sitting folded within her pants this entire time. She unfolded it, taking one last look before handing it over to Daniel. "…any chance you recognize who this is?"

Daniel took the photograph in his hand, but he did not have to look long before his face went white, a stern and intense look overtaking his usually welcoming and friendly expression. "Where did you get this?" His tone was serious, his eyes never breaking from the square polaroid in his grasp.

"I found it," Janene answered. "Well, Amon found it last night after the first break-in. It was lying on his bed. Why, who is it?"

Daniel didn't respond. He stared down at the photograph, squinting, wanting to be absolutely sure his identification of the woman in the blue dress was correct.

"Daniel?" Janene asked again, waiting on his response.

"Her name was Maria Mihailova," Daniel finally answered, pulling out his phone and taking a snapshot of the polaroid photograph. "I remember her quite well. I worked her case over a decade ago."

"Her case?" Janene asked, her heart rate elevating ever-so-slightly.

"I haven't thought about her in some time," Daniel answered, looking back up toward Janene and Daray. "And I've certainly never seen this photograph before."

"What happened to her?" Janene asked again, looking for more details.

"We don't know," Daniel answered truthfully. "She simply went missing, as if she vanished in thin air. There were no records of her leaving, no plane tickets, no CCTV footage, no witnesses, no clues in her apartment, *nothing*. I spent months on this case, every lead running cold, not that there were many."

"Who was she?" Janene asked, continuing her push for information, hoping there could be something that would connect with why it had been resting on her son's bed just after someone had broken into their home.

"She was an immigrant," Daniel answered, looking back down at the woman in the blue dress, the faded image something he had never laid eyes on during his months on the case. "She had escaped a tough situation in Syria, coming here on a visa, working as a secretary at the admissions office here at the University."

"And she just disappeared?"

"Poof," Daniel said, making a vanishing gesture with his left hand. "The case ran cold, and we had to move on."

"Any idea where that picture was taken?" Janene asked, hoping she could squeeze even the slightest bit more information from the photograph, having gotten farther than she ever could have expected when talking with Debbie in her state of raging insanity.

"I can't tell," Daniel replied.

"Let me see," Irene said, picking the image from his hand and studying each detail. "My word, she was pregnant..."

Daray's ears pricked up. He had been listening intently, upset with Janene that she had withheld the photograph from him, desperately wanting to get a good look at whom it was in the picture, waiting for his opportunity to snag the polaroid.

"Ah," Irene whispered to herself. "I think I know where this is."

"Where?" Janene and Daniel said simultaneously, Daray keeping his lips sealed, taking mental notes of everything they were saying.

"It's not far," Irene told them. "I'm surprised you didn't recognize the spot, Janene." She returned the photo to Janene, pointing to the rusted swing set that Maria Mihailova was holding onto. "That's the old swing at the children's park just up the road. We used to take Amon there when he was younger before they knocked it down for being too dangerous."

Janene scanned the picture, frustrated that she had not recognized it before. Irene was right. They used to take Amon there when he was just a little boy, taking turns pushing him on the swing as they gossiped, Amon always screaming to go higher and higher, the smile on that boy brighter than the sun.

"I remember that swing," Janene said, giving Irene a small smile of thanks. "I completely forgot about that."

"Interesting," Daniel said, taking out his notepad and scribblings a few minor comments to himself.

"What's interesting?" Janene asked, her mind spinning with information and details. She wanted nothing more than to go to the park to investigate, although it had already been such a long day, and the sun had already set long ago. She had no interest in going out alone at night, not with a maniac on the loose in their neighbourhood.

"Well," Daniel said, sliding his notepad back into his pocket. "If I remember correctly…that park was—or rather, *is*—right next door to the old Springs' household, isn't it?"

"Yes, you're right, dear," Irene confirmed.

Janene knew precisely who she was referring to. She knew it all too well, the story told to her many times by Daray. Allan Springs used to be Daray's old supervisor long before his research began on what he studied today. There had been what the townsfolk called a massacre. Allan was found mutilated and murdered in their basement. The murderer was never found—*another cold case, just like in the mystery of Maria Mihailova.*

"Why is that relevant?" Daray asked, taking the photo from Janene's hands, pausing a moment before looking down at it.

"Well, we know that Allan had taken on Maria as a client not long before she went missing and he was murdered." Daniel coughed, clearing his throat and continuing to speak. "We think he was helping her get through a few mental issues, but we were never really able to relate any of the details of his work to the disappearance of Maria. And of course, with Maria's disappearance happening at the same time as Allan's death, it made it very difficult to spread the manpower across both cases." Daniel paused, his voice sombre, reminiscing of cases gone cold. "Unfortunately we weren't able to solve either case. We got a lot of heat for that. Folks weren't happy."

"I wonder if it was all related?" Janene asked.

"It's very possible, and we certainly considered it," Daniel said, "But we never found anything else linking the events other than the fact that he had been acting as her therapist. Other than that one single connection, there was no concrete reason to think the cases were related—that is until you showed me that photograph just now. It would surely warrant further investigation if she were at the park next to Allan Springs' home right before her disappearance."

"Strange…" Daray said, finally looking down at the photograph, "Very strange…" He trailed off, doing his best not to hide his look of horror and disgust, trying his best not to reveal any cards in front of Janene, Irene, or Daniel.

It only took a single glance at the photo before his heart plummeted like a stone.

It only took a single look for his blood to run cold, the goosebumps on his skin peeking as if a winter's frost had raced through his veins.

He had seen the woman in the photograph before.

But not as she was when the photo was taken.

When he saw her, she wasn't smiling, happy, or even alive…

She was rotting, peeling, floating in the air as her icy stench filled the room, her skill exposed, her jaw hanging by the threads of her muscles and skin…

Daray had seen this woman before…thirteen years ago, in the basement of Allan and Erin Spring's home, something he had never shared with anyone to this day.

And he had heard the scaley whisper of her chilling voice only hours earlier, whispering the exact words he did not want to hear…

He had met Maria Mihailova before, but this photograph was the first time he had ever seen her alive…and he had a strong and adverse feeling that he would see her again…

…in a different form…

…rotting…

…decaying…

…dead.

15

I can't believe you didn't share this with me," Daray pronounced, his tone short and callous. Irene and Daniel had long gone home, and Amon had arrived home shortly after that, playing games in his room and ignoring the short-tempered fight nearing its end in the empty living room of the Horvac house.

"I don't understand why you're making such a big deal of this?" Janene stammered back, hours of fear and anger built up inside her, finally escaping through her lips. "We should be concentrating on how it got there…" Their words bounced around in their empty living room just as they would in a hallow dance studio.

"And how was I supposed to do that if I didn't even know about it?" Daray snorted, sipping his fifth or sixth beer, the alcohol proving a sufficient numbness to his lingering fear that remained deep within.

"I don't know if you noticed," Janene shot back, "But you're not exactly the easiest person to get a hold of these days."

"You could have texted me…"

"I did text you!" Janene exclaimed. "You never responded. And God knows you don't want to be disturbed when you're in your office."

That last statement drew silence, each of them taking a few long breaths, each of them a step beyond exhaustion. The fight had been going on for ten minutes now, and both of them were running out of steam and energy to continue their marital spat.

Janene was tired of this.

She was tired of being scared…

She was tired of feeling alone…

She was tired of being in the dark…

She was just tired.

And she didn't want to fight. They were supposed to be celebrating, cheering the end of a long thirteen years, the start of a new age for their family. But things rarely went as planned, and her life had been the farthest off the tracks it had been for a long, long while.

"So now what…" Daray asked, doing his best to sweep his frustration under the rug, the sight of the empty living room a constant reminder of what lurked in the shadows.

"I'm going to go to that park," Janene stammered, looking down at the photograph in her hand, the woman in the blue dress smiling back at her. "First thing tomorrow morning, before any of the boys in blue get there."

"And what is it you think you're going to find?" Daray said, with strong hints of sarcasm in his voice. "Do you think the intruder will just be there, waiting to be found or arrested? And on the off chance that picture was left behind for some ridiculous reason, do you *really* want to go there alone? Do you *really* want to face whoever is doing this to us…*alone*?"

"You're welcome to come with," Janene said, eyes never leaving the pregnant woman from the photograph.

"I…I can't," Daray said, searching for an excuse, not wanting to leave the house for any amount of time, not wanting any chance of something happening in his home where he didn't have some control. "I have…"

"…work to do?" Janene grunted back. "What could possibly be more important than this? What could possibly be more important than your own *fucking* family?"

"Why do you think I do what I do?" Daray retorted, referring to his long hours behind the desk, countless missed birthdays and anniversaries, and incessant nights spent at the lab studying and organizing his research. "If this research takes off and gets as much traction as they say it will, maybe you never have to work again. Maybe Amon is set for the rest of his days. Sure, the publication will make me nothing, but imagine if I wrote a book on it and sold it? We'd be set for life. *We...Us...our family...*That's what I do this for. That's why I make so many God-damn sacrifices."

Daray's words trickled off her like water over a duck's back, his statements as weightless as the single seed of a blooming daisy. Sure, Daray provided for her and Amon. He had always been generous with his money, as if that replaced all the moments he had been absent for the past thirteen years, but not for one second did Janene ever think that he was doing this research for anyone but himself. Their names would not be written down in the science textbooks. They might get a passing mention on his Wikipedia page, but that was it, not that Janene had any desire for fame or fortune. No, Daray had spent the last thirteen years in his lab trying to prove something, trying to prove that he could do what no one else had ever done, trying to prove that his name belonged amongst the great scientists of the past, trying to establish his legacy. Janene was okay with cooking suppers, taking Amon to practices, and doing everything Daray seldom missed, but she had no intention of dealing with any of his *bullshit*. Daray could miss as many significant occasions as he wanted, *but lying*—she would not tolerate it, *not for one moment*.

"You're not the one who sacrificed," Janene replied solemnly, sliding the faded polaroid into her pocket and making her way to the closet.

Daray tossed his beer to the ground, the bottle bouncing against the bare hardwood floors, the sound of glass against wood reverberating throughout the echo chamber that was their living room.

"And what the fuck does that mean?" Daray said, his mind fuzzy, his thoughts slowly bobbing back and forth in his mind, like the gentle sway of a metal canoe in the morning ocean tides.

"Whatever you want it to," Janene replied coldly. "I'm done."

"Where do you think you're going?" Daray asked as he watched his wife toss on his coat, marking her way to the front door.

"To the park," she said, turning her back to her husband.

"Are you nuts," Daray snarked, looking down at his watch. "It's quarter-passed-nine, and it's dark as hell. You won't find anything stumbling around in the dark."

"I'll take my chances," she said, making her way out into the cold air, more than happy to be anywhere but home right now. All day she had wanted nothing more than to be within the comfort of her own home, and now that she was there, she just wanted to be anywhere else. The presence of comfort and safety was no longer found within her own walls. Chaos and turmoil were now in their stead.

"Please, don't go," Daray called out...but Janene did not hear. If she had listened, she would have heard no anger or frustration in her husband's final statement. The drunken sarcasm had faded, the irritated tone no longer emerging from his lips.

They were replaced by fear...

They were replaced by anxiety...

It's not that he didn't want his wife to leave. He loved his wife, even if he was terrible at showing it.

It's not that Daray was mad at her for concealing the picture.

It's not even that he was frustrated with his wife in any way whatsoever.

Daray was afraid.

Daray was frightened.

Daray   just   didn't   want   to   be   left   alone.

16

Amon had been sitting on the edge of his bed, his door cracked slightly open, listening to his parents bicker and fight ever since he got home a few hours ago. He was used to them fighting, never aggressively or abusively, just verbally and constantly. He listened to Janene hop in her car and drive away, disappearing down the road and into the night. He listened to Daray slam the door once she left, standing by the front entrance for at least ten minutes before he picked up his glass bottle off the floor and tossed it into the recycling bin.

Amon had grown used to their bickering. Every year, there seemed to be just a little more, their arguments lasting longer, the silence between them longer still. They did their best to hide it from him, but thirteen-year-olds seldom miss much, their attention much more acute than what most parents gave them credit for.

He certainly understood that tensions were higher now, given everything going on. It had been startling, coming home to an empty living room and being told for the second time in two days that a stranger had come into their house and wreaked havoc in one way or another. It made him increasingly unsettled, knowing their family was being targeted. The first break-in felt random. The stranger could have broken into any of the homes in their neighbourhood, but it just so happened that the Horvac household was the unfortunate selection. But to see their home in absolute disarray for a second time…*that wasn't random*. That was targeted destruction.

Someone was targeting the Horvac family, and now his mom was out there, alone in the dark, a madman on the loose, the cops not having a single lead to work with.

Amon walked over to his blinds, peaking out toward the road where two police cars rested on the curb, each with sharp eyes intently watching every entrance of their house. That made Amon feel a bit safer, but someone had snuck in before, so who was to say they wouldn't do it again?

He didn't like thinking about it.

The thought of someone breaking into their home and hurting them seemed to run rampant within his racing mind, an apprehensive state of nervousness rushing through his bloodstream.

He hated feeling this way. Amon always prided himself on being tough and robust for his age. When his parents fought, he did his best not to let it bother him, burying the frustration and sadness deep within his body, not letting his emotions ever get the better of him. To Amon, showing one's emotions was to show weakness, and he hated feeling weak. He hated feeling inferior to anybody else. Maybe that was what it was to be thirteen. Perhaps he would grow out of it someday, but for now, he hated feeling lesser, in any way, mentally or otherwise.

He needed a distraction.

Amon needed to get his mind off the insanity that was taking over their lives.

The past twenty-four hours had been chaotic, everything falling into turmoil the moment his father decided to publish his research. The fighting, the long nights, the hushed mornings, the anarchy consuming the past few days—*his father's research always seemed to be at the heart of it all.*

Amon walked back over to his door, closed it shut and locked the deadbolt, one of the few pieces of security he had control over.

Yes, he needed a distraction.

Amon switched on his PlayStation and watched the television on his desk light up as he sat back in his green gaming chair in his tiny bedroom. There was one distraction that always brought him ease, that always seemed to make troubled days seem a little bit more swallowable, and that was video games.

So, on that note, Amon tossed on his Turtle-Beach headset, flicked the volume to full, and began to play, letting his mind sink as deeply into the first-person shooter as he could, ignoring everything else in his life to the best of his ability.

Time fixed all problems.

He just needed to let time pass.

And video games were the best way to watch the hours fly by.

Amon tuned out the rest of the world.

Amon tuned out his frustration, melancholy, and anxiety.

Amon buried the darkness deep within his mind.

17

The drive from Janene's home to the park wasn't far, less than half a kilometre, but it was long enough to cool her head and release a bit of the wrath that had built up deep within. She sat in the empty parking lot of the forgotten park, the darkness of the moon doing its best to shine through the thickening clouds, a thin drizzle obscuring the light's path.

She hated fighting with Daray.

She hated fighting at all.

Almost every argument could be avoided with clear and regular communication. That's what made every fight with her husband that much more frustrating. Their squabbles seemed to be a consistent and increasing problem over recent years because their most significant issue *was* communication. Daray was never around to discuss ideas or bounce thoughts off. Janene had become so accustomed to living independently that she rarely relied on Daray for anything related to her emotional or daily support. She loved him, but there was nothing worse than fighting over things that could easily be avoided, and their fights had undoubtedly taken their toll over the years.

Just a little longer, she had told herself in the months and weeks leading up to publication day.

Just a little longer, she had repeated to herself while sitting in the crowd during Daray's breakthrough presentation.

Just a little longer, she continued to reassure herself as she sat in her idling vehicle, her headlights shining toward the neglected park, the thick of the deep woods lurking in the background.

Just a little longer.

Janene nudged Daray from her thoughts for the time being, letting the task at hand distract her weary mind. The hour was late, and no one was around on this rainy evening. A light mist floated through the cool autumn air, sprinkles of water seeping down the windshield of her car as the wipers slowly batted them away. It had been a while, but she had been to this park many times over the years, taking Amon to play on the swings and letting him run off some of his endless energy when he was younger. She was surprised that she didn't recognize it right away upon seeing the polaroid photograph, but then again, it had been many years, and the park had changed quite a bit during that time.

The swings were removed years ago, the gravel beneath them long since overgrown by weeds and grass, the park signs graffitied or rusted, the old children's park lost to time—*though the park had not been abandoned without cause*. There was a reason nature had slowly taken back this tiny plot of land children used to run and laugh and play on, and that reason was what rested next door, what had happened thirteen years prior. *That reason was the former Springs household, resting adjacent to the park.* Janene could see the house from where she had parked, not a single light shining from the abandoned house, nor a hint of life to be found for the past decade. Thirteen years ago, the Springs used to call that house their own, and thirteen years ago, one of them had been massacred in the basement, the details left to the imagination of all those who pass by this dilapidated house at the end of the road. Few people ventured to the park after what had happened, not after poor Allan had been brutally murdered.

Janene stared blankly toward the deserted house, the home of Daray's old supervisor, the home that had barely had a single soul inside since that fateful day, except for perhaps a few daring teenagers or restless squatters. Almost a quarter of the roof's shingles had been lost to winds long past, the shutters were barely hanging on by rusty screws, and a small tree was even beginning to grow through the cracks of the rotten deck. The archway in the front entrance sagged downward, and a few of the windows had been smashed. The driveway was littered with cracks and weeds, and the lawn had been almost entirely taken back by the woods. The house slowly faded with time and age, as do all things. There had been a for-sale sign many years ago, but there weren't many people willing to move into a murder house, especially after the stories told by locals had spread to every ear within a hundred miles. There wasn't a household around that didn't know the story of the midnight massacre, of how Allan had been found butchered and mutilated in the basement, of how the cop who found him had to take months of leave upon finding his body, and how it took years of examination and investigation, only to come up with nothing.

No leads.

No arrests.

No suspects.

No fingerprints.

Nothing.

No one wanted to move into a slaughter home, the murderer still on the loose, the Springs house left to rot.

Janene was surprised they never knocked it down, but that cost money. It was far easier to let nature take it over, and it was cheaper to let time do its thing and wither the house away plank by plank, shingle by shingle, brick by brick. It was an eerie sight, the Springs household, sitting there almost as dark as night itself. But Janene wasn't here to recount the tale of Allan Springs. She was here to look for clues regarding the woman in the blue dress. She was here to try and uncover who had been terrorizing them the past few nights. She was here to finally put a rest to all the chaos that had been happening within their home, or at the very least, aid Daniel on his manhunt.

So, with that thought, Janene opened her car door, stepped out into the cool rain, and made her way toward the park, her car's headlights remaining on to light the path. The drizzle was refreshing, helping to combat her lingering exhaustion, helping to steer away any doubts or fears held within as she made her way into the forgotten park, *all alone*, the Springs' abandoned home watching her every step.

The terrain became rough the second she stepped off the pavement of the cracked parking lot. Long grass had overtaken the park, hiding stones, branches, holes, and other obstructions along the way to where the old swing set had once been. The trail that had once been here was long forgotten, nothing but weeds and brush left in its stead. Janene wasn't the best on her feet either, many years removed from her active days of youth, her fumbling feet doing her no favours as she nearly tripped several times as she pushed ahead.

"Christ," she cursed to only herself, nearly faceplanting into the grass, a branch jumping out and grabbing her ankle, nearly pulling her down to the dirt. She picked up the intrusive branch—the bark rotten and decayed—and tossed it to the side, clearing a path back toward the car just in case she needed to run.

She was cautious as she pressed onward, taking a few steps, scanning from side to side, looking for anything lurking in the shadows. *If the intruder did leave this photograph behind, then it must have been for a reason*, she thought, taking each step slowly and carefully through the overgrown grass. Janene knew it was a long shot to investigate the park. Still, she was at least happy to have some alone time, her mind slowly beginning to grow numb from the events of the day...*from*

Debbie...from Daray...from the intruder...it had all been too much...it had all been more than she was willing to handle...

Eyes up, she thought to herself, scanning the edge of the treeline beyond the park, following it all the way around to where the abandoned Springs house blocked her view. This part of the subdivision hadn't yet been developed, with nothing but trees and forest going on for miles beyond the neglected park. It was straining to spot anything in the dark, but from what she could tell, *she was alone* and hadn't yet decided if that was a *good* thing or a *bad* thing.

A good thing, she told herself, forcing away that eerie feeling rising up and into her spine back toward the depths of her soul.

You're fine, she whispered to herself again.

Janene pulled out the folded picture from her pocket, letting the car's headlights shine over the photograph of Maria in her blue dress, illuminating the image just enough for Janene to study where the woman had been standing all those years ago. Maria's hand had been resting on the slanted metal support pole of the old swing set, but the swings were long gone, removed by the municipality once rust and time had overtaken them. Fortunately, Janene had been here before, and she had a rough idea of where the swings used to be, having pushed Amon on them many times when he was only half her height. She paced out her steps, doing her best to position herself where Maria had been over thirteen years prior. It was difficult to tell in the dark, but after a couple of minutes of shuffling around, Janene thought she had found the right spot. She pushed some grass aside, locating an old concrete anchor left within the ground to which the swing's foundation used to be attached. There was a small metal circle remaining, filled with grass and mud, the rusted edge of the protruding metal sharp to the touch as if it had been lazily sliced by a metal-cutting saw. That was all the confirmation Janene needed to know that she was in the correct location. She turned and faced the forest, holding up the photograph to compare the treeline between today's reality and the reality of yesteryear.

The trees had grown so much in the past thirteen years that it was impossible to draw comparisons. However, it looked like at least a few older trees still resembling what they had been many years ago, the younger ones now taller and thicker, the eldest ones either fallen or long since rotted away.

What are you looking for, Janene? She whispered silently to herself.

What is it you're hoping to find…

Janene lowered the photograph back down to her side, scanning the area, slowly circling the park as if something were waiting for her—as if there were a single clue she was missing or some angle she could not yet see. She had absolutely no reason to think anything was waiting for her in the abandoned park, nothing but a lingering intuition that there was a missing puzzle piece, something that could explain who had been behind the intrusions, something to give a reason as to why someone would trash their living room without leaving so much as a note or trace of evidence behind.

A twig snapped, and Janene's eyes darted to the hidden darkness of the woods, scanning the treeline once again, the drizzle dripping from her lengthy hair, the rain slowly building in the thickening sky.

It was nothing, she told herself, releasing her gaze from the trees.

She could feel herself on edge, every natural noise amplified by her anxiety, alone in the park next to the house where the infamous midnight massacre had occurred.

You're fine, she whispered, the heavy beams of her lights from her car glaring into her face, her body casting scattered shadows on the trees behind her.

You're just fine.

She stood there for several minutes, examining the grounds, pushing away the grass, desperately hoping something would reveal itself in the night to give meaning to all that had happened to them.

But there was nothing.

Was there ever anything in the first place?

Janene was beginning to doubt there ever was.

It was a long shot, she woefully whispered to herself, holding her face to the sky, letting the soothing rain dance on her cool and tired skin.

Disappointment began to seep into her heart. She had *truly* hoped to find something in the park, *anything*, anything at all...but alas, there was nothing to be found amongst the overgrown grass and forgotten wilderness. Janene was confident she was in the right place, but her reasons for going there began to waver.

*Perhaps the photograph has nothing to do with this...*she thought to herself, holding up the polaroid of pregnant Maria in her blue dress, smiling toward the camera as if she wasn't about to go missing shortly after that mysterious photo was taken.

*Perhaps it was a fluke that the photograph ended up in Amon's room...*Janene pondered, her mind searching for reasons to support her doubt and disappointment.

The photograph rested in front of her eyes, the light of her vehicle's headlights shining bright, the dissatisfaction in her veins flowing strong.

Was there no reason for this madness?

Was there no explanation for all this devastation?

Was there no purpose to any of it at all?

Janene asked herself these questions, each question a statement of failure on her behalf, each answer lingering in the obscurity of the unknown. She hated the idea of waiting...*waiting for another attack on their home*...waiting for either the cops to catch the intruder or the stranger to break in once again and possibly do something much worse than simply breaking furniture.

What if they hurt Daray...

What if they hurt Amon...

Janene hated waiting around for the unknown to happen. She hated not being in control. *Perhaps that's why she became a teacher*, she thought, blankly staring at the square polaroid. It didn't matter. There were no more leads to follow. Only time could show the evolution of events to come. Only time would reveal the mysteries she sought to solve so frantically.

Janene hated not being in control.

But control was something she no longer possessed.

Her family's fate was in the hands of the police and the intruder, a thought that would keep anyone awake most nights.

It was getting late, and Janene had yet to locate *whatever* it was she was hoping to find within the darkness of the neglected park. She didn't want to go back home and fight with her husband again, but on the other hand, there was no reason for her to stay here any longer, no alternatives rising to mind, and no potential leads to her unsolved mystery.

It's fine. Janene told herself in silence, beginning to lower the photograph in defeat.

Time to go.

But fate, as it turned out, had other plans for Janene this night.

As she lowered the photograph, the headlights of her car caught a glimmer of colour dancing out from beyond the darkness of the thickening forest. Only her subconscious saw it at first, her mind catching up as her gaze was drawn toward the trees, away from civilization and the safety of her home.

Within the darkness, shimmering from the light of her vehicle's head beams, standing out like a thimble in the dirt, was a small flash of blue, waving in and out of existence as fast as one could blink, vanishing as quickly as a drop of rain. But it had lingered long enough for Janene to catch notice, her vision becoming drawn toward the secrets beyond the trees, her eyes scanning deeper into the woods.

"Hello?" she called out, too quiet for anyone to notice, loud enough to make her shutter at her own voice in the night's empty echo.

There was no answer.

There was no callback in return.

She wondered if it was just wishful thinking guiding her eyes rather than logic or reason.

Was she seeing things?

Was this real?

Just as she began to question her exhausted mind, in the flickering darkness, a flash of blue appeared from behind one of the thick pines once more, enduring long enough for Janene to know it was real, but disappearing too quickly for her to fathom what it was.

It looked like a piece of fabric, Janene thought to herself, taking one cautious step toward the trees. *Like a cloth dangling on the line.*

Janene took a few more steps forward, searching for what had drawn her attention so surreptitiously, her eyes drawing blanks as she scanned back and forth through the darkness.

"Hello?" she called out again as she approached the tree line.

No response.

Janene was not a stupid person.

She had seen enough horror movies and television shows to know that she should have never stepped foot into the shielded darkness of the woods.

But no problem was ever solved by walking away.

She would receive no answers if she turned tail and ran.

She would receive no fulfillment should she retreat, turning her back to the mysteries ahead.

Was it just as likely that nothing was waiting for her in the forest?

Was it possible that her exhausted mind had been playing delusional tricks on herself, leading her on a wild goose chase rather than showing her the truth of her reality?

Sure, Janene thought to herself before taking that final step over the threshold of the tree line. *But there was only one way to know for sure.* So with that—*against any sense of rationality*—Janene stepped into the darkness of the trees, the headlights of her car barely enough to guide her way, the drizzle of the night vanishing under the umbrella of thick branches and brush.

Janene fumbled around in the dark, where she thought she saw the flash of blue, searching around every tree, scanning the damp ground for anything that may resemble what she had seen.

But there was nothing.

Shades of fallen leaves, rotting sticks, logs, and dirt were all that she found as she inspected the forest floor, her footsteps crunching as she pushed the branches aside, the smell of pine and rotting leaves lingering in the air.

She pulled out her phone, flicking on the tiny flashlight, the light source barely enough to guide her path, but more than she had from the headlights of her car as she pressed onward through the woods.

"Hello?" she repeated a third time, once again receiving no response. A gentle waft whispered through the rustling autumn leaves, each breeze carrying with it a spray of damp air and the smells of pine, birch, and juniper trees. Whatever it was she had seen remained hidden, either hiding from Janene's curious gaze or never having existed in the first place. But as she lifted her phone's flashlight, scanning the deeper woods for the mysteries she sought, Janene once again caught a flash of blue, this time lasting slightly longer, but still not long enough to catch a good glimpse.

Janene pushed onward, stepping deeper and further into the woods, careful not to lose her way. Every direction was now beginning to look the same. The shine of her car's headlights had almost wholly faded within the thick of the trees.

What am I chasing, she wondered, pressing ahead into the dark.

A blue jay?

Possibly some garbage lost in the wind?

What?

Janene searched for reason among the flashes of blue, as humans tend to do, searching for meaning among that which they don't yet understand.

A collar on a cat?

A late-night butterfly?

These were all possibilities, but none of them seemed to satisfy her curiosity as she followed the flashes of blue deep into the subdivision's backwoods. Whatever it was, it was undoubtedly moving because every few steps, it would reappear, the blue flashes becoming more rapid the deeper into the forest she travelled, lasting slightly longer each time—*but not long enough to catch a good glimpse.*

It was too large to be an animal, yet it was moving.

It was too elusive to be a piece of trash or wrapper, yet Janene could not catch up.

"Is anybody out there?" Janene spoke softly to the darkness of the woods, carefully listening for any other footsteps surrounding her, hearing nothing but her own.

There was nobody.

No response.

No explanation.

Nothing.

Just constant flashes of blue, luring Janene deeper and deeper into the forest, Janene's apprehensive curiosity shoving her to follow, blinding her from any potential danger that may lurk in the night. But it wasn't just the existence of the flash of blue that enticed her to push ahead, despite every nerve in her body telling her to turn around and go home. It was the precise shade of blue that had caught her imagination and seduced her curiosity, reeling her further into the darkness against every natural instinct buried deep within.

She recognized the shade of blue.

She had seen it before.

She had seen it in the photograph.

It was the *same blue* from the picture...the *same blue* she had been staring at endlessly ever since Amon handed her the dreaded photograph...the *same blue* from Maria's dress, worn over thirteen years ago when her photo was captured a mere hundred yards behind her by the old swings.

Janene knew she was being stupid, illogical, and nonsensical.

She knew none of this made any sense at all.

And she knew she should have turned around and escaped the woods as fast as she humanly could.

But she couldn't.

She wouldn't.

Curiosity gripped and seduced her, forcing her to cut a path forward rather than turn tail and retreat.

Janene allowed herself to be lured, *step by step* until she had hiked a hundred yards deep into the forest, nothing but the light of her phone guiding her way and the overwhelming sense of inquisitiveness forcing her path.

It was only after about another minute of walking did Janene realize that the flashes of blue had halted. They had been appearing in the same general direction for so long that Janene automatically marched forward, blindingly allowing something she could not comprehend to guide her. But for the last thirty yards, Janene realized that the blue flashes had stopped, vanishing in the darkness and no longer guiding the way.

She suddenly realized how alone she truly was.

There were no buildings. There were no hints of civilization.

She was completely and utterly alone.

The woods seemed thicker…

 The air seemed colder…

The night seemed darker…

She knew that if anyone were waiting for her in the shadows of the looming forest, no one would hear her scream.

"Hello?" she called out again, her voice riddled with anxiety.

A cool breeze lifted through the air, dancing around the large tree trunks as the sound of branches and leaves shuffled in the wind, her hair blowing in her face as the forest temperature plummeted to a winter's chill.

She could feel the air on her spine and the ice on her tongue.

She knew she shouldn't have come this far.

She knew she had made a reckless mistake.

The smell of rotting leaves seemed to swell, rising from the ground as if the wind had disturbed the stench's slumber, surrounding Janene with the revolting odour of sulphur and decay. Janene held her hand over her nose, her exposed skin turning white and pale in the now-freezing air, her lips beginning to tremble and shiver, every atom within her body telling her to run…*run while she still could.*

But Janene would not flee.

Janene would not run.

She had to know what it was calling her deep into the woods.

She needed to know

She had come this far.

So instead, Janene tightened up her jacket, warmed her hands with her breath, blocked the smell of rotting stench from her mind, and continued her search for the mysterious flashes of blue.

But she wouldn't have to look far…

Janene scanned the ground with her phone, searching through the overturned leaves for anything that might resemble what she had been following deep within the forest. She used her foot to brush aside the sticks and stones that had rested amongst the decay, checking behind trees and within troughs for any clue within the dark, the rotting putrid stench only growing stronger as she disturbed the fallen wreckage — *the night only growing colder.*

It was only when she checked behind a fallen log, did she finally get a glimpse of something that didn't seem to belong amongst the rest. For every step she had taken within the forest, she had strolled over only autumn foliage, moss-covered logs, loose twigs and sticks, small stones, and stagnant water.

But there was something else...

Something that stood out from the aftermath of mother nature.

Something that didn't belong amongst the likes of the darkened forest.

And that something was a small piece of cloth, sticking out from the mud, only a few square inches protruding from behind a fallen log resting an arm's length from where the fabric lay.

And it wasn't just *any* piece of fabric.

The fabric was blue.

The *exact* blue Janene had seen flashes of, luring her deep within the shadows of the trees, enticing her far from the comforts of civilization.

Janene kneeled in the mud, resting her phone in a certain way that allowed the white light to illuminate the battered fabric.

She studied the blue material for a moment, noticing the rips and tears and faded mud spots, the water-soaked colour bleeding from the soft material protruding from the mud. It didn't take a scientist to know that this fabric had been stuck in the earth for a long time, likely resting here for years or longer, shielded from the sun within the veil of the forest, but exposed to the critters and elements that made their seasonal passage through the thick of the woods. The blue fabric was ripped, torn, shredded, and faded...*but more importantly*...there was no way this fabric had been floating around in the breeze, guiding Janene hundreds of yards through the woods. But it was also no coincidence that Janene had stumbled across this exact texture of blue deep within the forest, almost invisible to anyone who wasn't standing directly upon it.

She glanced around her, searching for what had guided her so deeply into the woods.

But she saw nothing but darkness.

From what she could tell, she was indeed alone.

Once she felt secure enough to drop her guard momentarily, Janene reached down and grabbed the fabric between her fingers. She felt the muddy material in her hands, the dirt and grime rubbing against her skin, the material nearly disintegrating in her hands.

Was it an old cloth? A towel?

It was too hard to tell.

The fabric had been sitting here for too long.

Time had clearly taken its toll.

Janene gave it a gentle tug, the threads of the fabric surprisingly not falling apart but also not coming loose from the softening mud, which had been dampened by constant rainfall dripping from the branches above. She had no idea why she was knee-deep in mud, far beyond the shadowed treeline of the suburban forest. Nor did she have any idea why she was tugging away at a piece of blue cloth in the thick of night, the foul odour of rot and decay intertwined in her breath. Janene had no clue as to why someone had constantly been terrorizing their family, ripping apart the threads of their sanity and tormenting them on multiple occasions for no reason.

Janene didn't know many things...but with some inexplicable rationalization...Janene knew that this was *precisely* where she needed to be. She had no reason to believe this other than what the gut feeling in her body told her. She had no reason to think this, despite every neuron in her brain subconsciously guiding her to this very spot in the woods.

And she had no reason to assume anything she did in the past few hours had any merit other than to calm her own self-interests. But here she was, deep within the woods, tugging away at a forgotten piece of cloth with frozen fingers, desperately heaving away at whatever remained hidden beneath the wet mud. And as for what happened next, no one could have justifiably brushed aside Janene's response to what was pulled from the mud on this long, exhausting night.

Janene tugged and pulled at the cloth, wiggling free what mysteries remained hidden under the mud's relaxing grasp, and once Janene was sure that whatever was buried below the ground was free enough for her to pry from beneath the earth, she rose to her feet, wrapped bother her hands tightly around the blue fabric, and yanked it with every ounce of strength still within her exhausted and frozen body.

It was heavy...It was muddy...

And it was something Janene would never forget for the remainder of her many sleepless nights ahead—because what Janene pulled from the mud was something she could have never imagined in her worst nightmares...

That something had a broken jaw, the bones twisted and turning off its worm-filled skull—that something had been buried in the ground for thirteen years, thought forgotten to time and age itself—and although there wasn't a single soul around to hear, no one could have justifiably brushed-aside Janene's endless screams of terror as she found herself face-to-face with the forgotten corpse of Maria Mihailova rotting amongst the mud and worms...

Janene screamed—Janene wept—and there was no one around to hear her cry.

Part III
Maria

18

...Thirteen Years Ago...

Allan was sitting in his office on the second floor of the Peterson building at Acadia University, sipping his twin coffee and watching the students through the window as they hustled to and from their respective classes, hundreds of eager youth zipping by one another up and down the steep slope of university hill. Allan enjoyed the view from his office, letting his thoughts wander in whichever direction it desired as he mindlessly stared out into the university wilderness, a form of short-spanned meditation between the busy workings of day-to-day life. Today was Allan's off day in terms of teaching classes, but that didn't mean he wasn't busy. There were hardly any days of the week where he didn't have at least *something* going on, especially recently, his wife a few weeks away from giving birth. There had been a lot on Allan's mind as of late, his wandering thoughts sifting through his mental to-do list as he watched the crowd of students slowly begin to thin out, indicating classes had begun, only the late strollers still lingering along the manicured paths.

He had to prepare a midterm for next week, he remembered, thinking of his 2123 Physiological Psychology class. He had most of the material already prepared from lectures in semesters long past. Still, he always liked to shake up the questions a bit just in case some of his students managed to find a copy of the previous year's tests, something they seemed more and more capable of locating.

He also had to submit a few revisions on several theses written by a few fourth-year students. He had only taken on four honours students this year, less than half of what he usually employed on an annual basis, but he knew there would be less time to devote to his students this year, his days and evenings taken up by more personal matters.

Then there was the meeting with Maria. She was supposed to pop by sometime soon for their bi-weekly session, something he had taken on as pro-bono work as a favour to the university. Allan was always happy to help when he could.

And lastly, he had to pick up a crib from Paula's Pampered Baby Shop in New Minas. Erin would kill him if he forgot again, the final touch to their baby room that had been sitting empty for too long. Erin was about halfway through her last trimester, her stomach beginning to look more like a watermelon than a grapefruit...*not that he was ever foolish enough to say that out loud.* They were starting to enter the period of excitement that comes with the days leading up to a newborn. The baby shower had been only a few weeks ago, and except for the crib, their home had already been prepared for the arrival of the newest addition to their family. *It was to be a boy.* The doctors asked them if they wanted to keep it a secret, but neither Allan nor Erin were strong enough to wait any longer. They had been dying to know and immediately folded upon the prospect of finding out.

"*A boy...*" Allan had said, holding his wife tightly in his arms while the doctor showed them the ultrasonic images, pointing out all the bits and pieces of biology—pointing at *their* son.

Some people would think they were crazy, trying for a child at their age. Allan was already forty-five, Erin only a couple of years younger, their bodies growing a several unwanted aches and pains, their skin showing a few more wrinkles than the day they met.

But those people didn't know what it meant to the Springs.

Those people didn't know what they had gone through.

They had gotten married when Allan was thirty-six with a beautiful ceremony in Mexico alongside immediate family and friends, and it wasn't long after that before they decided they wanted to add to the family.

Erin wanted three kids.

Allan wanted two.

So, they compromised and decided to try for three...

But woefully, the *powers-that-be* had different plans for their family.

The first miscarriage had been harsh...*brutal, in fact*...stretching their hearts to about as thin as they could stretch them. It was challenging to think about, a memory buried deep within Allan's mind. It may have been a long time ago now, but the pain's recollection never really faded...*not truly...*

Their baby girl was to be named *Alice*, after Erin's mother, with her middle name chosen as *Kelsey*, after a late Aunt of Allan's. *That was the name they engraved on the tombstone.* Allan didn't even want to do that, the anguish too arduous to cope with at the time. But Erin had insisted it was the right thing to do, as a way for them to try and achieve any resemblance of closure after losing their unborn child.

There was no funeral ceremony...

...no black suits or dresses...

...no cards...

...no condolences.

They did it in secret, *quietly*, and to this day, no one other than Allan and Erin knew where the tombstone lay. It helped...*a little*...but that sort of pain wasn't something that ever vanished--*not truly*. It stuck around, became engrained in day-to-day life, and became lodged in almost every decision made between getting up for work and going to bed late at night.

It took two years of recovery before Allan and Erin decided it was time to try again. Up until then, it almost felt as if they were trying to *replace* Alice rather than bore a new child of their own. Up until then, it was too tough even to consider the thought of trying for another baby. But after some therapy—sponsored by one of Allan's colleagues—they finally gave it another go. It took a few tries—*many in fact*—but after a bit of help from modern medicine, Erin finally tested positive, and Allan had never hugged her so tightly throughout their mournful marriage.

They finally had hope of being a true family as they had always dreamed of.

For the longest time, everything seemed to be going well.

Weeks went by…

…then months…

Everything was in order according to the many specialists they had conversed with. They even went so far as to drive to Maine, paying hefty tolls for American private healthcare, receiving one of the best pediatricians money could buy, who had told them that everything was on track, that the pregnancy was going smoothly, and that the baby was *healthy*. Erin took charge in designing the nursery, using her artistic talents to paint a mural of cartoon characters on the wall, the bright and welcoming colours the first thing anybody sees upon entry. They had purchased a fancy changing table, replaced the floor with a beautiful grey laminate, and filled the room with stuffed animals, toys, posters, and all the educational gadgets a growing infant would ever need.

Everything was perfect.

Everything was as it should be.

Then the unthinkable happened…just as it had happened before…*only later…much, much later.*

Allan could remember the hospital…

…the crying…

…the silence….

…the stale taste of sickness and sorrow…

After extensive blood work and tests, the doctors told them their stillbirth was linked to something called antiphospholipid syndrome, a nongenetic condition in which the immune system mistakenly creates antibodies that attack tissues in the body. It was a rare and hard-to-detect syndrome, one that they had been unaware of up to this point, the quality of tests at the time not quite acute enough to identify it. Of course, none of the details mattered anymore. All the trips, the expenses, the waiting, the *hoping…it had all been for nothing*…and once again…Erin and Allan were alone. The future they had dreamed about was a lost drop in an endless and barren sea. The door to the nursery remained closed.

Everything changed after the loss of their second child.

No longer were they cuddly and affectionate with one another.

No longer did they poke and prod and jest, enjoying the love they once had. The nights were colder, the distance between them expanding by each fleeting moment, as if they were no longer on the same path, as if they were on separate tracks, pointing them in different directions.

Allan did his best to console her, not because he wanted to, but because he felt like he had to. Erin had no interest in his companionship. For the longest time after the death of their second child, it was as if Erin had cut ties with any sense of emotion, any sense of humanity.

She still went to work.

She still went to the gym.

She was still Erin.

But despite the similarities, everything had changed. Everything they once had seemed to wither and fade. It took a very long time for things to slowly resemble the normality they once held when they got married.

Months...

Years...

Silence...

Resentment...

Those were dark days, days that had nearly destroyed the foundations on which their relationship relied, days that had Allan questioning the purpose of it all, and days that had Erin wondering what the reason was for continuing forward.

There had been fights...

There had been screaming...

There had been weeks-long stretches where Allan and Erin wouldn't speak to one another, Allan burying himself in his work, Erin doing the same, takeout dinners and separate beds becoming the pillars of their marriage, replacing the love and tenderness that had once been there.

Allan had fallen down a long spiral of self-degradation. He would dissociate, often disconnecting from the reality around him, regularly losing himself for days, not recalling what it was he was doing, where he was, or how he had walked several kilometres from his house without remembering a single step along the way.

His psychiatrists had told him it was his way of coping...his way of dealing with the harrowing pain that lingered with him around every one of life's corners. Dissociating was far better than living with the concept that everything Allan had worked for was for nothing. Detaching himself from reality was far easier than watching every one of his childhood friends start families of their own as Allan and Erin became left behind.

Whenever the pain became too much to bear, Allan would separate himself from the reality that tortured him so heinously...

Whenever the sorrow became too much to overcome, Allan would let his mind fold in on itself, burying anything that caused him anguish deep within his shattered soul...

And whenever the loneliness became too much to handle, Allan would bury his suicidal thoughts deep within the darkest corners of his heart, letting his mind go numb as a way to combat the tightening of the portentous noose.

It took a long time for Allan to become one with the nature of his own reality, and longer still for him to regain any resemblance of happiness in a life that seemed to be filled with nothing but a lingering void.

Therapy helped.

It may have even saved him.

He started remembering more, slipping back to the man he had once been.

Then, once he had regained a semblance of who he once was, he could finally divert his attention back to Erin and the marriage they had let rot and shrivel.

Allan was scared there was no returning to who they once were. He was terrified that their marriage was unsalvageable, that there was no hope of reigniting the spark of love they once shared.

But the flames had not fully been extinguished.

Now and then, a glimmer of what once was would shine through, providing just enough assurance for Allan and Erin to sludge ahead and claw their way to the next sunrise on the feeble promise that things could someday fade back to normal.

And after a while...*a long while*...things did indeed go back to how they were...

...Laughter slowly replaced silence...

...Love sluggishly substituted odium...

...And their gentle embrace gradually traded places with the waning hostilities that had lingered between them for so long...

But even after things slowly slid back to normalcy, even after they could smile and laugh with each other once again, neither of them ever brought up what had happened. It was as if they had been given a new beginning, on the pre-context that they never speak of the dark times again unless it was absolutely and unequivocally unavoidable.

Then a year passed...

Then two...

Then five...

Then before they knew it, seven years had passed since the beginning of the dark times, and their life was almost back to how it had been before losing their first child. It would never get back to one hundred percent. Allan knew that, and Erin accepted their truths, but it was as good as it could be, and Allan was thankful to have their lives back once again.

Erin had begun painting again.

Allan had regained control over his once-disturbed mind.

Once again, they were where they needed to be.

They were together.

They were happy.

But they were still missing one last thing.

Life was more than living out your final days on repeat, guessing at your purpose rather than genuinely understanding it.

That's—*at the very least*—how Allan felt.

It was as if a tiny void had pried its way back into Allan's heart—not consuming him like before, but injecting a nagging sensation that he never seemed to be able to abolish, like the drip of a leaky faucet into a deep metal sink.

They had considered adopting but had trouble finding a suitable fit. Their slightly older age had proved a significant factor by the time they had considered looking into the prospect of taking in someone else. There was also a greed aspect as well, and although Allan knew this wasn't the proper way to think, he still wanted a biological son of his own, a spawn of his own blood, someone He and Erin could give life to, created from the spark of their own love.

But they never dared try...

It was too difficult to discuss...even seven years later...even after all that could heal had healed, and all that could mend had mended.

They never tried...

They never considered it...

They were happy—maybe not as content as they could have been—but happy enough to get through the days with a smile on their face, which was far better than it had been in recent years.

However, life always has a way of tossing a wrench into the spokes of intention. Allan had been cooking meat for their weekly taco night, the smell of raw hamburger sizzling on the frying pan soaking the walls of their home. He accidently let the pan sit a little too long, the meat cooking a little longer than it should have. Erin was upstairs, folding the last load of laundry when the burnt smell had finally reached her—*and with it, an instant state of nausea*. Erin had sprinted to the washroom, holding back the urge to vomit as she stared down toward the toilet in a vaguely familiar stance, a stance she had found herself in just over seven years ago—*and again nine years ago*—a posture she had found herself in many times during the course of her two shortened pregnancies.

Erin didn't tell her husband right away. She wanted to be *absolutely* sure before ever daring to churn up the darker days barely beyond them, days that had stolen a piece of them, days that they had fought so tirelessly to be rid of.

She bought a pregnancy test...

Then she bought another...

Then she bought one more...

...all different brands...

...all top quality.

And they all pointed to the same thing...the same terrifying, wonderful, agonizing sign that Erin—once again—*was pregnant.*

That was just about eight months ago now...

...longer than either of her previous two pregnancies...longer than they had ever made it before. Allan had taken her to different specialists, ones that were more familiar with antiphospholipid syndrome, ones that could treat her in the ways she needed to be treated, that understood the intricacies and complications that could arise as a result of APS, and ones that could ensure the safe arrival of their son...whose name they dared not speak of until the day he was finally born into this roller coaster of a world.

Allan sat at his desk, staring blankly out the window, only a few stragglers left on the sidewalk, his mug now vacant of his coffee, his mind slowly drifting back to reality.

The last nine years had been a lot, almost more than he could withstand, but for the first time in a long, long time, things finally seemed to be aligning in the way he had envisioned on the day he got married, and although he was still nervous, that void he felt deep within his heart finally seemed to be shrinking, replaced by the prospect of raising his son, substituted by the speckle of hope that would once and for all shield him and his wife from the dark days that had nearly devastated them.

He loved his wife, and she loved him, and his only wish was that they could finally take that love and spread it to a child of their creation, something they had prayed for on countless shadowy nights, something that, for the longest time, they thought no longer possible in their future.

A knock on the door pulled Allan away from thoughts of the past, yanking his gaze away from the window and back toward his present reality, back toward his regular, daily duties under the employment of Acadia University.

"Come in," he shouted, letting the last few drips of his coffee trickle into the garbage can under his desk, wiping the mug with a paper towel and placing it face-down to let it dry for the next long day in his office.

The handle twisted, and in came a woman with a slightly darker complexion, a beautiful blue dress camouflaging the large baby bump on her belly, and long black hair swinging around on her shoulders.

"Ah," Allan said, re-remembering his appointment, immediately recognizing whom it was entering his office. "Great to see you, Maria. Shall we begin?"

19

Maria Mihailova sat in her usual spot inside Allan's office, the smell of coffee blending with the cool, damp air drifting in from his open window. She had seen dark clouds on the horizon, rain likely on its way, something she wasn't looking forward to on her walk to the bus stop if the rain did decide to split the sky.

"Hi Allan," she said, smiling toward him and making herself comfortable, as challenging as that was to do nearly nine-month pregnant, just a little bit ahead of Erin, not that it was a race or anything. Maria couldn't believe that any day now, she would be a mother...a single mother, which was obviously not the ideal case scenario she had envisioned, but a mother nonetheless. There wasn't a more significant gift God could give her—her years of prayer for a better future finally being delivered.

"How are we doing today?" Allan returned, his client for the past many months looking the best she's looked in a long time, their sessions together clearly making a difference, his work evidently doing some good in this chaotic world. "Big day for us, isn't it?"

"Good," Maria said, her thick Syrian accent distinguishable, even only speaking a single word. "Most good in a long time. And yes, it certainly is." Maria's English wasn't up to par yet, but it was close. She had been practicing ever since she was accepted as a refugee into the country six months ago. Allan was one of the first faces she became familiar with and blessedly continued to see.

"No trouble getting here?" he said again, keeping the conversation light before their session truly began, his mind still warming up from the fogginess of deep thought from his elongated stare out his office window.

"Busses are good. Much better than back home," she chuckled, her normally dry sense of humour seeping through. This was to be their twelfth and final scheduled session together, both agreeing to take a pause after the birth of her baby, Allan also to become a father shortly thereafter, each of their lives about to undergo drastic changes.

"I bet they are," Allan said, sitting up from his desk and making his way toward his 'therapy' chair, as his clients call it. Sitting behind a desk created an unwanted barrier between the client and the therapist, acting as a pedestal of superiority in a conversation, which wasn't the vibe a therapist wanted to create within the dynamic between the client and themselves. Instead, he sat next to the client in a small, green chair, resembling that of a Lazy-Boy recliner, except maybe with a tad more professionalism built in. Allan did his best to make sure his clients didn't see him as a superior or director of conversation, but more as a friend. He wanted to appear as someone who simply desired to listen to what his clients had to say, offering advice as if it were coming from a brother or father rather than a teacher or stranger. He was indeed a stranger to any person who walked through his office door looking for guidance, the barriers that came with it an obstacle to be overcome in all sessions for all clients.

And it worked.

Maria no longer saw Allan as a stranger.

The dynamic between Allan and Maria had grown far beyond that of a therapist and a client, and although it was entirely unconventional and outside the general rulebook of basic therapy, the similarities between Allan's and Maria's lives had caused them to grow much closer to one another than most other clients had before. Allan was one of the first friendly faces Maria had seen regularly upon her arrival in Canada, escaping war and seemingly never-ending conflict in her home country of Syria. Allan was the first person that genuinely listened to her problems, showing her that the struggles she faced were not the consequences of her actions but the consequences of fate outside her control. Maria had many demons in her past, and Allan helped her combat each of them one by one, showing her a perspective she had never thought of before, guiding her along a path that, before they met, she had never been able to see. And not only that, Allan had also helped her transition through the personal complications related to relocating countries. He helped guide her through the medical system, using his own previous experiences to steer her through the steps of pregnancy, helping her find suitable doctors, care, nutrition, and anything else she needed. He also helped her find funding for a more permanent residence, a small 1-bedroom apartment just a few kilometres down the road, close to a bus stop that could take her anywhere she needed within thirty minutes or less. And on top of all that, he helped her overcome the emotional and mental traumas that come with escaping war, abuse, and a darkened past. Allan may have been Maria's therapist, but he had become much more than that. He was a guiding star over the vast sea, a candle in the darkness, and the means to a fresh start she never thought she would have or deserved.

Maria watched as Allan perched himself in his usual spot in the therapist's chair, getting ready for their final session, opening his notepad, pulling out his usual silver pen, and noting the time and date before looking up at her with his usual welcoming smile.

"So…" he said, his usual word to mark the beginning of their one-hour sessions. "…what would you like to start with today?"

Maria smiled back, something she would never be caught doing in their first few sessions, something that now seemed to come with ease and regularity. "Honestly. I do not know," she responded, her accent thick and foreign.

"How far you've come," Allan smiled, scribbling down a small three-word note in his notepad before returning his eyes to his longtime client. "Well, why don't we slowly stroll through it all from start to finish, see if any demons we missed find their way to the surface? Just know that I would never ask this of you unless I felt you were in a place where I thought you were steadfast enough to handle it. You have come a long way, Maria. I don't think there's anything in this world you couldn't handle."

"What is—*steadfast*?" Maria asked, still picking up the pieces of English between the hustle and bustle of life, Allan a constant teacher for her, showing her the little nuances and difficulties that come with learning such a particular and complicated language.

"It's like being 'strong enough' or 'unwavering,'" Allan said, searching for a definition in his mind. "Essentially, it means I think you're mentally prepared to face what you may have found difficult to face before."

"Oh, thanks," Maria said, locking the word deep in her vocabulary.

"So, are you okay with walking through your past? A final recap on our previous eleven sessions?"

"I think so."

"Great," Allan replied, taking down another small note. "I'll let you begin wherever you feel is a comfortable place to start. And if you find it difficult to talk about anything at all, let me know, and we'll work through it step by step. No pressure."

Maria slowly let her mind dip deep into her past, recalling the major talking points of their last eleven sessions, recalling the memories that had handcuffed her mind within the narrows of lingering anger and endless despair, emotions she never thought she would be able to escape, feelings that would have stayed deep inside forever, if not for Allan and his wisdom.

There was a point in her life not so long ago that had pushed her to the precipice of what Maria thought she could withstand. The war in Syria had proved the climax of her troubles, but it was not the beginning of them. She thought back to their first couple of sessions together when her English vocabulary was only half of what it was now and when it was difficult for her to describe the pain she felt, to accurately articulate the desolation that had consumed her heart and soul, and the abandonment she felt from God and all those around her.

She had moved with her family to Syria from Latvia when she was very young on the promise of work and a better future, a wishful future that would not last the better half of a few terrible years. Her mother had died in a freak car accident shortly after arriving in the country, and her father, unable to withstand the pressure of living as a single father, ditched Maria for another family somewhere in Lebanon, leaving her to fend for herself from the age of thirteen, never once to be heard from again.

Maria had lived in the alleys.

She had lived in abandoned warehouses.

233

She had lived on the streets, begging for what little money was available in the pockets of passing strangers.

When she was thirteen, Maria could at least be spared the pity of those that walked by within the filth of the littered streets, tossing her the odd coin she needed to eat, handing over boxes of leftover meals and half-eaten sandwiches. For months at a time, Maria called the corner of a dumpster and dilapidated apartment building home, shielding herself from the rain with cardboard boxes, a torn orange tarp, and whatever else she could scavenge from the streets that had not already been claimed by the countless others that slept in the alleyways alongside her.

When her entire life was consumed by the need to eat, sleep, and survive, she had little time to worry about luxuries like education, friendship, and mental stability. Still, Maria had always been stronger than the rest. She always found a way to search for light in a place where so few could muster the strength to rise above what their surroundings made them. She used the orange glow of a flickering streetlight peeking through her ripped tarp to read books she rented or stole from the local library, following along with the rough guidelines and rules of middle school and high school textbooks twenty years out of date. Throughout the years, she would practice her writing by scribbling on the back of forgotten newspapers, writing poems and stories based on historical literature, and lighting them aflame afterward to use them as warmth in the Syrian winters when cool rains split the skies.

After a few years of begging, Maria had become decent at developing a routine, growing efficient in her daily search for food and sustenance. A local bakery a few blocks from where she slept would often spare her leftover bread and sweets at the end of long days, giving her enough to sleep with a full belly, and sometimes more so she could trade for other comforts such as pop or cash. A woman's shelter down the subway line would spare her a soft bed two or three nights a week, sometimes more in the winter, offering her the opportunity to shower and scrub herself clean within their communal showers away from the prying eyes of predatorial men, which she was lucky enough to avoid throughout her youth.

Over the years, Maria had tried to squeeze her way into a foster home several times, but there weren't many families that wanted to take in a teenager who lacked formal education, didn't have the previous experience of living within a typical family and didn't have any proof of identification except for the name she shared with those few willing to ask.

There were many hardships on the streets—the need to eat, drink, learn, and feel some sort of purpose. All of those proved a struggle, some days much tougher than the rest, some winters longer than others. But the most challenging thing she found about sleeping on a cardboard box was the need for companionship. It was a lonely life, begging on the streets, watching those fortunate enough to own their own clean pillow walk by, averting their eyes away from Maria, ignoring her existence as if she wasn't just another beating heart in a cold world. For many years, as Maria developed slowly into a woman from the turmoil of youth, she desired more than just to survive, more than just to live each day to the next. She had continued her self-education as best she could, reading stories of Shakespeare—*of love, heartache, romance,* and life.

It was these stories that often gave her the energy she needed to push through to another sunrise. The left-over baked goods were enough to allow her muscles and body to function, but the stories were what moved her heart, what gave her reason to eat and permission to survive.

But no one wanted to love a homeless seventeen-year-old girl. There were no romance stories with the woman who lived under a box. There were no tales of the knight whose heart was captured by the lady of the streets. The knights always fell for princesses, the ladies seen in the eyes of the public as being in a place of stature, purpose, and meaning.

Maria was certainly no princess, but her desires were the same as any of those in royalty, and she knew she deserved more than stale bread and lonesome nights. But what someone got versus what they deserved were often very different things. This was something Maria understood very well. She only got what she sought after—*if she didn't have it, the only way to get it was to take it for herself.*

Once Maria turned eighteen, she took what little coin she had saved over the years and purchased a single professional outfit, something from the thrift store that made her look like she hadn't lived the past seven years within the shelter of a forgotten alleyway. After that, Maria managed to fight for an extended stay at the woman's shelter, securing a bed at least five nights a week, as well as a permanent locker where she could store her newly acquired clothes without the worry of them getting destroyed by the elements, or stolen by others looking to replace their own shredded garments.

Maria used the communal computer for the next several weeks to apply for jobs. Specifically, she applied for jobs where she could utilize her writing ability without requiring her to hold a university or college degree. She lied about her age, writing down twenty-four, as no one would accept an eighteen-year-old in a professional setting but would at least accept a twenty-four-year-old in an interview.

The positions she applied to varied quite a bit, and seldom did they ever return her emails. She had no phone or home address, posing the address of the woman's shelter as her own, writing down a fake number to at least appear more professional. She banked on her emails being returned and knew that if she could get just a single interview, she would have a chance at a better life.

But it wasn't easy.

For weeks, Maria didn't receive so much as a rejection email.

For weeks, there was nothing but silence or automated "Thank you, but we're not hiring…" emails.

For weeks, her professional clothes sat in her locker, collecting dust, waiting for their opportunity to give her the future she deserved.

Then, after about a month of waiting, just as autumn was beginning to roll in, Maria finally got a response from a legal company looking for a secretary to fill in for a woman on maternity leave. The position was temporary, lasting no longer than six months, but it was something. And *something* was all she needed to get started.

The interview had been a smashing success, and Maria had made sure never to reveal her actual state of living to those looking to hire her. She told them she was currently living with her brother, looking to get some experience before applying to University, hoping to get some money as a down payment on tuition and other expenses.

After only thirty minutes of questions, they agreed to hire her on the spot. Perhaps it was her forced charm and presentation, or maybe it was the fact that there weren't many others willing to take on a position that was only temporary and paid so little compared to others in the same field.

It didn't matter.

What mattered was that she had a job. God had granted her an opportunity, and she had secured a chance for a better future.

The job itself was easy. Being homeless for seven years gave Maria a perspective not shared by most. Getting four extra hours of work dumped on her desk was nothing compared to sleeping in the freezing rain, shivering until all she felt was the faint beating of her trembling heart. Getting chewed out by a colleague for accidentally forgetting a page on a report was nothing compared to kneeling on the sidewalk, praying one person would drop a coin heavy enough into her paper cup so she could afford an afternoon bagel as her first meal of the day.

For six months, Maria did the job to the best of her ability, arriving early, staying late, enjoying the communal coffee and donuts left in the breakroom every day, always stashing the extra away, saving every coin she earned, never spending a dime on anything she didn't need. Then when six months passed, Maria was given her first blessing in a long time. The woman she had replaced, who had spent six months on maternity leave, had decided not to return, their family moving to Turkey on the rumours that a civil war might be brewing within Syria. Maria didn't pay much attention to that, not owning any property or assets or having anything to lose if missiles ever started flying. The business had decided to hire her on full-time, not offering her any benefits, but paying her twenty hours on the books and twenty hours under the table to avoid any taxation fees. Maria was okay with that. She had no long-term medical conditions that she needed to take care of, and wasn't in desperate need of any medication she couldn't get over the counter at the local pharmacy if she ever needed it.

The stars finally seemed to be aligning for Maria, and everything worked out as God had intended. Then after a few more months, God had finally revealed the next stage of his plan, giving her something she had long desired ever since she first began to rent those romance books from the local library, reading them from the safety of her cardboard box under the orange glow of the flickering streetlamp. The business had hired a new intern, fresh out of college, no older than twenty-five. His name was Aleksei, and he sat only a few feet from where she worked, their feet nearly touching as they faced one another eight to twelve hours a day, Monday through Friday. He had thick black hair, a thin beard, and a small scar on his cheek that he had gotten from his served time in the Syrian military. His teeth weren't perfect, but they were white, and he was strong. He had lifted weights consistently for the past few years, only recently taking a break to focus on his studies, the vestiges of sculpted muscle evident on his near-perfect frame. His eyes were brown, and he wore a suit made of fine material, much more expensive than what Maria had spent on her outfits, which now amounted to five, one for each day of the week, with the ability to mix and match a few tops and blouses.

Maria and Aleksei had gotten to know each other very well over the following weeks of his hiring, spending lunch breaks together, constantly talking throughout the day, Maria helping Aleksei with computing and Microsoft Excel issues, and Aleksei helping her with legal and technical nomenclature. Maria had never really spent this much time with a boy throughout her entire life, but she had imagined it, reading her romantic novels and stories, and even though it wasn't exactly like it had been in the fairytales, her time with Aleksei slowly seemed to be building a story of its own, a story where the woman on the streets finally gets her knight in shining armour, rather than the princess in the high tower. Of course, Maria never once divulged her past to Aleksei, always diverting the topic of conversation away from things related to her living conditions or family, constantly dodging questions that had the slightest chance of revealing who she truly was or how she had forcibly lived her life. If Aleksei ever found out who she was or where she came from, her chances of living within the fabled desires of her story would quickly vanish. Maria understood that, and wasn't willing to risk it—*not with Aleksei.*

But after a few months, their relationship would become more serious and intimate. They had decided to get dinner together, going on their ninth or tenth official date, when Aleksei asked her something she never thought was even possible for someone like her. They were at an Italian restaurant, a twenty-minute bus ride from the woman's shelter where Maria had been staying, enjoying a cozy meal of spaghetti and meatballs, garlic bread, and a bottle of red wine that would typically be way outside Maria's budget. His question had caught her off guard, her mouth half-full of pasta when he asked, Maria nearly choking on it as she processed the weight of his left-field request. "Are you interested in moving in with me?" Aleksei had invited her as the world came to a shuttering halt, and her mind became instantly flooded with a wave of emotion.

It was a prospect so out of the realm of what Maria had ever thought possible for her that—*at that moment*—she could not instantly come up with a response. It was like taking a kitten and giving it the controls of a spaceship.

A permanent roof over her head…

A bed she could call her own…

A boy she could spend her days with…

A life so far removed from what she had grown accustomed to…

Aleksei calmly and patiently waited for an answer while she processed every avenue in her mind, flooded with confusing sensations she had buried deep for so long, doing her best not to cry and embarrass him at the dinner table, holding everything in as not to show any weakness to her shining knight.

"Well?" Aleksei had asked after thirty seconds of pure silence, Maria's eyes wide and watery, the smells of the Italian restaurant floating through the air with tension.

Maria never answered, *at least* not vocally. Her throat had clogged with emotion, and every word inside her could no longer escape with her breath. All she could do was nod a gentle, nervous, steadfast *yes*.

"Great!" Aleksei had cheered, ordering another bottle of wine and giving Maria a long hard kiss on the cheek.

In such a short amount of time relative to the past many years, Maria's life had gone from absolute low to absolute high, all her problems now memories of the past, her future now in the palm of hers' and Aleksei's hand.

Maria remembered the first tour of his 1-bedroom, 600 square foot apartment, a castle compared to the nightmare she called home the past many winters. She remembered the look on his face when she showed up with a single suitcase half-filled with clothes, a few textbooks, and some notepads. Maria had lied to Aleksei, telling him that she sold most of her other belongings or donated them to goodwill shelters. Maria also remembered that first night spent under their roof, cuddled tightly under the warmth of soft sheets and a heated room, snuggled tightly with Aleksei the entire night under the comfort of his protection and the embrace of his companionship. For the first time in Maria's life, things seemed to be finally working out for her. The darkest corners of her existence were replaced with light, God finally answering her many nights of hopeless prayers.

But God always seemed to have an interesting way of turning one's life inside out, pulling the strings of destruction on what should have been a perfect relationship, putting into motion events far out of the control of a woman barely escaping the clutches of homelessness and poverty. "God always seemed to have a sense of humour," Maria had told Allan during their seventh session together. And little did she know, God had prepared two splinters along her path, two reckonings that would prove more than Maria was ready to handle.

The first reckoning was the war. Tension had reached its bubbling point between Rebels and the Syrian Arab Republic, the powers finally collapsing in on themselves with a manner of destruction and chaos hardly fathomable unless witnessed by the naked eye. Missiles frequently raced across the skies, raid sirens were a constant state of reality, and regular explosions deafened the ear with undesirable consistency. The war had started in southern Syria but spread everywhere quickly, inching closer and closer toward their little piece of heaven. Businesses were closing, friends were getting shipped off to war, and families were retreating into other countries, fleeing the constant waves of destruction coming down at them from the colliding militaries as their forces inched closer night after night. Bombs fell, tensions rose, and the dream of peace became harder and harsher each day as war replaced tranquillity, and gunfire replaced peace.

The second reckoning was a final sliver of humour sent down to Maria from God above, something that was begotten from nightmares during the midst of a generational war. Maria spent many years alone on the streets, and even though she did her best to keep her education up to snuff, there was only so much one could learn without being guided by those that were worth looking up to.

Maria never had any teachers.

Maria never had any heroes,

And more importantly, Maria never really had a mother.

She remembered her, and there were undoubtedly memories of happiness and embrace between her and her mom when Maria was very young. Still, the instruction and guidance one receives from a protective parent was never truly present in Maria's life.

She never learned that the most crucial person one should protect is their own self.

She never learned the secrets that a mother's love could teach, or the warmth a mother's protection can bring.

And unfortunately, Maria never learned not to be completely coerced by a man unless she was *absolutely* sure he was the one for life.

Maria loved Aleksei. He was the first to show her warmth, kindness, a home, and many other things along the way. But Maria's mother was never there to warn her about the forthcomings of a man, about the tricky ways he might seduce her into thinking he is her everything, and all else is folly. And lastly, Maria never learned how to protect herself against getting pregnant.

The war had scared Maria.

The war had scared Aleksei.

He had military experience and knew it would only be a matter of time before he was shipped off to the front lines should the war extend any longer.

They had taken solace in each other's arms, Aleksei pulling her close, Maria entranced by the comfort of his welcoming embrace. In war, many things become hard to find. There is that which is obvious, like food, clean water, electricity, and other targets of war. But there is also that which those within the first worlds could never truly understand—things like public events, soccer matches, movie nights, and other related activities seemed to disappear first, the pleasure and happiness of humans no longer necessary in the grand scheme of war. And atop that, the access to things that would typically be so regular and abundant seemed to go next. Batteries were no longer available, the production and import of clean clothes faded away, and more crucially, access to contraception was no longer seen as a fundamental human right but now an afterthought to the tides of full-scale war.

Aleksei had already used what few condoms they had left, and Maria's money was too tight to afford birth control, even if it were available. But yet, there were few sources of pleasure in a world where bombs falling from the sky was a daily occurrence. When one cannot outsource their desire for happiness, one must look inward to find purpose within a world of turmoil. Aleksei provided that purpose, offering Maria a brief source of comfort in a country where comfort was no longer a priority. Many times, Aleksei had given her relief from the fears of war, and even if only for a little while, it was enough to block the images of the dead broadcasted over local television.

But comfort did not come without a cost, and the irresistible pleasures of flesh on flesh did not come without natural consequences. Within a few weeks, Maria began to feel sick, her body reacting to things in ways unfamiliar to her, in ways that made her ill to her stomach, in ways that would hold her over the toilet for long hours as Alexsei held her long black hair away from her mouth.

There were no doctors available. Most of them were taken as a resource of war or had long since fled the country. But Maria was not stupid. She knew what her body was telling her. She had read the textbooks, and she had understood the signs.

Maria was pregnant.

In the midst of the war, Maria was to be a mom.

It was an emotion one could only understand if standing in Maria's shoes, lingering somewhere between excitement and unfathomable despondency. She had only just escaped the clutches of living on the street, and amid war, she was to be with child.

Aleksei would comfort her, holding her tight, telling her everything would be okay and that by the time the child could walk, the war would be over, and they could be the family they saw on the television—happy, together, and hopeful of the future.

His hope had been misplaced.

It only took three weeks and a stray bullet to make it clear that there was no happiness left in Syria for Maria, no hope of a future, and no reason to stay.

Aleksei had been on his way home while trying to secure a few meals for their family when a passing military vehicle shot up the streets, a bullet connecting with his spine, killing him on the spot. Maria only figured that out a few hours after the shooting, when she went looking for him, only to find his body pulled to the side of the road, a bullet hole in his back, his eyes lifeless and empty, along with the hope he had given her.

It was at that moment—when Maria flipped over the corpse of the father of her child—that she had decided to close herself off from the world.

For the sake of the baby, she had decided to leave the country, packing everything she owned into her tiny suitcase once again and making her way toward the Lebanese coast, where she luckily managed to secure a boat to Canada that was funded by the UN relief efforts, her pregnant state as a single mother all the convincing she needed to escape the terrors that remained behind in her home country.

After a few long weeks, she had finally arrived in Nova Scotia, finding a place for her and her child in Wolfville and securing a job as a secretary for the University of Acadia that was funded by student-led Syrian relief efforts. Shortly after that, Maria met Allan, and throughout many weeks of necessary therapy, she slowly divulged her story of madness and heartache, a story one could only believe if they had witnessed the exhausted, battered, and defeated look upon Maria's war-torn face.

It took many months, but slowly and surely, Allan's work with Maria allowed her to feel again, to find hope once more, and to believe that there was a future for her child that wasn't as bleak or worthless as the past she had endured herself. She could talk about the past, not as something she deserved, but something she endured and survived, something that became a part of her but *did not* define her.

Maria could step forward into her future, knowing that her child would not have to endure the same hardships she endured herself, that within Canada, there was hope—hope that no one born in Canada could *really* understand—*not as Maria understood it.*

Allan had shown her kindness beyond what she had ever known, truth beyond what she had ever believed, and hope beyond what she had ever thought possible.

Her son had a future.

Her son would have a mother.

That was all that mattered to Maria Mihailova.

She would devote her every breath to ensure that those two things would be the center of her child's left, no matter what it cost her or what it took.

Her child would have the future she never had.

Her child would truly live.

That was all she cared about in this world, *or the next.*

20

Allan's notepad was full by the time Maria had finished reciting her life story. He had heard it all before, the fragments of her past slowly developing over the previous eleven sessions, but this time he was no longer jotting down notes on the details of her tale but rather on the manner in which she explained them. Maria no longer told her tale from the point of view of a victim but instead rehearsed it as if recited by someone else, as if she had been a bystander along the entire way, observing but never enduring. The traumas that had once encapsulated her in despair and sorrow no longer held her captive but were instead the pillars in which she used to rise above it. Her teenage years on the streets were that of a different Maria, a version of her that Allan no longer saw. Maria was now a woman at the reigns of her future, standing in the place of one who was once held back by the shadows of her past, and although the pain of losing Alexsei was still there, she now had the tools required to deal with any darkened thoughts that rose from the depths of her years in Syria, and the capacity to rise over any lingering depression or overwhelmingly negative thoughts.

Suicide was a word she had used many times when referring to her teenage years, but that word was no longer something that bore any significance to her, except for the realization that she had overcome the worst of times.

War was a concept Maria had often discussed, yet now the reality of war was a foreign concept to her, something she no longer saw fit to bare any meaning in her or her son's life.

Loneliness was a feeling Maria once used to describe her daily routine, a sensation soon to be replaced upon the birth of her child, never to be experienced again.

These were the notes Allan had written down in his notebook, among others, as Maria softly spoke through the tension points of their last eleven sessions, ending her tale just as the hour of their twelfth and final session expired. Allan realized he had barely said anything the entire time, allowing Maria's thoughts to flow through, her achievements to shine, and her past to fade. It was always a great sign when the client did most of the talking, Allan thought to himself, dating the notepad and jotting down some final closing scribbles. A vocal client demonstrated that they wanted to improve and were there with purpose and desire to become the best possible version of themselves. Therapy was sort of like going to the gym. It's something that was difficult at first, but once they forced themselves to go a few times, it became more manageable, more routine, the clients often allowing their nervousness and anxieties to slide away, opening themselves to the emotions and pain that had held them hostage for so long. In Maria's case, she had only taken about a session or two before she was completely ready to divulge her past. Allan had attributed that to her son, Maria wanting to make sure she was in a good mental space upon the birth of her child, forcing herself to face the demons before her son's arrival.

And face them she did.

There will always be adversity, and there will always be new challenges to overcome, but after their twelve sessions together, Allan was fully confident that Maria was in a place where she could handle anything that came her way for the sake of her son, and the sake of her mental well-being.

Allan was proud of her. He was proud of himself.

And most importantly, he was proud of the connection that had grown between them, their pasts entirely different, their lives now intertwined forever in the name of personal growth and self-improvement. Allan had shown Maria a lot, but in return, Maria had given him a perspective he had not previously appreciated. Most of his clients were locals, students, and educated adults, all with similar pasts and parallel traumas. Maria's suffering was at a whole different level, her pain putting into perspective the troubles of his own life and his ability to overcome them. If Maria could conquer homelessness, starvation, war, and desolation, Allan could surely face the pains of his own life and overcome the loss of his previous two children, the void between him and his wife, and the dark days of his recent past.

For the sake of his child-to-be, Allan could—*and would*—be better.

Signing his name on the bottom of the notepad, he the lined yellow page and handed it to Maria, letting her read about her accomplishments and achievements from the perspective of her longest-standing Canadian friend and therapist. Generally, he didn't share any of his notes with clients, but she deserved to read what he had noted down. She deserved to know how far she had truly come.

"I'm quite proud of you," Allan told her, giving her a long, assuring smile. "You're an amazing woman, and I'd wager that the best parts of your life are yet to come."

A gentle tear ran down Maria's skin, dripping onto her blue dress as her long black hair rested on her shoulders, her hand brushing away the joy that leaked from her eye.

"I owe you so much," Maria told him, honestly and gracefully.

"You owe me nothing," Allan replied. "You have given me more than you know."

"Do all your clients cry as much as I do?" Maria joked, grabbing one of his many sleeves of Kleenex and holding it to her face.

"Not many of my clients have gone through as much as you have," Allan said. "But yes, I'd say about half cry as much as you do. You can always tell when a client enters my office wearing sunglasses that it's going to be an emotional session."

"I should remember to bring glasses," she responded, slivers of her Syrian accent seeping through.

"You won't need them," he said, standing up from his green therapist chair. "This was your last session. And I believe you've achieved what you came here to do."

"I'm happy about that," she gleefully wept. "But I'm sad I will see you no longer."

Allan laughed. "You do realize only about forty people live in this little university town, right? I'll probably see you every other day." Of course, there were more people than that, but it did seem that he constantly ran into the same locals, most often the ones he didn't want to run into, often his clients or their spouses.

"Good," she said, standing up along with Allan. "I hope to see you often."

"I'll make sure of it," he said, showing her toward the door. There were rules in place that forbid the personal connection between client and therapist outside of session hours, but Allan was happy to make an exception for Maria. In part, he felt responsible for her wellbeing, the same way he hoped he'd feel for his own child in just over a month. He wanted to ensure the rest of her days were full of laughter and joy, the days of her past remaining in the past, as they deserved to stay.

"Well," Maria said with a final goodbye, "...I better get going."

"How are you getting home?" Allan asked, placing his notepad on his desk and making his way toward the window to close it.

"The bus leaves in forty-five minutes," Maria returned. "I thought I'd just wait for it to come by."

"No need," Allan countered. "I'll drive you home."

"That is...*okay*?" Maria asked, her accent once again dripping through.

"Of course," Allan replied. "You're nine months pregnant. I can't have you out sitting in the cold waiting for a bus now, can I?"

"Thank you," Maria said. "You are too kind."

"Don't mention it."

Allan grabbed his coat, stuffing his laptop into his bag and his keys into his pocket. He did a final scan around his office to make sure everything was in order, then turned toward the door, leading Maria slowly out of the room, her sluggish pregnant walk vastly different from the day their sessions began, her belly only a tiny bulge at the time, barely noticeable under her springtime sweaters.

Allan's car wasn't too far away, his parking spot located just behind the building, which was one of the greatest benefits of being a tenured staff at Acadia University. The other was the amount of leave he was able to procure. Allan planned on taking nine or ten months off once the baby was born, none of the other staff showing any objections to his desires. They all knew what had happened the previous two times the Springs family tried to have children. If anyone deserved to stay home and enjoy their time with the little one, it was Allan and his wife, Erin.

Allan's house was only a few minutes from the University, and everything in the town was within fifteen minutes or less unless he got caught in the rush hour traffic on the stretch of road between New Minas and Wolfville, which could easily add another thirty minutes onto the drive. Fortunately, being a professor and practicing therapist at Acadia University came with the additional benefits of making your own hours, which allowed Allan to come and go outside the usual nine-to-five grind, his schedule his own for the making, another one of his favourite perks of the job. Maria's apartment was another ten minutes beyond Allan's subdivision. Allan had helped select where she would reside upon her arrival from Syria, selecting a cheap option which still allowed for amenities such as in-suite laundry, decent building security, and a newly renovated kitchen and bathroom—*an enormous step up from a cardboard box in a war-torn city*. It was also decently far enough away that not many students would reside in her building, which meant there wouldn't be many late-night parties or rambunctious young adults keeping her baby up at night.

Allan helped Maria into the passenger seat, sliding the chair back to make room for her belly, holding her hand as she slowly eased her way into the car.

"Careful now," he said, ensuring she didn't bump her head on the way in. "There you go."

"Thank you," Maria returned, immediately fastening her seatbelt, her motherly instinct already strong in the forefront of all her decisions.

Allan carefully closed the passenger door, walked around the car and hopped into the driver's seat.

"Mind if we make a pitstop along the way?" Allan asked. "I just want to drop something off at the house and would rather not have to double back."

"Of course," Maria responded, more than happy not to be waiting for the bus.

"Perfect. Thanks." Allan had planned to stop by the clinic and pick up some routine blood-work results for Erin, but didn't overly like the idea of leaving his work laptop and notes in the car while he spoke with the doctor. His laptop had been stolen a few years ago from his office by someone he presumed was a desperate student looking to get a leg-up on the upcoming April exams. The theft had resulted in the loss of months of research and countless notes on his clients at the time. Fortunately, his computer had a password he knew no one would guess, so the information was at least protected, but the laptop was never found, and his work was lost forever. Since then, Allan had always been cautious with where he left his electronics and research, never leaving anything out of sight, always keeping it within a safe place—*as well as a backup*. So instead of leaving it in the car, he thought he would drop it off at his home office before making his way toward the hospital, dropping Maria off along the way.

"Ready?" he said, looking over to Maria resting in his passenger seat.

She gave him the thumbs up, and they were off, their twelfth session now a distant memory, the day's work complete. Autumn had begun to roll in, making the drive very pleasant as the late-afternoon sun slowly shifted across the sky, reflecting off the bright reds, oranges and yellows emanating from the season's leaves, rain clouds beginning to form in the distant horizon. Allan watched as Maria marvelled at all the bright colours, realizing this was most likely the first time she had ever seen them in such quantity, their spectacular shades vast and endless across the hilly Nova Scotia horizon. Allan made another mental note, his mind wholly acclimated to the beauty of autumn, her perspective a fresh look on something he now took for granted after many years living in such a stunning province.

"Quite a sight, isn't it," Allan said, gesturing toward the horizon where thousands of trees showcased their bright autumn colours.

"God is good," she said *powerfully*.

Allan was not a religious man, but on this, he agreed, smiling as he observed the beauty of nature either chanced to them by physics and time, or gifted to them by the grace of God himself. It didn't matter what they believed; *one simply couldn't deny that view.*

It only took a few extra minutes to arrive at Allan's place. He slowly pulled into the driveway as Maria continued to stare out the window toward the children's park, where an empty swing set stood near the forest's tree line boasting its autumn foliage.

"I'll just be a moment," Allan said, hopping out of the car, carrying his leather briefcase and notepad into his home. The house was empty at the moment. Erin was out with her sister gathering things for the baby, like clothes, diapers, and whatever else they already didn't have. Allan never argued about buying anything for their child to be. They had waited long enough, and Erin deserved every ounce of happiness their child could bring them. She could buy a golden crib for all he cared, as long as she came home with a baby in her belly and a smile on her face. *That's all that mattered.* That's what it would take to steer the void in their hearts away, replacing it with the love they deserved and the joyfulness they had long awaited.

Allan was out of the house in under two minutes, closing the door behind him, locking it up and making his way to the car. Though he quickly noticed the car was empty, the passenger door left ajar. It only took a moment to find Maria standing blissfully in the park, gazing out toward the horizon of the hills, the fresh air only accentuating the chirping of young birds and the rustling of wind over fallen autumn leaves. Allan held back a moment, enjoying the view, enjoying this moment Maria was experiencing.

There was no war. There was no loneliness. There was no hunger. There was no pain.

Allan observed as Maria stared out toward the wilderness with inspiring simplicity, her long black hair blowing in the wind, her blue dress matching that of the distant sky. It was one of those moments he wished could last forever, a truly blissful feeling of ease and contentment, a feeling that almost made every bit of pain this world had to offer fade away and disappear. *Almost.*

Allan walked over to the passenger seat, opened the dash of his car and pulled out a tiny polaroid camera, one his wife had purchased many years ago that had probably only ever taken six or seven pictures during its entire life. She had wished to capture moments of their second child, but the dark times had taken the joys of photography away from them, the camera a relic of painful memories.

But as Maria had shown him, those painful memories were things of the past, things that—*although important*—were not worth suffering over for the remainder of their days. Maria had shown him that life was still worth living, even if there were times that consumed the very essence of his soul, even if there was a moment in his life where he considered what the point of pushing forward even was. This moment was perfect. And for it to be captured by the *very camera* that had acted as a reminder of the dark times for so many years, left forgotten in the dash of his car and untouched for many years—*it made it that much sweeter.*

Allan walked over to the children's park with the polaroid camera, Maria standing with her hand on the swing as she stared out toward the park.

"Maria," Allan called out to her. "Smile."

Maria only stared at the camera a moment before releasing the most beautiful smile Allan had ever seen outside of his wife, and with the simple click of his finger, the moment was captured, the gears within the camera twisting and turning as the photograph popped forward from its tiny slit, blank and undeveloped.

Allan pulled the photograph from the camera, shielding it from the sun as he handed it to Maria, her prominent smile enduring. Allan had helped her find that smile during their twelve sessions, an accomplishment he was most proud of across his entire career.

"Here," he said, writing the initials 'M.M.' on the back and handing the photograph over to Maria. "Something to remember this day by. A photograph to mark the beginning of your new life."

Before Maria could answer, Allan's phone began to ring in his pocket, the peace and tranquillity of the autumn breeze broken by the electronic sounds beckoning him to answer.

"I'm sorry," he said, pulling out the phone, not recognizing the number that appeared on the tiny screen. "I should take this." Allan walked away from Maria, letting her gaze toward the colourful hillside just a little longer as he answered the call. "Hello?" he answered, waiting for the voice to speak as he slowly made his way back toward the house. Little did he know that the voice on the other line would destroy all hope he had achieved over the many years of therapy and self-actualization. It was to be the phone call from hell itself, the devil on the other line, telling him his time on this earth was over, that Allan was to join him in purgatory for the rest of his days.

The second Allan answered that call, his life was over…the darkness overtaking him as it had long ago…

21

Maria watched from the playground as Allan slowly walked back toward his house. She didn't mind waiting. The view of the autumn horizon was stunning, and the fresh air was healthy for her baby, kicking within her belly now and then as a reminder that he was still there. It wouldn't be long before he was ready to meet the world.

Everything was turning out better than Maria could have ever dreamed.

Her baby would not know hunger.

Her baby would not know war.

He would have a shot at a life she never had and the opportunity for a childhood she merely dreamed of while sleeping on the streets of Syria. It was amazing how life could change in such a short amount of time. Two years ago, she had been sleeping in an alleyway. Now, with the help of many foreign aid workers, Allan Springs, and a lot of luck and good timing, Maria was sleeping in her *own* apartment and working for salary leagues above what she had earned in Syria. Sure, she wasn't making nearly as much as most families in Canada, but it was more than she had ever imagined she would have and more than she ever thought possible for someone with her background.

Maria's English was coming along nicely, and she was starting to adapt to the strange customs of Canadians.

Their love for hockey. Their inhumane ability to not allow any amount of cold weather to bother them. Their passion for the sticky substance they put on pancakes.

Canada was a strange place, but she loved every bit of it, and she knew her son would too. This was a place of hope. This was a place where her son would have a life free of the terrors that had troubled her, and she would make sure she was alongside him every step of the way, never abandoning her child, never leaving him to fend for himself as Maria's parents had done to her.

She was going to be a good mother. A great mother. The best of the best.

Maria turned to look back toward the autumn leaves, the thick forest behind Allan's house a blessing, God's gift to the world. She didn't know if she would ever be able to afford a home like Allan and Erin's, but she was more than happy in her single apartment with clean running water and a roof over her head—*a luxury compared to what she had grown up with.*

The view over the hills was spectacular. There seemed to be an astonishing view of endless colour and charm everywhere she looked.

That was what it meant to live in Nova Scotia.

That was what it was to live in peace.

The baby kicked inside her again, with force, Maria whispering down toward her belly to try and sooth her unborn child. She had read somewhere that talking to an unborn baby helped to put them at ease, creating the bond between mother and child before they were even born.

"Shhh," she sang, the fresh breeze blowing her dark hair across her face as she whispered alone to the baby from the center of the children's park, a place she hoped to bring her child once he was big enough to ride the swings and run freely on his own. "Esi Mierā," she said in Latvian—the language of Maria's parents—then mentally switched to English. "Be at peace."

The baby kicked again, and Maria felt the cramps and pains in her chest grow as she walked over to the swings, carefully sitting down and holding her belly as her son seemed to squirm inside her. "Esi mierīgs," she caressed. "Be calm."

The wind seemed to be picking up ever so slightly, gusts of cool air carrying the damp smell of autumn over the park, the dying blades of grass swaying back and forth in waves, the empty swings swaying with them.

Several cramps began to rise within Maria's stomach as if a gear left dormant had suddenly decided to start spinning inside her, softly churning up her organs, her breathing growing shallow to try and ease the pain.

Then suddenly, alone within the whispering wind of the children's park, Maria felt a damp liquid trickle down her legs, her dress moist in the groin area, the cool air pressing against the dripping liquid.

She knew immediately what it meant.

The motherly instincts inside Maria told her precisely what was happening.

Her water had broken. Her baby was ready to be born.

Maria carefully rose from the swing, a steady stream of water oozing down her skin as she turned toward Allan's house, preparing her voice to call for him, to shout for assistance upon the arrival of her baby boy.

But Allan wasn't at his house.

Allan was standing at the edge of the park, staring directly at her, an unfamiliar look gleaming from his eye, his cell phone clenched in his hand.

She wondered how long he had been standing at the edge of the grass line where nature ended and the concrete civilization began.

"Allan…" she grunted, surprised that he was standing silently only a few feet behind her, never announcing his arrival. "…my baby…he's ready…"

Allan did not respond.

Allan barely even looked down at the water soaking Maria's blue dress.

Allan's eyes hadn't blinked, his body a statue in the autumn breeze, his teeth slowly grinding back and forth as if he were lost in a cloud—*or stuck in a nightmare.*

"Allan?" Maria groaned again, the cramps beginning to rise within her once again, the birthing process beginning its course. "I need your help. Please."

Again, Allan did not answer.

Maria didn't know it, but the kind, generous, and compassionate man she had come to know and cherish over the past six months and twelve sessions was no longer there—*at least not where it mattered.*

The man before her was an empty vessel of the Allan Springs who had guided and protected her these past months.

The man before her was a broken man, a lost man—*a man on the verge of performing unspeakable horrors.*

The man before her, a ghost of whom Allan Springs *used* to be, was the harbinger of death, the slayer of good fortune, and the last man Maria should have ever been with at this very moment.

Maria didn't know it, but the man standing before her would be the last face she ever saw, the last voice she ever heard, and the final cruelty she would ever know.

The devil hid in the shadows of what she believed to be pure, and the devil's name was *Allan Springs.*

The crisp autumn breeze blew across Maria's face…*one final time.*

22

ello?" said Allan Springs as he stepped onto his porch, just out of view of Maria, still basking in the glory of the Autumn views. For a moment, there was no answer, just a few seconds of silence that made Allan believe that a telemarketer had somehow gotten ahold of his cell number, as they always somehow found a way to do. The silence held for two or three seconds before he called out again....

"Hello?" he repeated. "Anyone th—"

"Allan," the voice spoke from the other side, cutting him off.

"Speaking," Allan replied.

"Allan Springs?" the mysterious man continued, his voice deep, his tone flat and to the point.

"That's indeed my name," Allan spoke, waiting for the man to continue.

There was silence again, lasting only a second or two, the man's breath releasing a clear sigh from the other side of the line, a sound Allan had become familiar with during his therapy sessions with clients over the years, a sigh that was only released when his client was about to talk about something difficult or troubling.

Allan's heartbeat raced just a little, a dribble of anxiety pressing through his veins as if he knew he was about to receive terrible news—not that he could have ever predicted the bombshell this stranger was about to deliver. No man, woman, or child on this planet could have withstood the words Allan Springs was about to hear.

"Hi Allan," the voice said, silence replaced once again by the man's deep and trembling voice. "This is Joel Perry, a nurse at the Kentville Regional Hospital." There was another pause, but it was only brief. "I'm here with Officer Martin, Are you alone right now?"

"I am," Allan said, forgetting Maria for the moment, his ears locked in on Joel's voice. He had met many nurses over the years but couldn't place a face on Joel, the man remaining a stranger, except for his name.

"There's been...*an incident*..." Joel spoke, clearly holding something back, clearly choosing his words as if they were being read from a script.

"An incident?" Allan asked as his heart rate increased further, his anxiety beginning to fold inward on himself.

"I'm afraid I can't speak to it over the phone. Are you able to come into the hospital?"

Allan had no desire to deal with red tape or formalities. He knew there were security risks when dealing with medical cases over the phone. He knew that better than anyone, being in the profession he found himself in these past decades. But Allan had no interest in waiting. He had no interest in spending the twenty-minute drive to the hospital imaging the worst.

"Joel. What happened?" Allan asked firmly. He would get his answers now, not later.

"I'm sorry, but I..."

"Listen," Allan spoke, cutting him off, "you tell me now, and you tell me straight. I'm not driving ten feet toward the hospital without knowing what it is I'm driving for. Understand?"

There was silence, and Allan knew that meant Joel was processing his terms. He didn't dare assume the worst, which was unfortunate because what Joel was about to tell him was far worse than even Allan's darkest fears.

"There's been an accident," Joel spoke, finally giving in to Allan's demands, breaking the hospital's restrictions on over-the-phone conversations. "It has to do with your wife."

Allan lowered the phone from his ear, staring blankly toward the street, his head beginning to spin, his vision beginning to blur. He felt the darkness slowly seeping back into his mind, the same darkness that took years to conquer, the same darkness that had almost ended his marriage and his life. It began to whisper to him, muttering horrid things...*awful things...*

She's dead.

You're alone.

She's gone.

You failed her.

It was a voice he had not heard since the loss of their second child, a voice he thought he had rid of once and for all, one that had remained dormant in his mind for so long, slowly slithering back once again. Allan forced the whispers from his thoughts, pushing away the void of darkness with all his might, using everything in his therapist's toolkit to try and keep the demons at bay, to allow him to at least finish his conversation with Joel.

Maybe it wasn't that bad.

Maybe she just broke something, or is in shock.

Keep it together.

Keep it together for Erin.

"Is she..." Allan struggled to finish the sentence but forced himself to continue, even if it took the last of his mental strength. "...*alive.*"

"She's in critical condition," the nurse said bluntly, barely a split-second between Allan's questions and Joel's answer. "But she's barely holding on." The first of two pillars holding Allan's world above the dark came crashing down. His head was spinning, and the world seemed to be collapsing in on itself, but he held on, just long enough to ask a final question—*a question no father-to-be should ever have to ask once, let alone for a third time.*

"Is the baby—*alive?*" Allan asked.

Silence returned his answer.

Silence was all Allan needed to hear to know his life was over.

The second pillar began to crumble.

Allan didn't push for an answer. He already knew what Joel was going to say. He almost expected it—*as if it were meant to be—as if he was meant to live within the veil of shadows—as if it were a sinister plan long-laid out by the powers-that-be.*

Joel continued to speak, but Allan barely heard a word. Joel's voice created sounds and noises that formed words, but Allan was in no state for the sentences to take shape inside his withering mind.

"Their car was sideswiped," Joel said distantly, Allan's phone pressed against his ear, his thoughts tumbling deep into the void. "It rolled twice before coming to a stop. She doesn't have long. And I'm so sorry, Allan, but they couldn't save the baby. The impact on her stomach was too heavy for the fetus to withstand. The heartbeat was lost before she was even out of the ambulance. I'm sorry. I'm so, so sorry. Did you want—"

The voice at Allan's ear trailed off, Joel continuing to speak, Allan no longer able to hear it. The words were hazy, as if emitted from the opposite end of a subway tunnel, bouncing around in Allan's mind, echoing with meaningless chaotic harmony as the void grew and grew—*and grew.*

He dropped the phone from his ear, letting his arm rest limply at his side, the phone clenched within his trembling fingers.

He's dead.

It's over.

You deserve this.

You failed them.

The whispering voice inside his head spread across the darkest corners of his mind, Allan putting up no resistance as the corruption rapidly spread like an inescapable infection, blanketing his every notion in shades of unbearable insanity.

He's dead.

You're a failure.

Erin's dead.

The darkness has returned.

Allan knew he should fight, but he was tired.

Allan knew he should resist, but there was no fight left inside him.

Kill yourself.

Hang yourself.

You can do it now.

You can do it in the garage.

Allan didn't move, for he lacked the strength.

Allan didn't hang up on Joel and try to get to his wife before the end, for he lacked the courage.

There's no purpose.

What's the point?

You're a failure.

You're worthless.

A gentle breeze kissed Allan's skin as it blew by, but Allan was no longer there to feel it.

The birds sang their late-afternoon song as the danced raced across the darkening sky, but Allan was no longer there to hear it.

His body was still, his feet unable to move, the gears of his mind ceasing to turn. His consciousness was deteriorating deep within, surrounded by shrouds of darkness, collapsing in on itself as the deepening void rapidly consumed everything that made Allan who he was. The inexorable dissociation was taking over, and Allan Springs swiftly slipped away into madness, plummeting further than he had ever fallen before.

You should kill yourself.

You'll never be a father.

Your purpose is meaningless.

You can do it with some rope.

Joel's voice called from him from the cell phone in his hand, but Allan was no longer there to answer it. It rang and re-rang several times, the vibration in his hand numb and empty, like the distant buzz of a stinging bee.

All Allan could do was be still.

All Allan could do was let the void seize his very soul, twisting within himself as everything he had ever worked for disintegrated in a single ninety-second phone call.

She's gone.

You couldn't protect her.

You're worthless.

You can do it in the garage.

Allan thought of his first child...of the tombstone they had erected in his honour, how it now laid vacant, overgrown by weeds and autumn leaves, soon to be forgotten as the slow passage of time trickled onward.

He thought of his second child...of how it had nearly destroyed their dwindling marriage, of how only after years of therapy and many sleepless nights, did they manage to push through the dark times, barely salvaging a glimmer of what Allan and Erin used to be.

And now...Allan thought of his third child...lost not to medical conditions, but to fate, as if it weren't meant to be...as if this was the final sign from God, telling them there was to be no happiness in their future, no purpose in their lives, no children to pass the torch to.

You don't deserve children.

You're a failure.

You're nothing.

You can do it with a rope.

The whispers within Allan's head hastily took over, leaving no room for thoughts of his own, carrying his consciousness far away and completely taking over his mind like an intrusive weed within a dying garden.

Kill yourself.

You can do it right now.

Look to the trees.

You can do it in the forest.

Allan took a step forward, not of his own accord, but of the cravings of his twisted mind, the corruption taking complete control, Allan no longer at the helm of his desires.

Keep walking.

Straight into the woods.

No one will care.

You can do it in a pond.

Allan stepped off his porch, his phone still in hand, the whispering darkness guiding his every step, his mind lost to the wilderness of the void.

Walk forever.

This is it.

There's no more purpose.

You don't belong here.

Allan marched past his car, the passenger door left open, the quiet hum of the engine outside the realm of what he could comprehend. The world seemed to swirl and twist before his eyes, his vision blurred and wavy, his senses numb and depleted.

You couldn't protect your child.

Never look back.

Keep walking forward.

You can do it in the woods.

His twisted mind commanded him to continue, and Allan willingly submitted, with no hope left within his dwindling soul, no purpose left within his empty heart. Allan walked across the pavement, slowly making his way toward the sidewalk, stepping beyond the concrete and onto the dying autumn grass, oblivious to the world around him, oblivious to Maria, sitting on the swing before him, her bright blue dress dull from the sight of his dazed vision, the smell of autumn's decay odourless in the wake of his nullified senses.

And although he was staring right at Maria, he did not see her…

Although she was calling out to him, he did not hear her…

And although she was clearly distressed, he simply did not care…

Leave her.

Walk into the woods.

Lose yourself forever.

You can do it in the trees.

Allan hesitated a moment, as if an unwinnable war was waging within his wilted mind.

He saw Maria.

But he did not acknowledge her.

She was standing before him, yet she was miles away.

And although his mind was empty…

And although his heart was gone…

…Allan did notice one thing, the subconscious thoughts of his scattered mind locked upon Maria, as if the darkness had shared with him a twisted secret, telling him there was something to be gained standing in Maria's presence.

She tried to say something to him, but Allan did not hear. All he saw was the water soaking her blue dress, dripping down her legs as she struggled to stand, her hands gripping the swing set tightly, the voices continuing to whisper deathly commands he dared not disobey.

This is it.

You're purpose.

This is how you become a father.

Take her into the woods.

Allan continued to linger as Maria pleaded for him to listen. There was a war waging in his mind, a battle between fruition and detachment, darkness and light—between what was right *and what was necessary—what was logical, and what was nonsensical…*

Look at her.

It's yours for the taking.

That's how you'll save Erin.

This is how you do it.

Allan took a slow and steady step toward Maria, never blinking, never wavering, his eyes locked upon the bulge in her chest, his heart blackened by the loss of his third child.

God wants this.

It's meant to be.

This is how you save Erin.

You must take her into the woods.

Allan was in no state to distinguish right from wrong, good from evil, or horror from enlightenment. Allan was no longer himself but the shade of a broken creature as the threshold of what he could withstand had finally eroded—*the dam had burst, the waves crashing through crumbling walls.*

Allan marched forward until he was hovering directly over Maria, possessed by the void that gripped him so viscously. Darkened thoughts were his master, Allan merely the puppet.

Grab her.

Take her into the woods.

You can do it in the trees.

You can do it with a rock.

Allan clenched his fingers around Maria's long black hair, yanking her to the ground as she screamed and hollered, no one around to hear, the secluded woods at the forefront of Allan's twisted vision.

Take her now.

This is how you save your marriage.

You can do it in the trees.

You can do it with a rock.

Maria bit, kicked, punched, and screamed, but Allan's senses were numb. He didn't feel a thing. With one hand, Allan dragged Maria by the hair, with the other, her wrist. She was too weak to fight, too distraught to make sense of the madness that had taken over the very essence of Allan Springs. Allan let the twisting whispers guide his every motion, the darkness hauling Maria out of the park and into the woods, the void dragging her a hundred yards beyond the tree line where even the sky could not peak through the thickness of the woods.

This is it.

You can do it here.

No one will ever find her.

You can do it with a rock.

Allan had no idea what he was doing.

No conscious part of Allan Springs had any comprehension of the broken decisions he made. The void had mesmerized him, his dissociative sanity curling to madness, psychotic notions dissolving the last bits of Allan's contorted mind.

No one can hear her scream. No one will know where she is. This is how you save her. You can do it with a rock. You can do it with a rock.

◇◇◇◇◇

Maria fought. Maria screamed. Maria cried. But there was nothing Maria could have done against the raw strength that had overtaken Allan's soulless body.

She shouted for help to come.

She pleaded for God to save her.

Neither answered...and neither came.

She looked up at Allan from the deep of the woods, his face blank and emotionless. Maria no longer recognized the man that had taken care of her these past six months.

She didn't understand.

She didn't know what had happened to Allan.

The kind and gentle person she had known was gone.

A monster had taken his place, as if he were possessed.

The last thing Maria would ever see was Allan Springs hovering over her pregnant body, holding a rock the size of a grapefruit.

Allan raised the rock high into the air, then let his arm come crashing down with as much force as the darkness would allow, the stone connecting heavily with Maria's jaw.

It only took one swing.

And Maria was no more.

Allan   had   done   it   with   a   rock.

Part IV
Hidden

23

Janene Horvac sat in the back of an ambulance at the edge of the neglected park, her body trembling and shaking, a silver weighted blanket wrapped around her as the bright blue and red flashing lights of four police cars, two ambulances, and a single firetruck split the night. Their sirens were silent, but their presence was known across the entire neighbourhood. Most police officers were one-hundred yards beyond the tree line, propping up their floodlights and mapping out the surroundings around the corpse Janene had uncovered...the body in a weathered blue dress...*Maria's body...*

Janene struggled to string any of her thoughts together, the image of rotting bones amongst the mud and leaves scorched into her mind, her exhausted state of being mudding the waters of sensibility. She held in her hands a cup of warm lemon water, the paramedics telling her to sip slowly and focus on keeping the water level with the horizon, an exercise that would help alleviate the tension of what she had just uncovered.

When she dialled 9-1-1, Janene could barely compose a single coherent sentence. She managed to stumble out her location and some minor details of what she uncovered, but that was it. Never in her life did she think she'd discover something to this degree. She was a schoolteacher. She was no detective, no investigator. The only dead body she had ever seen was at an open-casket funeral for her grandmother, and that was more than enough for her never to want to see another corpse.

Janene took a sip of water, letting the warm liquid trickle down her throat, warming her from the inside. The blanket around her shoulders was heavy and comforting, the floodlights shimmering on the wet pavement as if a late-night sun rose over them. Somewhere within all the commotion, Janene could hear her name being called. It sounded distant, her mind still wandering through the events of this tumultuous day, her ears picking up the sounds of her name but not yet responding to it.

"Janene," the voice called out again, sounding more present, natural, and direct. She looked up at the man standing before her, holding a notepad, wearing casual jeans and a brown leather jacket. She recognized him immediately, having seen him just a few hours earlier in the emptiness of their living room.

"Daniel," she said barely stumbling out the words, looking up from her seat on the edge of the ambulance. "Keeping you busy, aren't I?"

"It's all right," he said, forcing a smile and sitting beside Janene in the ambulance. "I don't mind. Besides, once I heard your name on the radio, I got here as soon as possible."

Janene suddenly felt a burden, as if the disturbance of Daniel's night off was her fault—like she had inconvenienced everyone by dialling 9-1-1 and reporting the body. She knew that was illogical, but then again, she was barely thinking straight, her mind scarcely able to string two-and-two together.

"I'm sorry," she said automatically.

"Nonsense," Daniel replied. "You did the right thing."

"By going into the woods at night while there's a crazy person on the loose breaking into our house and threatening our family?" Janene responded, taking another sip of water.

"Well…I didn't say it was *all* the right thing. But I'm glad you called us. The rest doesn't matter."

Janene could see a few officers rolling out the police tape, blocking off the entrance to the forgotten park and creating a primitive perimeter around the entire scene.

"Do you mind if I ask you a couple of questions as a formality?" Daniel asked, clicking his pen, still holding a welcoming expression on his face, doing an excellent job of making Janene feel comfortable despite the chaos.

"Can I ask you something first?" Janene replied, taking another sip of steaming water.

"Of course."

"Is it her?" she asked, taking out the photograph from her pocket and staring at it one last time, the image of Maria holding the corner of the swing set, smiling, completely unaware of what it was that was about to happen to her. "Is it Maria?"

Janene could tell that Daniel was hesitant to answer, but after only a moment, he gave in, the benefit of being friends with the sheriff paying off.

"It's still too early to tell," he said, jotting down the date and time at the top of his notepad. "But it certainly looks like it. We'll have to run some tests to be sure."

"How could this happen?" Janene wondered as she thought of the horrors Maria must have endured to end up where she did. "And right next to Allan and Erin's old home. It must be related…right?"

"I really can't speak on it, Janene. But your guess is as good as mine."

"I know. It's just...this sort of stuff shouldn't happen in our little slice of the world, you know? It's hard to fathom." Speaking it out loud helped Janene process, helped her be at ease with all the chaos, even if the chaos seemed to be unending.

"People are capable of doing terrible things," Daniel said, the cool night breeze slipping between the emergency vehicles. "I've seen quite a bit of it over the years."

"I can imagine..." Janene answered, her imagination trailing off.

"Mind if I ask those questions now?" Daniel returned, drifting back on topic.

Janene nodded, ready to help her friend in any way she could

"What were you doing in the park tonight?" Daniel asked.

"I just...needed to get out of the house," Janene said, not mentioning the fight she had with Daray right before she left. "Irene recognized the park in the picture, so I thought I'd come here and have a look around."

"Did you expect to find anything this late at night?"

"Not really. I don't really know what I expected. It was more of a shot in the dark than anything. I was just looking for answers as to why someone would break into my house and trash the place."

"You should leave that for us..." Daniel said, speaking now as a police officer, as well as a friend.

"I know..." Janene followed up. "But it's hard to sit still when stuff like that happens...you know? Especially after finding that photo in Amon's room. *My son's room.*"

"I understand," Daniel replied, finishing his note and preparing for the next. "And where did you go once you got here? What did you do once you arrived at the park?"

278

"I just walked around the grass, where the swings used to be, then slowly made my way into the woods where...where I...*found her.*"

Daniel scribbled some quick notes before moving on to his next question. "And why did you go into the woods? The body was a hundred yards deep, and it was pitch black. It was a lucky find to stumble across her."

"I..." Janene paused a moment. She didn't end up over Maria's body on purpose...*she was guided there*...by something she could only describe as a blue flash drifting through the air, like the north star guiding her way. Janene had no idea what it was she had followed deep into the shadowy woods. She thought it might have been her eyes playing tricks on her, the moonlight shimmering off something concealed within the forest.

But why was it moving?

Why did it veered away from her as she walked?

Janene decided to keep that from Daniel as well...at least until she had time to process whatever she had seen. Enough had happened already today...and she didn't want to sound crazy...*not to Daniel.*

"I just walked around the trees..." Janene lied. "...I didn't realize how far I'd wandered in. I used my phone to light the way and stopped when I saw something blue sticking out from the dirt. It was pure chance that I found her. Just blind luck."

Janene looked off toward the tree line, a pair of cops walking across the threshold of the trees, one holding a camera, the other a heavy-duty flashlight. The sound of generators rumbled around her, dozens of extension wires twisting and turning toward the woods to power the floodlights and other gadgets needed to properly conduct their investigation.

Daniel jotted the last of his notes, closing his notebook and sliding it into his breast pocket. "That enough for now," he said, his police senses telling him that Janene had been through enough already today, the body not going anywhere anytime soon. "I'll stop by if I have more questions."

"Am I a suspect?" Janene asked, feeling silly to ask but still curious nonetheless.

Daniel laughed, quickly reeling back his reactive gesture, thinking it might be inappropriate given the circumstances of the evening. "For a body most likely thirteen years old? No, you're not a suspect, Janene. I'd like to think my longtime friend isn't a murderer."

Janene forced a small smile, still holding the mug of steaming water tightly with both hands, her tremble almost completely evaporated from her fatigued body. "Okay," she said, not pushing any further.

"Come on," Daniel said, I'll give you a ride home. "One of my boys will take your car back later."

"I'd appreciate that," Janene said, standing up from her perch on the back of the ambulance and tossing the weighted blanket to the vehicle's floor for the paramedics to deal with.

As Janene followed Daniel toward his unmarked cruiser, she looked back once more toward the woods, the commotion, and the scene of the crime. She wasn't any closer to figuring out what was happening inside her home, but at least the mystery of Maria's disappearance had been solved, the discovery of her body the mark of a newer investigation. Janene scanned the tree line as if she were searching for something, wondering what the flash of blue was that guided her through the night to Maria's corpse.

Did she imagine that?
Was it really there after all?

Janene had no idea. The threshold between reality and imagination seemed to blend more easily in her exhausted state, her body ready to collapse onto her pillow, her mind prepared to place this day far behind her.

She turned away from all the commotion, not wanting to think about the events of the day any longer, not wanting to think about whatever it was that led her to Maria's rotting body. Daniel opened the side door of his cruiser, helping Janene slowly settle into the passenger seat, closing the door gently behind her as he made his way toward the other side. Janene rested her head against the seat's cushion, thankful she didn't have to drive. She was beyond any state of enervation she had ever felt before and in no condition to be behind the wheel of a car, even if their house was just around the corner. She closed her eyes, letting the blue and red flashing lights fade away, allowing the image of Maria's corpse to dissolve deep into her mind, accepting that this day was finally over...*finally done with...*

But she was wrong...

...Janene didn't know it yet...but the worst of it all had yet to come...the eye of the storm passing by, but the remaining terrors yet to commence...

...And deep within the forest's shadows...beyond the naive eyes of those that lived and breathed...a phantom lurked and observed them all...stalking Janene back to her home...in the dark...in between what's known and what's hidden...a final reckoning to be had this night...

24

roplets of rain battered against Amon's bedroom window as the wind began to soar, the sky starting to open, and the night's veil of shadow well underway. But Amon didn't hear the breeze, the rustle of tree branches rubbing up against the house, or the rain bouncing off their shingles above. He was deep into his videogame, his eyes glued to his monitor on his desk, his noise-cancelling headphones blocking out any sound from the real world, leaving behind only the noise of war, gunshots, respawns, and explosions as he mowed down his digital enemies. Amon wasn't an avid player of war games. He usually preferred RPG classics like Skyrim or God of War, those games taking over one hundred hours to finish, sometimes more if he was going for one-hundred-percent completion trophies. But today, Amon wanted something to distract his senses, something to help him forget about the intruder, his parents fighting, and the photograph he had found lingering in his bedroom.

There was no light in his room other than the gentle glow from his monitor lighting up his youthful face as faint shadows flickered against the walls of his tiny room, Amon's silhouette shimmering in the dark, his body blocking the light that failed to pass around him. If anyone didn't know about the events of before, one would assume this was a typical day for a teenager, getting home from school, tucking himself in his bedroom and playing video games late into the night. But today had been far from average, Amon doing his best to block out the anxieties that pressed their way to the forefront of his thoughts, videogames providing ample opportunity for distraction.

He didn't know where his parents were.

His mom had left after their fight, never telling them where she was going, not yet returning from wherever it was she had gone. Daray hadn't yet spoken to Amon either, although Amon guessed he was down in his office, blocking himself off from the world, burying himself in his work as Amon did with his videogames.

It didn't matter.

Amon was happy to have some alone time.

He enjoyed being by himself. He was used to it, being the only child that he was. It was sort of bred into him, and even at thirteen, he cherished his time alone. It's when he was able to think best. Even under the distress of the chaotic online war game, Amon found that his thoughts were continuously drifting from topic to topic, his attention never staying put for more than a minute, attacking the events of his life from all angles while he played.

He thought of his parents, wondering if they would have a divorce or not and what would happen to him if they did. Daray wasn't *really* his father, not biologically anyway, so would his mom have priority for custody, or had Daray been around long enough to have an equal say? Of course, he didn't think his parents would get divorced, but it was always a constant lurking fear, one he never really talked about with anyone—*because who would listen?*

He thought of the intruder…about why someone would want to cause so much distress to the Horvac family? Amon figured it had to do with something related to Daray's research. Perhaps someone was upset with what ramifications his father's work had on their ideologies? Amon was only thirteen, but he was more intelligent than he let on. He always prided himself on being slightly more intelligent than his other friends—perhaps another perk of being an only child, outside of the extra Christmas presents and an unshared bedroom.

He thought of his mother, and how she didn't seem to be quite herself these days. Even Amon had noticed her extended bath times, the extra meals per week that were delivered instead of home cooked, and the increasing number of mornings where she would skip a shower to prolong her sleep for another thirty minutes.

He thought about other things too, his mind quickly stumbling from one topic to the next, then back again, as if on a loop, like a wild dog let loose in a chicken coop. He thought of his friends, his assignments due on Monday, what he wanted to do with his life, the next videogame he wanted to play, and whatever else found its way to the forefront of his thoughts. It was easy to get distracted while gaming, Amon often losing his train of thought while pressing his advantage in a game of 6v6 team deathmatch, picking up another idea as he waited for the next lobby to form. That was the beauty of gaming. It proved a great distraction from undesirable notions.

Amon intended on playing until two or three in the morning, keeping himself distracted until the lull of sleep took over. He had no intention of interacting with the outside world this night. Unfortunately, fate had no consideration for the intentions of a thirteen-year-old boy.

Just as he got his seventh kill in the latest round of team deathmatch, he noticed his breath slowly forming thin clouds between himself and the monitor. Amon also noticed the muscles in his hands tightening as if he had pressed them in the winter's snow. It was difficult to play video games with cold hands. Reaction time slowed, making it more challenging to reach the required buttons to execute the desired motion. Once his Amon's current match was over, he backed out of the lobby and took his headphones off, letting the room's silence overtake the ringing in his ears. He finally heard the rain bouncing off the roof, the wind whistling through the tiny creaks of their old home. The weather was beginning to pick up, the autumn night's temperature dropping, his visible breath a sign that winter was just around the corner.

Amon rose from his desk, tearing his eyes away from the monitor and toward the window. *It was closed.* That was surprising, Amon thought, considering the temperature of his room. But then again, their house *was* old, and Daray always held off turning on the heat until it was absolutely necessary, their oil-burning furnace costing them more and more with each season's passing. But Amon had no desire to freeze tonight, so he walked over to the thermostat by his door and raised it to a more comfortable temperature, placing his hand by the radiator to feel the heat slowly emanate. The hot air was gentle, but somehow the cold was still more prominent, his breath still noticeable before his nose. Amon knew it would take a little while to get warmer, so he would just have to deal with cool fingers until he was comfortable enough again to play games.

But among the cold, there was also a gentle smell of something foul. It was faint, but he could still smell the nasty odour. It was as if something had died inside their furnace over the summer, the smell only now being released from the radiators. He looked around his dimly lit bedroom, wondering if the smell was coming from somewhere within. After a moment's search, he opened his backpack, unzipping the nearly unused flap at the front and finding an entirely browned banana, squishy to the touch, its smell overtaking the cold upon opening his backpack.

"*Gross,*" he whispered to himself. He considered taking it down to the trash and cleaning it out, but he didn't feel like running into either of his parents at the moment, so instead, Amon zipped the backpack back up, tossed it in his closet, and pushed the door closed. *A problem for tomorrow,* Amon thought silently to himself, making his way back to the gaming chair, sitting back down and tossing a nearby blanket over his lap, the heat not yet taking over the cold, the lingering smell of rot not yet disappearing from the stagnant air within his room. *It would leave soon enough,* he thought to himself as he tossed on his headphones, grabbed his controller, and turned his attention back to the screen. But as he tried to dive back into his digital distractions, Amon noticed that none of the buttons on his controller were working, and the audio in his headset was glitching, skipping with similar harmony to that of a scratching record. He tried mashing all the buttons, but the frozen image on the monitor wouldn't budge. Amon switched the monitor on and off again, but once the screen's glow returned, the same frozen image glared back at him.

"Dammit," he swore to the emptiness of his room. His game had never frozen like this before, but it wasn't an uncommon occurrence in the world of video games. He lowered his hand and held the reset button on his PlayStation, the screen flicking to a blank white as the gaming console slowly rebooted itself. Amon stared mindlessly at the white screen as his PlayStation restarted, impatiently waiting for the game to come back on—*the distractions to avert his attention once more.* He did his best to halt the invading thoughts creeping back into his mind—thoughts of the intruder, his parents, and the darkness surrounding him in the basement the previous night. Amon tried redirecting his thoughts to other distractions, focusing on anything other than the lingering anxieties that gripped him so tightly.

He listened to the repetitive tic of his clock on the wall.

He heard the wind whistling through the cracks of their old home.

He watched the rain tap against the glass as increasingly heavy gusts swirled through the air.

He regarded his breath as it rose into the chilly evening air, the heaters not yet strong enough to block out the cold.

He felt the cold air press against his skin as his muscles remained tense and slow.

He smelled the lingering decay, seeming to grow stronger, even after tossing his backpack behind closed doors.

Amon waited…and his monitor remained white…seconds passed…a minute passed…two minutes…the screen remained white.

It was taking forever, Amon thought, waiting for his PlayStation to reboot. It had never taken this long to reset before—*but again*—it had never frozen on him before, not like this…so he decided to wait a little longer, his thoughts creeping back, the events of the day crawling through his mind once again.

Who would attack them?

Who would terrorize them?

Why did they deserve this?

The screen remained white, the sharpened shadow of his body lingering against the wall behind him, following his every move.

Were they targeting all of us—or just Daray?

Was it because of his father's work at all—or something else entirely?

Would they attack again—or was that it?

Amon loathed being left alone with his thoughts. Despite his best efforts, he couldn't shake that uncomfortable sensation that harsher events were on the horizon, and although he had no reason to believe it, he felt like the worst of it was yet to pass.

He felt like there was still damage to be done.

Were they still in danger?

Was he still in danger?

The screen remained white, the empty light of his monitor filling the room with a bright glow mixed with muddled shadows.

It was silent.

Amon was waiting.

Amon was alone.

Only after another minute in solitude Amon began to hear the gentle calling of his name, rising amongst the hushed stillness as he awaited his gaming console to complete its endless reboot.

"Amonnn..." it breathed, as quiet as an empty breeze and as gentle as a mother's whisper.

"Amonnn..." it beckoned, emanating from nowhere, stretching across the cool and rotting air.

Amon's guard rose high, his headphones still tight against his head, his ears not yet attuned to the calling of his name amongst the flame of dancing shadows. He had thought he imagined it, his eyes still locked on the glowing white screen, his fingers clenching into a cold, tense grasp.

"Amonnn..." it whispered from the shadows, the voice bleeding from the walls closing in around him.

Amon closed his mind and listened, thinking the voice was simply a figment of his imagination, his endlessly running thoughts playing a trick on his wary mind.

It's just the wind, he told himself repeatedly, wanting nothing more than his game to turn back on and distract him from his overly active imagination.

It's just the wind.

It's just the wind.

"Amonnn..."

It's just the wind.

It's only the wind.

"Amonnn…" The voice said, louder than before, too loud for the wind to be a viable explanation for the voices he heard from the seclusion of his bedroom.

Amon ripped off his expensive headset, letting it drop to the floor, the plastic on the left ear cracking as it connected with the wheel of his gaming chair. He didn't care. His heartbeat was beginning to match the sound of constant rain pattering off the shingled roof, his breath growing colder, the smell of decay rising through his nostrils.

Amon didn't return the call of whatever it was that beckoned his name.

He knew better than that.

He just waited—listened—the monitor glowing silently—the shadows on the wall watching his every move.

For a moment, there was only silence. It lasted long enough to make him think the voice had somehow originated from his headphones, perhaps a malfunction of the reboot or even a glitch in his tired mind.

Perhaps he had played enough games tonight…

Perhaps he had…

"Amonnn…" The voice ripped his thoughts in half.

Amon jumped from his chair, rising to his feet as he scanned the shadows around his tiny room, his eyes darting to each corner, desperately searching for the source of the voice…

He didn't move…

He didn't budge…

He remained still…as did his haunting shadow…silence resting between the repeated calls of his name from the dark.

"Amonnn…" it called out…too loud to be the product of his imagination… too shrill to be anything but real…

Amon's eyes warily shifted toward the right corner of his room...toward the rotting smell—*toward his closet...*

He stepped away from his desk, his headset on the floor, the blanket resting beside it. His shadow followed him along the wall as Amon stepped toward the corner of his room, eyes locked on his closet, the doors shut, hiding whatever had been calling his name...or *whoever* was calling his name...

Again, Amon didn't call out.

He didn't dare respond to the whispered calls.

He thought of the intruder...of how he had never been found...and stared at the closet doors...eyes wide...ears locked...every bone in his body tingling...every muscle under his skin tight and tense.

He waited for his name to be called again...but the voice did not call out...

...ten seconds felt like a lifetime...

...twenty seconds felt like an eternity...

...thirty seconds felt even longer...

Amon anticipated his name to be spoken...but the call never came...

Silence overtook anticipation, his shadow waiting patiently alongside him.

...forty seconds passed by....

...fifty....

...a minute...

Amon didn't budge...

Amon didn't move a muscle as he awaited what lay hidden behind darkness...

...But he wouldn't have to wait much longer...

Amon's twin-closet doors slammed open as if a battering ram had bashed them from within the tiny walls of his square closet. The left door slammed against the wall, a woosh of rotting wind forcing itself upon Amon's face and body. The right door bounced off its hinges, tumbling to the ground, smashing the monitor as it fell, the screen's white glow replaced with shattered glass and utter darkness, Amon's shadow vanishing in the night, the room bathed in the pitch black of a moonless evening.

Amon fell back as the unbearable stench of icy rot engulfed him. The edge of his bedframe caught the backside of his knees, Amon tumbling onto his ass, landing on the corner of the mattress where the photograph of the woman in the blue dress had rested less than a day earlier. Amon's breathing grew unfathomably shallow, his eyes wide with adrenaline, his muscles paralyzed in fear and anticipation. He stared forward, eyes never blinking as they did their best to adjust to the blanket of darkness, his room engulfed by the pitch-black void of autumn's moonless night.

He waited for the intruder to reveal himself…

He waited for the source of the voice to press forward and do whatever it intended to do to him…

But he saw nothing…

He heard nothing…

Only darkness consumed his senses….

…ten seconds…

…twenty seconds…

…nothing…

The air seemed to freeze around him.

The smell of rotting decay seemed to spread across every inch of Amon's darkened room.

And although Amon could see nothing before him…he knew with certainty that he was no longer alone…

…and the approaching absence of silence would confirm his worst fears…

From under the veil of looming shadows, Amon heard the jagged breath of something hiding within his tiny closet. The breathing was not unlike that of a dying beast, grasping for life, each gasp raspy and broken, each gulp of air shallow and distorted.

...Amon couldn't see the hand before his face...but he could hear the intruder...in his room...breathing alongside him somewhere in the dark...their intent unknown...Amon awaiting what was to follow...

Then after the eternal passing of rotting time, the voice spoke out once more.

...There were no more whispers...

...There were no more names...

It was a woman's voice—spoken with complete clarity—a voice raspy and broken—their breathing torn and gruff...

She only spoke one word...

One word was all she needed to say...

"Runnnn..."

She did not have to say it twice.

Amon did what he was commanded to do--*he ran*—retreating straight out of his bedroom, down the stairs and toward the basement where he prayed Daray would be working—*never looking back*—never questioning what had lingered in the room alongside him...

It didn't matter.

Amon   would   find   out   soon   enough.

25

aray waited.

   Daray paced.

   Daray stirred.

   And Daray waited some more.

He sat alone in the solitude of his office, his door closed, every light on, every neuron inside his brain firing with full force. If someone were observing from the outside looking in, they would have seen a man resembling someone that had nearly succumbed to unsettled madness, walking circles around his desk, picking books off the bookshelf, flipping mindlessly through the pages, then placing them back, and circling his desk again. Of course, anyone in his position would be doing the same if they knew what awaited them between the thinning shadows of known and unknown realities.

   He considered running but knew that would do him no good. He had worked too hard and spent too many lonely nights getting to this point in his career. Running would forfeit all he had earned, all he had researched, all he had achieved. Unfortunately, the alternatives were equally as grim. No matter how many circles he walked around his desk, how many neurons fired across his troubled mind, or how many books he flung across the room like a Yankee's pitcher, every solution he derived ended the same way—*the end of his legacy.*

   Running begot failure.

   Staying begot death.

   Fighting begot the same.

   He knew what awaited him amongst the smells of rot and freezing air. Daray knew what end loomed near. He had seen what the spectre had done thirteen years ago in Allan's basement. Daray had witnessed the horror of splintering bone and oozing blood mixed with beastly screams of death and anguish. His supervisor had cruelly perished at the ghostly hands of what Daray had been trying to study these past thirteen years, the creature from beyond raising his research to new heights—at a cost, as Daray was only now beginning to comprehend.

He picked up a book from his shelf, scanning the cover, distracting his restless mind, desperately searching for nonexistent answers, doing his best to escape the intrusive thoughts of death and shattering bone. *It was no use.* No matter how many words he read or diagrams he studied, he could not let his mind wander from the horrors that awaited him, the horrors he knew he could no longer escape. He slammed the book shut, hurling it toward the far wall, denting the gyprock, the pages falling to the ground amongst the dust.

The clock ticked on the wall, time passing ever slower...the seconds dragging ever longer...

Tic...Toc

    Tic......Toc

        Tic.........Toc

Daray ripped the clock from the wall and slammed it into the floorboards, batteries, gears, and plastic exploding in arbitrary directions, time still creeping forward.

He sat back in his leather chair, pressing his head against the back, forcing his eyes shut as he searched for elusive answers.

He could drive far away—but that would bring questions...questions that would lead to investigation...investigation that would lead to the discovery of...*things he did not want discovered...things that would bring his research to ruin...*

He could stay and fight—but how did one fight that which awaited him amongst the rot? He had uncovered the idea of existence beyond that which was known to humankind, but beyond that, he was as much in the dark as the next fool, wandering reality without a clue of what it all meant.

He could try and reason with it—but that was a hopeless thought. A ghost held no concern for the worries and cares of the corporeal. *Especially Daray…*

He could kill himself—that thought had crossed his mind quite a bit. He could clean up his research, tie up loose ends, then toss himself into the icy waters of the Bay of Fundy, cement block tied to foot, concerns lost forever. This idea seemed to be at the forefront of all possibilities. It was certainly better than letting the spectre decide his fate, his bones splintering, his body breaking crack by crack. It would undoubtedly preserve the legacy he had worked so long to achieve. But Daray was a coward. He hadn't the strength to take his own life, nor was he ready to greet what awaited behind the veil of the beyond. There was *surely* an answer besides death, an answer Daray seemed unable to discern, an answer that eluded his disturbed and troubled mind.

He stood from his chair, circling the room once more, tossing another book toward the door, the spine splitting from the pages, loose paper floating to the floor in all directions. Daray stared at the bookshelf for a moment, weighing his options and pondering his past decisions that led his family to this point.

Would Janene suffer the same fate as Allan?

She was innocent.

Did she deserve such an end?

Was what she deserved even a consideration in events to come?

And what of Amon?

He was only thirteen, his unstained hands barely of this world.

Would he suffer the consequences of Daray's actions?

If Daray revealed himself, his past, and his research, surely that could save Janene and Amon, *couldn't it?* One would think that the promise of protecting his family would be enough to force Daray's hand. Still, it would mean the end to everything he had accomplished, not to mention his contribution to the world, society, and science. Humanity only ever progresses on the heels of preceding discoveries. How many lives could be saved, studies be had, papers be written, and discoveries be uncovered simply because of Daray's research and the breakthroughs he had accomplished in his field? Daray had unveiled the secrets of the human soul...that was not something one brushed aside when considering their next move, even if it jeopardized the safety of one's family. Daray was a scientist, it went against his very purpose in this world to do anything that might risk the integrity of his work. Sure...*he had lied a bit...he had altered the data just a little...but he had to...nobody would accept the truth...nobody would accept how he came up with his conclusions.* The methods used may have been unconventional, but that didn't mean his work was any less absolute, less reputable, or less worthy of the praise and recognition he had long awaited—*and deserved.*

No—*he could not reveal his secrets...*he could not forfeit the work he had achieved or the advancements he had uncovered for the sake of humankind and society.

He would not.

He could not.

He will never.

*Still...*that left him in the predicament of trying to avoid his torturous demise, for which he had zero solutions.

It didn't matter.

He was out of time.

She had come.

The rot came first.

The rot *always* came first.

Daray thought it might be in his head playing tricks on him, his anxiety-ridden mind forcing the sour smell of sulphur and corpses up his nose, but the scent had quickly grown too strong for that to be the case. Daray stopped in his tracks behind his desk, not moving, not thinking…just waiting…listening…*suffering*…

The rot rose throughout his office, replacing every cubic inch of stale air, bleeding through the walls and filling his room with the smell of a thousand rotting corpses.

Daray's door remained closed…*but it didn't matter*…

Daray's lights remained brightly on…but again…*it didn't matter*…

He knew it was too late…he knew he had already gone too far down the rabbit hole…and he knew his time was up…he just wasn't ready to accept it…

Daray reached down into the lower drawer of his office desk and pulled out a small black shoebox, placing it by his closed computer as the rotting odour grew stronger…*and stronger*…

He flipped open the lid and reached his trembling hand inside, pulling out something he had long wondered if it would have been better pointed at his head than hidden in the depths of his office desk…

From the shoebox, Daray pulled out a silver Ruger GP100 revolver, the cylinder loaded with .357 rounds, the serial number filed away. He had ordered this gun in secret many years ago from an unreputable website, hiding it away from prying eyes, never once removing it from the box in the desk, breaking every rule in the book by owning and keeping a loaded, unlicensed firearm.

He didn't care...

He knew that someday it might come to this...

He didn't even know if it would work...

But he wasn't going to go out without a fight...

Daray sat down at his desk, his trembling hand holding the heavy revolver, the barrel pointed toward the door, having no other intentions but pulling the trigger the second the ghastly spectre made its appearance.

He had imagined this day to come for a long time, praying it never would arrive but knowing it may. He doubted bullets would matter against a creature already departed from this world, but he was a scientist after all...theories only held substance if they were tested...and he planned on testing this theory with every *God-Damn* round in the chamber—*every round but one...*

The revolver held six .357 rounds. The first five would be for the monster that had mutilated Allan thirteen years ago. That would be enough for Daray to know whether weapons of one world could banish a creature from the next. And if that didn't work—*well*—he would have to find that little bit of extra courage after all, because he had no plans on letting that creature tear him limb from limb, screaming in agony as he felt the bones within his body splinter, fissure and break.

It wouldn't be long now before he got a chance to test his theory. The smell of rot had grown fiercer than he had ever smelled it before...more pungent than when the creature had torn up his living room...and more potent than how it had been thirteen years ago...

And the room was beginning to grow cold, as if a winter's frost was slowly crawling through the walls of their home, stretching across every tooth and nail, the warmth quickly disintegrating away. Daray could see his breath form before his face, his hands tremulous as they gripped the cold steel of the heavy revolver.

It wouldn't be long now…

Minutes…

Seconds…

An eternity subject to the absent tic of his smashed office clock.

Daray waited; the barrel of his revolver pointed directly toward the unlocked office door. There was no sense locking it anymore…he knew there was no delaying a creature such as this…walls and doors had little meaning to a spectre.

He waited…and waited…*and waited*…the smell driving him mad with anticipation, the temperature dropping leagues below freezing. Ice began to form across the top of his forgotten mug of coffee, the metal of the fun icy to the touch making it difficult to grip…but he stayed his hand…*he would not be lowering the gun this night…*

The whispers came next, fading in the like unavoidable approach of night, darkness to fall thereafter.

"*Darayyyy…*" The voice whispered…quietly…softly…leaching through the walls as if they weren't even there.

Daray didn't respond.

His purpose was clear.

His eye was locked on the iron sights of the revolver.

"*Darayyyy…*" The voice hissed, calling for him, hope seeming to fade with each sinister whisper.

"*Darayyyy…*" The voice breathed once more…each call louder than the last…the crackling voice of the ghostly woman creeping in through the cracks of reality, stretching across Daray's quivering mind as he awaited his chance to take the shot. Deep within...Daray knew the gun wouldn't help...but logic and reason always have a way of fading in the concealing wake of blind hope, and that was all the desperate scientist had left...*blind hope, six bullets and the aspirant prayer that his legacy wasn't about to go down with him.*

"*Darayyyy...*" The woman's voice addressed him from the void, beckoning for him to join her, raspy and torn as if spoken from the rotting throat of a forgotten corpse.

"Come on then!" Daray finally responded, screaming at the walls and giving into the madness, slamming the grip of the gun on the desk, desperately awaiting his fate. "Show yourself, you bitch!"

For a moment, there was only silence amongst the rot and cold...*the seconds seemed to tic faster now.*

"*Release...*" The voice continued, shifting her ghastly tune, the whispers bouncing around the room as the lights slowly began to flicker and wane.

"Fuck you," Daray responded, barely able to draw breath, his lips rapidly turning blue, the trembling barrel of the gun barely holding true to its intent.

"*Release...*" the voice murmured, whispers fading into screeching shouts, every individual object within Daray's office beginning to tremble.

"I will not!" Daray shouted, standing up from his desk, holding the gun with a white-knuckled grip, the barrel still pointed toward the door, his finger ready to pull the trigger on a split-second's notice.

But only silence fell upon his forsaken office...
The voice did not respond...
The trembling of the room seemed to fade...

All Daray could hear was his struggling breath and the chatter of his juddering teeth, the silence mimicking that of the void from which he knew the spectre came…

There was no warning for what happened next.

It happened all at once…

…so suddenly…

…so viciously…

…as if ignited by the spark of a single grenade…

Every textbook, novel, paper, and thesis in Daray's office flew from the shelves with the force of a thousand cannonballs—paper and ink shattering into pieces as they connected with each other, slamming into the floor, the wall, the ceiling, Daray, and everything in between.

Every light burst into splintering pieces, showering the air with thin shards of glass as it rained jagged crystals from the ceiling above.

Every floorboard seemed to rise from the earth as if an earthquake had erupted from beneath the ground—the wretched chaos centralized locally within Daray's God-forsaken office.

And lastly, the office door was hurled off its hinges, flying toward Daray as he narrowly dodged the soaring chunks of wood splintering toward him with rigid force. Daray didn't think as he jumped to the side, dodging every bit of anarchy that flew through the rotten air, his frozen white finger squeezing the trigger as he fell to the ground, the single shot of a .357 magnum blasting through the air toward the empty doorway.

◇◇◇◇◇

Amon never saw it coming.

How could he have known what was about to happen?

He was about to knock on the door when it was sucked in toward the office from its hinges, the loud eruption of a gun severing Amon's own fears and unsettled notions.

Amon never had time to react...*to think...or to cower.*

He didn't even know what it was that connected with the upper portion of his chest.

All he knew was that he felt something rip through his body, tearing apart whatever it shredded through inside his teenage body, knocking him flat on his back as the prodigious agony forced his mind to go blank, his thoughts collapsing in on themselves, darkness consuming his mind as he lay motionless, blood pooling out onto the basement floor, his reality closing in all around him.

Everything went black.

Everything went dark.

Everything was dark.

26

anene watched from their porch while Daniel drove away in his ghost car, waving goodbye as the increasing rain fell from the sky, the winds rising on this cold and dreary night. She watched Daniel drive down the hill and out of view, turning the corner on the main drag and disappearing into the night.

She thought of Maria, her body resting under the mud and trees for thirteen years, a case unsolved for so long, uncovered by the mystery of a forgotten photo, a photo now impounded as evidence as her case reopens under Daniel's watchful eye. Janene thought of the pale shade of blue that had guided her through the darkness of the woods, with no explanation besides her own exhaustion and random chance.

She knew there was more to it than that.

There had to be.

Her heart told her so.

Her soul told her so.

But she was too tired to try and analyze the pieces.

She just wanted this day to end.

She wanted it all to end.

Janene would not get her wish.

She had barely closed the door behind her when she heard the gunshot split through the silence, her heart dropping deep within her stomach at the sound of the blast.

For a moment, *she did not move*—as if her mind's processing power had slowed to a near halt, her thoughts catching up with the gunshot echoing somewhere inside her own home.

Her ears rang, her mind sputtered, and the rain dripped from her hair as she stood at the entrance of her home, the living room vacant of furniture and life, the peace of their tiny home ripped in two. It wasn't until she heard the second gunshot, did she charge into motion, her feet running faster than her thoughts, her body automatically running toward the source of the shot against the whims of every nerve in her instinctual body.

There was only one reason she ran forward rather than retreating, one reason she sprinted towards unknown dangers rather than racing outside to alert the cop cars guarding the streets around her home—*and that reason was Amon*. Motherly instincts drew stronger than any other feeling known to humanity, and Janene *knew* that her son was in danger.

She didn't know how she knew.

She couldn't explain it.

But she knew Amon had been home, and now there were gunshots within their walls—she didn't need to know anything else.

Her son was in danger.

Janene needed to save him.

That was all she needed to act.

Janene had no idea where the gunshots had originated, the loud blast echoing through the house from seemingly every direction, bouncing off the walls like that of a cave. She was about to sprint toward Amon's bedroom when she heard the third gunshot, followed rapidly by a man's scream...*Daray's scream*...emanating from the basement, where a fourth shot swiftly followed the third.

Janene didn't think.

Janene didn't consider her own safety...her own safety didn't matter.

Janene sprinted down the stairs toward the basement with little concern for herself, her mind spiralling with visions of the worst...images of an intruder holding a gun, gunning down her family, doing to them that which had done upon Maria thirteen years prior. She had no reason to think that, but that is all that ran through her mind as she barreled down the stairs and into the basement...*into the all-encompassing dark...*

A fifth gunshot ripped through the air before Janene reached the bottom of the stairs, the sound of the blast louder than ever before, her ears practically deaf as she reached the basement, a flash of dread immediately stretching across her horror-stricken face.

Janene saw nothing except what lay on the ground before her in a pool of blood, the body still, fingers twitching ever-so-slightly.

She didn't see the bullet holes in the wall.

She didn't smell the rotting stench or feel the freezing air.

Janene only saw her son lying on the ground, still as a corpse.

A flood of emotions flashed through her adrenaline-filled soul, her entire body shaking on the verge of collapse, a billion thoughts cramming their way through her tormented mind.

"Amon!" she cried out hysterically as she rushed over to her son, not caring for her safety, not looking for the shooter or her husband.

Those things didn't matter.

Only her son mattered.

She threw herself onto the floor beside Amon, whose blood poured from his right shoulder, hiding the bullet hole in a pool of red. His clothes were soaked, and his eyes were unresponsive.

"Amon!" she cried out again, brushing her bloodied hands through his hair, having no clue what she was to do.

This wasn't a sight meant to be seen by a mother. No mother should ever have to question whether their son is dead or alive...no mother should ever have to let that wonder slip through their tortured mind. Janene could barely control her shaking hands or keep her gaze locked upon her motionless son lying wounded on their basement floor.

"Help!" she screamed, pleading to God, to herself, to anyone within earshot of listening.

She wasn't thinking.

She was screaming.

It was all she could do.

"Please, help!" There was no one to hear her pleas...no one to answer the call. She looked down at his chest, relieved to see that he at least still drew breath, his chest rising and lowering ever-so shallowly, his eyelids weakly twitching.

*Amb....ambulance...call...call an ambulance...*She forced the thought through the tears, the panic, and the crippling fear of losing her baby boy. *Wh...Where is a...a phone...?* Her thoughts were clustered and choppy, the gears of her mind barely able to spin.

The...office...phone...ambulance...Daray's office...

Janene quickly jumped to her feet, her hands bloodied, her son's breathing shallow. She knew Daray had a phone in his office...and she knew she had to call an ambulance...those were the only two thoughts in Janene's mind...those were the only two thoughts that bore any meaning in her forsaken reality.

She hadn't noticed that the office door had been blown off its hinges.

She hadn't noticed that the entire basement had been ripped apart into chaos. Books were lying everywhere, all wall hangings had been knocked to the ground, and hundreds of torn pages were chaotically covering the floor.

She hadn't noticed any of it until she stood up and stared into the office to see Daray standing behind his desk...*holding a gun*...the barrel pointed toward the empty doorway. It all processed slowly across her mind...ideas barely palpable among her distressed thoughts...but slowly, Janene began to connect the pieces...

...*Amon was shot...*

...*She saw no intruder...*

...*Daray was holding a gun...*

It all slowly clicked...it all slowly pieced itself together...

"What...what did you do...?" Janene managed to spit out in the form of furious whispers, her eyes still focused on Amon's breathing, her hatred now focused solely on her husband.

There was no answer.

It looked as if Daray was trying to speak, trying to utter simple words, but no voice broke the silence. He muttered meaningless whispers to himself, the gun raised at eye level, never lowering...

Janene took a step forward...repeating herself with ferocious intent, her incensed eyes now locked upon her husband's wandering gaze. "What did you do!?" she shrieked, not caring that the barrel of a revolver was pointed directly at her temple, not caring that with the flick of her husband's distressed finger, her life would be over in a matter of microseconds.

Daray croaked out a pathetic whisper, barely loud enough for Janene to hear...

"She...She...She..." He repeated himself like a madman, his eyes wild and loosely straying across the room as if he were searching for something within the rotting darkness of his office—a rotting odour that Janene was only now beginning to smell.

"Daray..." She cried out, pleading for an answer and the truth as to why her son lay motionless on the ground with a bullet wound in his shoulder.

"*She...She...She was...She was here...*" Daray muttered, barely able to speak.

Janene didn't know what her husband was saying. Words from behind the pointed barrel of a smoking gun seemed to have a tinge of madness along with them, and Janene was in no state to converse with insanity.

"What are you talking about..." she said, taking a step into the office toward Daray, eyes focused on the gun, shoes crunching on shattered glass and torn books. "We need to call an ambulance!"

Daray did not respond.

His eyes were barely focused on Janene at all.

They weren't even focused on Amon.

His gaze drifted over Janene's left shoulder, growing wide, the aim of the revolver following his stare.

"Daray!" Janene cried out, the air on her tongue freezing to the touch, the smell of decaying rot rising in her nostrils. "Please..." she cried, pleading for answers, begging he would drop the gun and let her call for help.

Daray did not provide the answer she sought.

He provided no resemblance of sanity or the man she had known these past thirteen years.

His eyes remained wide and lost.

The gun, which she had no idea where he had acquired it, was still pointed straight and true.

He spoke two words...two words that became the difference between the reality she knew and the reality she would come to know—two simple words that would split the very foundation of the beliefs she held of the universe.

"Turn…around…"

She didn't want to at first…did not want to turn her back to the man holding a revolver, the man that barely resembled a shade of her husband. But he was no longer staring at her. From the looks of it, he hardly even recognized that Janene was in the room. Daray's eyes were focused on something behind her.

Something wretched.

Something in the shadows, amongst the freezing rot.

Janene spun around.

Janene screamed in terror.

It prowled behind her, lurking in the dark, as real as anything else in this world, as visible as Daray, or Amon, or Daniel, or Irene…blackened feet drifting inches above the ground over Amon's pooling blood…a rotting stench steaming from her decaying skin…peeling flesh and a torn blue dress wavering from her body like moulded strains of cheese stuck to a rusty shredder.

The ragged spectre in drifted through the air…

She glided mere inches from Janene, blocking the only exit out of the office, blocking Daray and Janene from their only means of escape.

Janene's breathing became shallow and sporadic, her chest tightening, her body on the verge of collapsing— *something she would have done if her son's life didn't rely on her very survival.*

She stared up at the horrid creature's face, her jaw swaying back and forth on strings of rotting muscle, her eyes black and hollow, rotten and lost, patchy black hair oozing from her exposed skull, resting on her shoulders as she wandered ever closer.

Janene stepped back, retreating behind the desk next to Daray, next to the man that had shot their son.

Sulphur and rot continued to linger in the stale air...

An arctic freeze overtook the non-existent warmth of the blackened basement...

Janene and Daray were alone...trapped in the office by a creature not of this world but of the next...*and although it took a moment*...Janene realized exactly what it was that floated before them—or rather—*who it was*...

She had just found her body an hour earlier, lying forgotten amongst the mud, wearing the same blue dress that appeared on the creature before them...the same blue dress that had been in the picture found in the photograph on Amon's bed...

Janene spoke the spectre's name, the words escaping her tongue the minute the dots connected...

"...Maria..."

Janene couldn't help but stare at the incorporeal monster before them...a shade of the woman that once was...Maria's ghost, somehow lingering in their reality, *real*...a memory of a lifelong past, yet lurking before them all the same.

Janene stared at her rotting skin...her swaying jaw...her blackened hair...her exposed skull...all matching the body she had found partially buried in the mud...Maria's body...thirteen years neglected.

"How...is this possible..." Janene muttered with jagged whispers, her voice trembling at the sight of Maria, Daray's answer remaining silent.

Maria's ghost didn't budge. She remained in the doorway, blocking the only exit, impeding the possibility of saving Amon, preventing their only way out of this God-forsaken basement.

Janene quickly realized that the *'how'* didn't matter.

Maria was before them.

Of that, there was no denial.

The means of her resurrection—should it be called that—mattered not when staring face-to-face with a ghost.

Maria was there.

Maria's ghost was real.

Questions jumbled around in Janene's head, each weighted with unbearable emotion and fear, each bringing with it an avalanche of unfathomable notions. Each question bounced around Janene's mind, all deserving of an answer, none worthy of being asked.

How is this possible?

Who did this to you?

Where did you come from?

These were not the questions one asked when faced with the insurmountable reckoning of reality before them. There was only one question that would bear any meaning, one that might give Janene a chance to save her son, and one that may prevent a fate that Janene assumed would not result in a happy ending.

"Why are you here, Maria?" Janene asked, barely able to form words, the view of her son's shallow breathing enough to draw strength as she struggled to veer her gaze away from Maria, lingering inches off the ground before them...her dead gaze locked upon the Horvacs...

For a moment, no answer was returned...

Janene didn't even know if Maria could hear her...

Maria's ghost just continued to stare at them with rotting eyes, blocking their escape, unfazed by the gun Daray held firmly in his grasp.

But after a few seconds—*each second suffering longer than the last as Janene watched her son gurgle and struggle for shallow breath*—Maria finally gave her answer, looking not to Janene but at Daray, scowling at him from across the room, her putrid hand pointing to the bookshelf to his left.

"*Release...*" Maria spoke, her voice raspy and hollow, her jaw swinging by the tissues of her rotting skin and muscle, the voice coming from someplace deep within her forgotten soul.

"What...?" Janene responded, not understanding, not having a single clue as to what Maria was trying to tell them.

Daray did not respond.

But Daray knew what the creature was asking.

Maria was asking for his end.

The destruction of his legacy.

The desolation of his family.

"*Release...*" The spectre screamed, every speck of dust and debris trembling on the office floor, Maria drifting ever closer, the rising stench forcing Janene's eyes to water.

"*I don't...I don't understand...Please! My son!*" Janene pleaded and cried, but the ghost seemed to have no interest in the worries of the land of the living. The spirit drifted ever closer, approaching halfway across the room, Maria's arm outstretched as if reaching for them both, calling for them to join her in whatever darkness awaits beyond...

"*Release...*" It spoke again, louder, harsher, deeper...the bones of her fingers protruding from the peeling skin of her decomposed hands, Maria's thirteen years of rot and decay ever visible on the otherworldly memory of the rotting corpse before them.

"I don't understand!" Janene cried out, wanting nothing more than to get help for her son and to be free of this madness once and for all. "Please, I don't understand..."

"I do," Daray said, finally shattering the encompassing madness that seemed to cloak his fractured mind.

He looked over to Janene, her eyes frightened and lost.

He looked over to Amon, bleeding out on their basement floor.

His legacy wasn't worth the lives of his family.

In what he assumed would be his final moments, Daray could not allow his family to suffer.

"I understand." Daray lowered the gun, resting the silver weapon against his hip as he stepped to the left. The ghost halted in its tracks, its outstretched arm still pointing to the bookshelf, its rotten gaze following Daray's every move.

Daray stepped toward the creature before them, carefully keeping his distance, his eyes never breaking away from the spectre's sullen gaze. Janene watched as he reached into the third shelf of the bookshelf, pulling something that looked like a tiny lever, something that would have usually been hidden behind dozens of textbooks, the sound of a metal latch clinking from behind the bookcase. Then—*with little ease or effort*—Daray gently pulled on the corner of the bookshelf, the unit swaying open as if it were on a swivel, a hidden passageway revealing itself amongst the darkness of the room, a dim white light glowing from beyond the new opening within Daray's office.

Janene had never known that was there.

In thirteen years, she had barely ever stepped into her husband's office, it being the one room he always said he wanted to himself to work in private. She had always respected his boundaries. It was *his* house, after all. Janene and Amon moved in with him just under thirteen years ago, but Daray had been there several years before that. But not in all that time had she ever suspected he was up to anything else within the secluded confines of his private office.

She couldn't have been any more wrong.

"I...I don't understand..." Janene said, watching as her husband revealed a secret door within his office, the bookcase swinging open, the rotten corpse still floating alongside them, watching the Horvacs with unknown intent.

"I know," Daray said, stepping back toward the desk with a dispirited look, gun still in hand. "Go." He motioned for Janene to enter and explore whatever he had kept hidden all these years.

"Please..." Janene said, trying her best not to stare at the abomination next to them that was Maria. "...please help me understand..."

Daray did not answer.

He looked defeated and broken, never raising his eyes to meet his wife's, a single tear dripping down his pale cheek.

"Daray...?" she asked, pleading for answers.

"I uncovered what no one else could," Daray muttered, absent any emotion. "It cost me everything. Go. It'll be okay," he said plainly—*despondently.* "Please, just—*go.*"

Janene knew her husband.

He had known him for thirteen years.

The man that stood before her was a pale shadow of the man she knew.

Her husband was caring.

Her husband was intelligent.

Her husband was proud.

She sensed none of these qualities as she passed him toward the enigmatic passageway.

Maybe he had been overtaken by fear—*as she was.*

Maybe he had become engulfed by shattered realities—*as she currently felt.*

But in the end, it didn't matter how they felt. All that mattered was getting through this so she could save Amon. All other feelings remained numb and secondary when her son's life was on the line. All other emotions remained buried under a mother's protective instincts. Janene took one final look at her husband, who was gazing at their bloodied son, a wound of Daray's own creation, a consequence of his despicable actions.

Janene knew she didn't have much time.

Janene knew she needed to get help as soon as possible—*if Maria would only allow her such amenities.*

Janene needed to push ahead.

Janene needed to push onward.

She stepped foot into the secret passageway, leading to a set of stairs that curled below the foundation of their house, a small spiral staircase long hidden beneath the earth.

She pushed ahead, leaving Daray alone with the monstrosity that was Maria.

Reality seemed be collapsing all around her.

But Janene closed her heart to it.

She needed to press forward.

She needed to save Amon.

That was the reality.

That was all that mattered.

27

elease.

Release.

Release.

The words raced around in her mind as she descended the spiral staircase one step at a time, the echoes of her footsteps bouncing around the narrow passageway.

What secrets had Daray kept from them?

What remained hidden beyond the very floorboards she had called home for so long?

What lingered in the dark below?

She would find out soon enough.

Janene didn't dare turn around. The wretched stench was enough of a reminder that Maria's putrid spirit still lingered, waiting for Janene to uncover what remained hidden below.

How was such a thing possible?

How was any of this possible?

Questions that would need to be pondered at a later time.

If she were to escape this at all.

A dim blue glow guided her way down the spiral stairs, beckoning for her to unearth what awaited below. The walls were carefully constructed from stone and brick, the narrow passageway barely wide enough for Janene to squeeze through as if she were descending deep into a forgotten mineshaft. Homemade bulkheads supported the ground above her head, preventing the collapse of her home's concrete foundation. Several heavy-duty power cables ran down the steps beside her, Janene having to watch her step as she sunk further beneath the ground.

What unknown hell was she about to walk into?

Her body trembled as she pushed forward—*but for the sake of her son, and the sake of her sanity, Janene pressed onward.* She counted the remaining steps as she marched further into the bowels of what remained hidden, doing her best not to slip into madness, her lucidity waning thin.

"Four..." she spoke softly to herself as a means to calm her troubled heart, the tremble of her lips audible as her voice echoed through the narrow corridor.

"Three..." the room was beginning to come into view as a dim blue light shimmered from below.

"Two..."

Could she bear to see what Daray had kept from her all these years?

She had no choice.

This was for Amon.

Her son depended on her.

"One—oh my God..."

28

*H*ello…?"

That was the first sound Janene heard as she entered the underground chamber beneath her home, the walls a mix of mud and carefully assembled brick, loose wires strung across the ceiling, connecting strings of hanging fluorescent lights across a tiny space barely larger than Amon's bedroom. To the right was a large pile of scientific equipment and machines, matching that of what she had seen in Daray's lab at the University upon her few visits over the years. To the left was an assortment of books, DVDs, vitamin bottles, video games, magazines, playing cards, toys, yoga mats, and other miscellaneous items that looked like they had been stolen from her son's room.

And all of this…*everything she saw*…was behind a thick wall of transparent plexiglass with marble size holes poked in a diagonal pattern across the seven-foot high, eight-foot-long glass wall, acting as a barrier between Janene—*and who remained imprisoned behind it…*

…trapped between stone and glass…

…buried deep below the threshold of their home.

Janene disconcertingly stared at the blue eyes gazing back at her from behind the enclosed glass confinement—*the eyes of a boy no older than Amon.* He was wearing jeans and a simple grey t-shirt. He had no shoes and no socks, his bare feet pressed against the dirt floor. His skin was as pale as the distant moon, his frame thin and feeble, his wrists boney and weak. Janene felt her entire body tense at the sight of the trapped child—her hands clinched tight enough to press coal into diamonds, her teeth clamped into one another near enough to crack a tooth.

Her body shook…

Her muscles solidified…

No words could form as she stared into what she could only describe to herself as a cell…*a cell for a child…hidden below her home…*

Janene began to hyperventilate.

The room was spinning.

Her vision became blurred and distorted.

She could feel her intestines rising into her throat, her body not strong enough to keep down the vile substance pushing itself into her mouth.

Janene bent over and puked out the entire contents of her queasy stomach, spitting orange and yellow bile all over the tiny floor on her side of the plexiglass.

What was Daray doing down here…

What had he done…

"Are you okay…?" The boy behind the plexiglass asked, his voice quieted like a whisper, his back pressed against the far wall of mud and brick.

Janene wiped the vomit from her lips, forcing herself to stand upright as the room continued to spin, her balance barely able to regain control.

"Am I…what?" Janene managed to reply, not understanding what was happening or who was talking to her from within the cell.

"Are you okay?" The boy asked again in a gentle, yet shy tone, as if he were just another one of Amon's friends, talking to Janene with polite manners. "Where is papa?"

"I'm…*fine,*" she answered, confused and lost. A thousand thoughts crammed themselves across Janene's wary mind as she did her best to grasp the situation. She scanned the tiny cell, a mockery of a child's room if she ever saw one. A small cot acting as a bed was tucked away in the far corner. There was a tiny TV on a small bookshelf filled with board games, video games, books and other distractions. Along the ground was a grass-like mat placed over a heavily packed dirt floor, the turf mat mimicking the type of material expected to be seen on an artificial football field, the same kind of material Amon plays on amid busy summers. Pressed against the wall were old movie posters and pictures of nature. One image wrapped within a wooden frame showed a simple illustration of an unknown coastline, while another presented a photo of rolling hills among a setting sun. A simple exhaust fan hummed on the ceiling, a visible silver tube running up into the ground, presumably leading somewhere above.

What the hell had she stumbled across?

What sort of evil was this?

Janene looked back toward the boy with pale skin, his back pressed against the far wall, visibly scared eyes staring back at her—as if he had never seen another face before today, as if he had been down here alone his entire life.

Whose child was this?

Where had he come from?

Did Daray kidnap him?

What was going on?

Janene forced her fear to the darkened corners of her mind, doing her best to hide the look of disgust from her face, even if it was all she knew at this very moment, even if terror and revulsion were all she felt among her shattered heart.

She had spent her entire career working with children, teaching them—*helping* them. *Surely this was no different*, she told herself, desperately looking for common ground between what she knew and what terrified her beneath the subfloor of her own home.

She could do this.

She had to…for Amon.

"Who…*are you?*" Janene asked, her trembling voice barely able to speak, her stomach hardly able to fight the urge to turn and vomit once again at the sight of the half-filled chamber pot tucked under the child's bed mere feet from where he was standing.

"My name is *boy*," the child answered, clearly frightened at the sight of Janene.

"*Boy?*" Janene asked, distraught at the heartlessness of his name.

The boy hesitantly nodded, keeping himself as far away from Janene as he could within his tiny glass confinement. "Who are you?" he asked. His english was perfect.

"My name is Janene," she stuttered, doing her best to keep her voice calm and soothing, unsure if she instead sounded like a frightened beast to the child, her mind unable to overcome the quivering fear that blanketed her every thought. "How long have you been down here?"

"Where is Papa?" the boy asked, averting the question, his voice carrying through the tiny holes of his confined cell.

"Who is 'Papa?'" Janene asked, already knowing the answer but praying she was wrong.

The boy didn't respond.

The boy just stared at her—his skin pale, his eyes blue and wide.

Janene took a cautious step toward the cell, the glass thick and robust, a small door locking the child within. "Who is papa?" she asked again, keeping her voice as calm as she humanly could—as if she were talking to one of her own students. The boy declined to respond, the humming of the overhead fluorescent lights the only sound within the hidden chamber below Daray's office.

"I won't hurt you," Janene said, kneeling on the compacted dirt floor and putting her hand against the glass. "I promise. Please, tell me who Papa is."

The boy was hesitant, studying her every move, protecting himself in the distant corner of the glass cell. But after a moment, he finally caved to the soothing voice Janene tried to project.

"Daray," the boy said with elegant ease, completely tearing apart the last decade of Janene's life.

What monster had she shared a bed with all these years...

What monster had helped raise her son...

How could she have been so blind...

How could she have been so oblivious...

How could anyone be so immoral?

She shook the thought from her mind. She could reflect on how oblivious and ignorant she was after the face—*but right now, Amon needed her.* Janene's son was hurt, and she needed to get back up to him as quickly as possible. She suddenly thought of the words Maria's rotting spirit had spoken to them within the putrid cold of Daray's office. They didn't make sense then—*but they did now.*

Janene was slowly connecting the pieces together.

Release.

Release.

The ghostly words rattled around in her mind.

Janene knew what she needed to do.

She reached over to the tiny glass door and twisted the lock, the door popping open as the pale child retreated to the furthest corner of the room, curling into a near-fetal position.

"No!" the boy screamed, finally raising his voice above a whisper, burying his head in his knees and shoving his back tightly into the stone wall.

"It's okay..." Janene assured, kneeling near the entrance of the glass cage, not daring to move any closer for fear of scaring the traumatized child. "I won't hurt you. I swear. You can trust me."

"You can't touch me!" The boy said, beginning to sob hysterically. "I'm contagious! You'll die!"

Janene was aghast at the boy's response.

What lies had Daray whispered in this poor child's ear?

Had he been experimenting on the boy?

And for how long?

How long had the boy been locked beneath the earth...

...unable to feel the warmth of the sun against his skin...

...unable to hear the song of the birds as they danced across the sky...

...unable to experience the laughter and friendship of other children...

...unable to enjoy a life he could call his own...

No more.

This boy was to be Daray's lab rat no longer.

It was time to set him free.

"It's okay..." Janene softly spoke. "You don't need to be afraid any longer. You're not sick. I promise you that. It will be okay."

"But papa told me I'm sick. That's why I need to stay. Papa needs to find a cure. Where is papa? Where is papa?" The boy's voice had sunk back to a whimpering whisper. Tears flowed across his pale-white skin as he rocked himself back and forth, clearly convinced by the deceptions and wretched lies Daray had told the poor child.

Janene was sick.

Janene was disgusted.

How could she not have known about this?

How could she have been so naïve?

Was this how he had uncovered his secrets?

Was this how he was able to do what no one else had ever done before?

She didn't care.

It didn't matter.

It was time to end this.

It was time to release this young boy from the torturous bonds placed upon him by her vile husband.

Janene took a long, calming breath, allowing her fear to become slowly replaced by compassion, the desire to help the boy outweighing the horror she felt within.

"Come with me..." Janene insisted, holding out her hand into the glass cage. "...come with me...*and I promise you*...it will be okay...You're not sick. Let me help you."

"I can't..." the pale boy cried, coddling himself in the corner as his tears dropped to the dirt below his feet. "...I can't...I can't...I can't..."

Janene forced an amicable smile as if she were staring at her own son—as if Amon himself had been locked within this poor child's tiny glass cell.

"Yes..." Janene said, keeping her hand outright, "...you can do it...*I promise*. Everything will be all right. You can finally be free."

The child raised his eyes above his knees, staring at Janene from the corner of the room.

If there was any fear within her eyes, she did not show it.

If there was any dread hidden within her heart, she did not share it.

And if there was any trepidation left within her battered soul, she concealed it wholeheartedly.

Amon's life depended on it.

As did the boy with pale skin.

Janene knew there was no getting by the spectre without the imprisoned boy by her side.

She knew what the creature above wanted, above all else.

Release.

Release.

"Take my hand," Janene tenderly invited, pleading for the child to leave this appalling cage behind. "Take my hand, and I'll show you the world."

The boy studied her from across the room, the gentle humming of electric light filling the lingering silence as she awaited his response. She smiled toward the boy, a single tear sliding down her cheek, barely able to stand herself, scraping her heart for every last ounce of strength that remained within her exhausted soul.

Then, for the first time in what felt like an eternity, a miracle finally arose.

The boy slowly slid from his spot in the corner…

…If there was any fear within his eyes, he did not show it…

…If there was any dread within his heart, he did not share it…

…And if there was any trepidation left within his forgotten soul, he concealed it with all his heart…

The boy reached out…

Janene did not move, for she did not want to frighten him, but she could tell the boy was ready to leave, even if he was scared out of his skin.

The child rose to his feet and stepped away from the corner of his cell, cautiously making his way over to Janene.

Step by step, the boy walked across the tiny room until he stood right before Janene,

Janene knew he was scared…

She knew he was frightened…

But that didn't stop what he did next.

He didn't merely take Janene's hand and exit the room.

He instead wrapped his arms around his entire body, squeezing her tightly as he cried over her shoulder, sobbing uncontrollably as Janene returned the embrace, holding him tightly for a moment, letting him release every bit of emotion he held deep within.

"Come on," Janene said as she lifted the young boy into the air just as she would when Amon used to cling onto her shoulders years ago, although she realized how grossly underweight the boy was, lifting him off the ground with surprising ease. "Let's get you out of here."

Janene took each step slowly…careful not to bump the frightened child against the walls or ceiling of the spiral staircase, cautious not to do anything that might frighten the shuddering child.

"It'll be okay," Janene reassured the pale-skinned boy as they made their way to the top of the stairs, Daray's office coming back into view. "But I need you to do something for me," she said, stopping before she brought him out of the hidden chamber once and for all. "I need you to close your eyes. Can you do that for me?" Janene didn't know how the boy would handle seeing the creature waiting atop the stairs. She knew the only place he would feel genuinely safe was that wretched prison cell, and she didn't want him running back there on account of Maria's terrifying soul haunting Daray's office, not when she was so close to setting the child free—not when she was so close to getting back to her own child.

"*Okay…*" the boy gently agreed, obeying to her simple request, allowing Janene to lead him out of the hellhole below.

Janene was hardly holding herself together.

But from the broken void in her heart, she found the strength to carry on...

For carrying on was the only that could save her son...

And even when faced with dueling realities, Janene knew what she had to do.

And atop the stairs, Daray was waiting for them, face as pale as snow, a revolver in his grasp.

29

Janene stared down the monster that was her husband, Maria still drifting close by, blocking the exit—*blocking the only path between Amon and his salvation.*

Janene didn't know what to feel.

Nor did she know what to think.

She only knew that she was disgusted by the man before her—an empty, soulless and vile excuse of a human that she had the misfortune of spending the last thirteen-plus years of her life with. She may only be a school teacher, but Janene now knew in her heart that her husband was evil, and she wanted nothing more than to be out of his sickening sight once and for all.

"How could you..." Janene said as she reached the top of the spiral stairs, barely able to make eye-contact with Daray, but holding herself strong, not letting him see the tears that were building behind her fury.

Daray didn't answer.

He couldn't answer.

How could anyone explain locking up a child.

How could anyone justify such a heinous and despicable act of evil.

"A child..." Janene hissed, barely able to form words. "A little child..."

She wanted to kill him.

She wanted to take that gun from his worthless grasp, place it to his skull, and pull the trigger.

She had sacrificed *everything* for that vile man, and now here she was, pulling a child from an abysmal cell underneath their home, her son laying on the ground with a bullet wound just outside.

"How long..." Janene said, her teeth grinding against one another like glass, the boy in her arms clamping his eyelids shut as instructed, the wretched stench of Maria's floating corpse flooded the tiny room. "How long was he down there."

Daray didn't answer.

His eyes were shallow.

His breaths were short.

"How *GOD DAMN* long!" Janene screamed, shoving her hand into Daray's chest, her husband barely reacting to the show of aggression.

"...thirteen years..." he murmured, his pathetic voice barely able to muster the words of his unspeakable act.

Thirteen years.

That boy had been down there...for thirteen years...

The entire room was spinning.

Janene propped herself against the wall with her shoulder, never letting go of the boy, never allowing his face to point in the direction of Maria or Daray. No boy should see such wicked things.

She wanted to ask a thousand questions.

She wanted to understand how he could be so cruel...so evil...

She wanted to grasp how he could do something so horrendous to someone so innocent, and still somehow put a smile on his face for the rest of the world to see.

And most importantly, Janene wanted to comprehend how he could do such a thing to her and Amon—how he could keep such an wicked deed under their roof for so long, without ever displaying an ounce of remorse or regret. How could someone be so cold—so broken—so soulless.

There were a thousand questions—a thousand doubts...

But there was only one thing that mattered—Amon.

She turned to face Maria, who was floating above the rubble and chaos scattered across the office floor, still blocking the only exit out of the room.

"I didn't know..." Janene softly spoke, terrified of what the spirit might do to her, and what might happen next. "Please believe me...I didn't know."

Maria didn't budge. Her jaw hung by the threads of her rotting skin, her black feet and tattered blue dress drifting inches above the floorboards.

"I released him," Janene pleaded, her lips trembling in the freezing air, her pathetic husband cowering behind her. "It's okay now. I swear it. He'll be protected. I promise."

Again, Maria's ghost didn't budge.

It glared down upon them with rotting eyes as if casting judgment upon Janene, deciding what it would do next, determining her fate with enduring intensity.

"Please..." Janene softly pleaded as the dots slowly began to connect within her mind, realizing whose thirteen-year-old child she was holding in the darkness of Daray's office. "I saved your son. Now I beg you. Let me save mine."

The creature hovered a moment longer, its beady rotten eyes never drifting from Janene's own horrified gaze. Seconds passed in silence...but Janene had said enough...and she would be given her response promptly.

After a moment's hesitation—*a moment that felt like a lifetime for Janene*—Maria slowly drifted off to the side, clearing the only exit out of the room, forming an unobstructed path to Amon who was still laying on the floor, his breath shallow—*but he was alive.*

Janene's fingers trembled in the cold. Her nose was overwhelmed by the powerful stench of sulphur and rot.

But she no longer saw Maria as a threat or something to be feared. From mother-to-mother, revenant-to-reality, she somehow knew that Maria was on her side, just as Janene was on hers.

Janene began exiting the room, never looking back at the pitiful beast that was her husband, never allowing him to see the tears race down her cheek—*never granting him that satisfaction.*

And as she left, she looked up at the ghost hovering before her, and spoke three simple parting words, ones she would never regret for the end of her days.

"He's all yours."

Janene would never forget the sound of the trigger, clicking and failing to fire on the six-and-final shot. Nor would she ever forget the immense sound of Daray's screams as his bones splintered and burst from within his body, brought to an end by a deafening pop and crunching thud.

Janene never looked back, but she knew what would await whoever it was to arrive first on the scene. She imagined it would look something similar to what was found in Allan Springs homes, thirteen years ago.

And she would never forget the boy, whispering "goodbye mommy," as she helped both Amon and the former-prisoner up the basement steps of her home to a better life.

Janene would never forget any of those things.

But she was more than content to put it all behind her.

Janene had survived the chaos.

They had survived Daray.

They had survived it all.

Epilogue

Dear Daniel,

I know it's been a while since we last spoke, but honestly, I'm still trying to process everything that happened back in Wolfville, and although I still don't understand all the bits and pieces, I think I'm finally ready to at least try and move on. There have been some updates on my end, and I'm sure you've read the news and seen the stories, but I wanted you to hear it in my own words—you deserve at least that.

But first, Amon is doing great at his new school. Vancouver was the best place we could have moved to, far from those that knew the deeds of his father, far from horrid memories desired to be forgotten, but still close enough to the ocean that it still feels like home. He's made a few new friends, is doing great in all his classes, and is even getting back into sports now that his injury has fully healed. He sends his regards…in the way one might expect from a teenage boy…you know how it is…

As for Daray's work—well—you probably know all this, but in case you don't…all his papers have been scrubbed from the records. It turns out he lied about most of the details, all his research solely based on a single "patient" (for lack of a better word) rather than hundreds of volunteers as he had published. Apparently, all that data had been fabricated, his real work occurring in that horrible place beneath his office. I'm still getting constant calls from reporters and journalists, both from the scientific community and otherwise…but I've said all that I can say. I've made it clear that I'm no longer interested in talking with anyone. I don't care if I ever think about that monster for the rest of my life.

I'm glad he's dead.
I hope he rots in the ground.

I also received your last email. I'm thrilled that you've found a home for Thomas. I like that name, 'Thomas.' It suits him well. It's the name of someone who will accomplish great things. I'm sure of it. I know it will be a while before he can genuinely fit within society, but I have faith that his path will straighten itself, and he will find peace. I would have loved to take him in, but I think that would be too much for us to handle, and from what I hear, things are going well. The professionals will take good care of him. I'll leave all the important decisions up to the therapists and doctors. I have done my part.

As for what happened…

Janene retreated from her keyboard a moment, pausing her typing as she thought about what she was going to write next. She had never told anyone about Maria—not Amon, not Thomas, not the reporters…*nobody*. If she even breathed the words 'ghost' or 'spirit,' the lawyers and journalists would have torn her apart, and after everything that happened, Janene never wanted to risk losing custody of her son. Amon was all that mattered in this life, and she would do whatever it took to protect him from the harshness of the world—*from people like Daray*—from people that would tear them apart for the sake of a more exciting story, left to be written in whatever way that gave them a larger paycheque, no matter the cost. *No*—Janene would never talk about what she had seen—*not truly*. No one would ever believe her, and there was no gain in treading on things left misunderstood.

Janene knew Daray's work was accurate.

She knew he had used the poor boy locked in the basement to uncover secrets of what lay beyond--*Maria's secrets*—but she was just as happy to see every bit of his work rot along with him. Maybe someday someone would rediscover that which we knew little about, but as long as it wasn't Daray's name written down in future textbooks, she was content. Daray would be forgotten, and his legacy would be lost with the passing of time.

Janene rested her fingers back on the keyboard, finishing her email to Daniel, finishing this never-ending tale once and for all.

…As for what happened…I hope you uncover more details about how the boy came to become locked away as he was. I know the leading theory is that Daray killed Allan and Maria. That seems to add up, given what he's done. And I know that you were able to confirm that Thomas was indeed Maria's child. If you ever come up with anything else, please, let me know. Apparently, you found evidence that he was going to 'erase' any trace of his work. It keeps me up at night, thinking about what that means. I'm glad it never came to that.

Janene thought about Maria, and about the timing of her appearance. She must have sensed her son was in danger. Why she didn't show up for thirteen years, that's anybody's guess. Who was Janene to question the nature of the beyond? Only Daray knew the details of what rested beyond the threshold of life and death, and his knowledge died with him.

Thomas was safe now, and Daray's repulsive experiment was over.

Maria had gotten her revenge.

It was all over, and Janene was grateful for that.

Lastly...I wanted to thank you for pleading my sanity to the courts and separating my name as far away from my ex-husbands as possible. I know if it were not for you and Irene, I may have found myself in my own cell, and for that, Amon and I will be forever indebted. I wish we could have stayed in Wolfville with you both, but it was a chapter in our lives we needed to put behind us. Amon deserves a future where the misdeeds of my former husband do not torture him, and although I know there is still a long and bumpy road ahead of us, I think we will be all right. So again, thank you, and know that you and Irene are welcome to visit us whenever you'd like. Thomas too.

I wish you the best in the case of Maria Mihailova.
I know you will uncover the truth of what happened to her.

She deserves peace.

We all do.

Sincerely,
Your   friend,   Janene.

Turn the page for a sneak peek at
Book II of The Twisted Boeman Collection

Twisted Shores (Preview)

I t was dark in the room when Bill awoke. The grogginess took a second to fade, his surroundings slowly shifting back into focus. It didn't take Bill long to realize he was no longer lying in the discomfort of his makeshift bed under the stairs.

He...*was he standing? He was.* In the centre of the Bernard and Marion's basement, feet planted on the concrete floor....*and he was alone.*

Bill scanned around for the rest of the group, *but they had all vanished*, absent from their resting spots in the dark. Empty cushions replaced where Buck and Marla once sat, the washer/dryer was vacant of Colton, and the supporting metal pole was no longer host to its two prisoners.

Did everyone leave? Surely not.

Where would they go? Why would they leave him behind?

Everything around him seemed darker than usual, more ominous than it should. It was strenuous to see to the far walls, and everything looked bleak and grey, *all spectrums of colour absent from the plain basement.* Even Bill's clothes were different shades of grey, matching the aesthetics of his surroundings. And even though it appeared so, *it didn't feel like he was alone.*

Bill had felt this way before.

It was silent, not even a breeze was blowing outside, the dim whistle Bill had fallen asleep to completely gone. Not even the gentle hum of the electricity buzzed, only silence...*followed by more silence.*

But that didn't last long either.

From the tenebrosity surrounding him, phantom whispers began filling the stale air.

"Kill them."

The whispers' direction altered rapidly, arising first from his left, then his right, then from everywhere else.

"Kill them all. Kill him."

The voices were indistinguishable from one another, interchangeably alternating in an infusion of men and women, children and adults. And they were growing louder. Building upon one another voice-by-voice.

"Kill her. Kill him."

Bill forced his hands over his ears to try and block the amplifying sound, but that didn't seem to do anything. The cries continued like they were trapped within his head...*clawing to get out.*

"Kill them. Kill her!"

Louder and harsher, the voices grew, each one more substantial and more onerous than the last, near to the deafening point.

Unbearable.

Yet inescapable.

Bill tried to run away, to turn and dash up the stairs away from the crazed voices, but his feet were anchored to the floor, like they were nailed to the cement below. With no hope of breaking free.

"Kill them! Kill them all!!"

Bill wanted to scream among them, to shout for them to stop. But his voice came up empty; his lungs exhausted from verse. He closed his eyes, suctioned his hands to his ears as stiff as he could, and fought off the voices as best as he was able. He thought they would never end, trapped in this nightmare, forever intertwined with the whispers.

But then the voices halted.

From nothing they arrived, and from nothing they returned.

Instantaneously the voices teetered off, leaving him alone once again amongst the darkened silence as the ringing in his ears staggered gradually away.

Was this a dream? A nightmare?

It felt so real.

Without warning, a woman's terrorizing scream burst from his right. Bill looked over swiftly to see Marla lying on the ground, hands tight to her fleshy neck. She lay flat on her back, her eyes bulging out of her head, her legs flailing and thrashing rapidly on the concrete ground. Her hands clawed harshly at her throat; her tongue wiggled back-and-forth out of her mouth like a worm poking its head from the sand. She looked as if she was choking, like someone was sitting on her chest, holding her to the cold floor and strangling her with ghostly hands.

But it was just her.

Bill tried to get over to Marla, needing to reach her, *wanting to save her*! But he was powerless to watch, an arm's length mile away while she silently perished in front of him.

Another single scream erupted to his left, opposite Marla. *It was Colton*, lying flat on his back on the dryer. It was as if he just appeared out of thin air, his fate tied with Marla's. His hands were at his neck, eyes rupturing from his sockets,

345

feet dangling from the dryer as he suffocated from nothing in a noiseless frenzy. The solo scream echoed around in Bill's mind, but the room remained hushed as his companions helplessly suffered.

A third screech, this one much deeper and more resonant, exploded to his right once again. Lying alongside the gasping Marla, was Buck, tongue wagging back and forth in his mouth as the heels of his boots scraped against the floor. His hands were to his throat, and silent empty gasps flowed from his crippled windpipe.

Another pair of screeches exploded in front of him, *weaker*, yet just as terrifying. Bound to the pole that had only moments ago been bare, was the old couple, back-to-back, the old lady convulsing violently, legs quivering as she struggled to breathe. The older man cracked his head back and forth rapidly against the metal pole, splattering grey blood down the corroded metal surface, covering his balding head in the gore.

Bill, incapable of moving, watched as everyone around him needlessly suffocated, an unthinkable force butchering them before his eyes. He tried with all his might to move, grabbing his legs with his arms, tugging at his feet unsuccessfully as they remained stuck like cement. Bill tried to scream, to struggle, anything that could get him even an inch closer to the others.

But he failed.

Endlessly, he failed.

One by one, everyone around him stopped struggling, and the flailing turned to stillness, the gasps to oblivion. One by one, each one of his companions drew their last, silent breath, then collapsed on the spot, motionless, quiet, *gone*. Once the last twitch faded from the old man's bloodied neck, Bill found himself alone again, now surrounded by death in the reticent darkness.

It wasn't long before a slight cold breeze brushed against the back of his head, raising the thin hairs on his neck. A frozen chill sunk to the bone, and his heart pounded within his chest as he felt the invisible clasp around his feet simply lift away, allowing him to turn and face the garroter. Slowly and shakily, Bill turned, eyes unsuccessfully fighting the urge to gaze toward what his curiosity could not ignore. His feet allowed to rotate by whatever invisible force had held him captive seconds earlier.

Hovering at the bottom of the stairs amongst the death and despair, was *the shadow*. It floated mere feet in front of Bill, humanoid in form, but pure evil in presence. Bill felt the fear and dread float off from the Entity, filling the room with a malevolent darkness. The whispers hastily returned, briskly drowning out the silence once more with their wicked words.

"Kill them. Kill them."

Bill felt his hand rise from his side, uncontrollably.

He tried to resist but lost all function as The Entity began to take control.

"Kill them. Kill. Kill."

The nefarious chant repeated itself as Bill's fingers grasped around his Adam's apple. Slowly his grip tightened as he felt the final oxygen in his lungs become consumed. Fear and panic built up inside him as he found himself unable to breathe, *unable to fight*, as the darkness rippled in. His peripherals faded away until the last thing he saw before himself was the shadow, barely hovering above the ground before him. It approached threateningly, *yet slowly*, as it wavered within reach. The creature stopped an inch before him

347

as Bill felt his consciousness start to drain and drift. Just before all strength and cognizance dissolved, he heard the Entity utter in a gentle, low-pitched scratchy voice, barely audible, yet unforgettable:

"...I...Fo..und...you..."

The Writer's Embrace

For more up to date information regarding new editions to the series, novels, short stories, and more, visit www.thewritersembrace.com, home of A. Ryan MacGibbon.

The Writer's Embrace is an ever-evolving writing community designed and maintained by the author of The Twisted Boeman Collection, and a place where fellow writers, readers, and followers can:

- Find up to date information regarding the release of new books and novels.
- Read blogs and informative pieces written by the author.
- Read raw short stories and poems directly from the author.
- Learn more about A. Ryan MacGibbon.
- Communicate directly with the author through our contact pages.
- Write your own stories and poems and discuss them amongst peers in our **Free Writing Forum**.
- Enter Semi-Regular Contests, offered on-and-off depending on time availability.

The site is entirely free and welcomes writers and readers of every background!

www.thewritersembrace.com

The Twisted Boeman Collection

The Twisted Boeman Collection, envisioned by A. Ryan MacGibbon, comprises a series of standalone novels that delve into the diverse and chilling realms of horror. Each book is a unique foray into different sub-genres, crafted to offer readers a pulse-pounding journey from the first page to the last.

Book II – Twisted Shores

Originally released as a stand-alone, this remastered version of Twisted Shores is sure to have the reader at the edge of their seat as Bill Shapely goes toe-to-toe with the *Entity* and his army of twisted maniacs, all under the Twisted Boeman's malevolent control, all forced to obey his dark commands. Will Bill survive, or will he lose his mind alongside the rest of Sydney, NS?

Book III – A Shadow in Time

The *Entity* strikes again, but this time with completely different intent. Kelly Christopher, a cop in Halifax, NS, sees undeniable video evidence of himself shooting a cop—*but the thing is*—he has no recollection of the event whatsoever. Soon events start becoming twisted, the Entity makes his appearance known, and Kelly finds himself lost in time, frantically struggling to survive, and desperately seeking to clear his name.

About the Author

A. Ryan MacGibbon's roots are deeply embedded in the rugged beauty of Cape Breton Island in northern Nova Scotia, where he was born and raised. His formative years by the elegant Mira River set the stage for a lifetime of curiosity and exploration, leading him to Acadia University for a B.Sc.H. in Physics and subsequently to McGill University in Montreal for a M.Sc. in Particle Physics. A seasoned professional in data science, Ryan dedicates his leisure time to crafting enthralling novels and short stories or enjoying the company of friends and family in the lively quarters of downtown Halifax. His literary debut, *Hidden*, marks the beginning of *The Twisted Boeman Collection*, a series of standalone horror novels that introduce readers to the darkest corners of his mind. Ryan currently resides in Halifax, N.S., where he shares his life with his remarkable family.

Reach out at www.thewritersembrace.com.

@thewritersembrace

:)

www.ingramcontent.com/pod-product-compliance
Lightning Source LLC
Chambersburg PA
CBHW050541260626

47157CB00002B/387

* 9 7 8 1 7 7 7 7 8 0 2 5 8 *